Bound

Jodi Raimondi

PublishAmerica
Baltimore

PublishAmerica has allowed this work to remain exactly as the author intended, verbatim, without editorial input.

ISBN: 978-1-4489-6243-3
PUBLISHED BY PUBLISHAMERICA, LLLP
www.publishamerica.com
Baltimore

Printed in the United States of America

DEDICATION

This book is dedicated to my mother, Pat and my father Joe Gallipani.
I miss them dearly, thanks for everything, I know you would be proud.

Acknowledgment

I'd like to acknowledge, Donna Starke, I know you are going to be alright just keep climbing that hill and you'll get to the top.

To Jessica Strickland, you're finally in the loop.

And of course my family, Gene, my husband, and my three children Tina, Jillian and Joe, I love you all.

And to JZ and Mary J, For keeping me in an "Empire State of Mind."

Bound

1

Homeward

There are times when a story needs to be told by *all* who had a great impact on it. That is why I, Danny Marcello, (only Dianna, with the exception of my creator, Sebastian, have the privilege to call me by my given name, Danato. Not even you-the reader, can call me by my given name.) decided to continue our saga. Dianna did a good job telling you about how we met and how we became bound to one another, but there is so much more to the story. Nothing is ever as simple or as perfect as it seems. Witches and vampires have hurdles to jump and crosses to bare also. Therefore, the best place for me to pick up the story would be where Dianna left off.

I departed from Dianna's ransacked apartment from the previous night—and what a night it was. I gave her a sworn promise of returning within a few hours after taking care of some business. Dianna didn't need to know that the business I was referring to was—*Joe.*

The matter of Joe still needed attention. Dianna belonged to me, regardless if we were together or not. This was a known fact among all our kind. Once another being is marked by a vampire's scent and blood, they become that vampire's sole property forever, unless they are released from the vampire's possession, not just from their obligation. Unfortunately for the victim, they are unaware of that fact as it's happening. Just about everything in a vampire's world is sacred and eternal. Joe attempted to rape and possibly murder my future mate at the time and my marked possession.

What he did to Dianna was an act of betrayal against me. I'm his creator. To be disloyal or to cause a malicious act against your creator is a serious offense in our world. It is forbidden for us to kill our own kind without extreme consequences. This was one of the exceptions to the rules. There wouldn't be any retaliation against me if I decided to kill Joe because of his disloyalty. Another exception would be killing what we call "loners"—a vampire who chooses to exist without a clan; one who walks alone. Loners choose to be outcasts and therefore our rules don't apply to them. That's why when I ripped off Jason's head with my bare hands, I didn't have to worry myself about being judged or shunned within my world. Jason chose his own fate when he tried to make Dianna his prey.

She belonged to me.

I left Dianna's apartment two or three hours before sunset. Joe is anything but stupid. He was well aware that this wasn't over and I was going to confront him. Joe would be awake and out of sight as soon as the sun set, so I had to act fast. With the help of Dianna's magic, she made it a cloudy day for me to walk the streets unharmed by the sun's rays. She didn't know why I asked her to do the task but she did as directed.

She learns quickly.

I arrived home to find Sebastian and Helena playing cards while the others were resting. Sebastian was wearing his white silk smoking jacket with matching silk pajama pants and Helena was dressed in Richard's old blue flannel shirt and her cut off denim shorts. The first thing Sebastian did was look at his watch to check the time when he noticed me barge in through the door.

"Where's Joe?" I said in a quiet, serious manner.

"He's in his room," Helena answered and pointed down the hall.

I pulled off my coat and threw it on the floor before I torpedoed down the corridor to Joe's bedroom. Sebastian and Helena both jumped from their seats and immediately followed behind me.

"What the hell is going on now?" I heard Helena whisper to Sebastian.

Sebastian didn't take any time to answer her question. He motioned down the hallway to keep up with my stride. Sebastian hasn't moved that fast in years. He must have known that this wasn't going to be one of our typical adolescent brawls in the living room.

I imploded Joe's bedroom door.

Joe was resting on his back silently in his oversized bed. He instantly woke up when I clutched him by the throat, pulled him out of bed and threw him across the room and into the wall. I didn't give him any time to speak, I picked him back up and pinned him up against the wall before I belted him in the face. His head slammed hard against the solid cement, his eyes bulged and both his feet were dangling off the ground.

"I want you to give me one good reason why I shouldn't fucking kill you right now!" I demanded. My eyes were glowing sadistically red and Joe struggled to speak,

"Wha…be…because…I…I…didn't kill her!" He cried as he tried to remove my hand from his throat, unsuccessfully.

"You have to do better than that!" I ordered, and slammed him against the wall again, much harder than I did the first time.

"Dan, let him speak. He can't answer you while you're holding him so tightly," I heard Sebastian's voice from Joe's doorway. I turned to acknowledge him, still holding a tormenting grip on Joe's neck. Helena stood motionless, her eyes saddened and her mouth dropped as she witnessed something that has never happened within our clan before, *a betrayal.*

"Dan, please, listen to me…" Joe begged. I slowly turned back around and loosened my grip from his neck, but I still didn't let him down, "I could have killed her at anytime, even when you were in the room. I had more than enough time to do away with her—but I didn't because of my loyalty to *you*," he said, anxiously.

With him still tight in my bruising clutch, "You have women falling at your feet, you can have any woman you want, why her? Why did you go after her and don't fucking lie to me!" I scolded and slammed him up against the wall one more time so he would know that I was serious and that death was still a possibility for him.

He was winded and scared when he spoke, "I…I…it was her blood.

I've been addicted to E.B for a while now and my supplier cut me off temporarily. I only wanted her blood," he huffed, trying to stretch the muscles in his neck to escape my grip, "I did what I did out of desperation. I never wanted to hurt her, and more importantly, I didn't want to be disloyal to *you*. I was coming down from the sensation of E.B and the craving was unbearable, so I went to Dianna to satisfy it."

I looked at him with a lot of uncertainty. However, I was still willing to hear his story.

"Where were you getting enchanted blood? And remember, I'll know if you're lying."

"Put me down and I'll tell you, I'll even show you," he pleaded. Red flames were still sparkling in my eyes, I put him down and let go of his throat. I waited at a halt and stood close to hear his story. By this time, the entire household was awake and standing inside Joe's room inaudibly awaiting the outcome.

Joe wisped his pin straight—mid back length—pitch black hair into a ponytail as he started to tell me his side of the story. His periwinkle summer blue eyes were almost white, it was either out of fear or out of desperation for his next fix…or perhaps both.

"There are two old spinster witches living in Midtown. They allow us to drink from them in return for the orgasmic pleasure of a vampires bite," Joe informed me as he was rubbing his neck for relief.

"How can that be?" I questioned. "How are you able to stop drinking without draining them?"

"They charmed their own blood for protection. After about a minute or so of drinking, the sweet taste becomes bitter and sour and then you have no choice but to stop, it's unbearable, it tastes like…death."

I somewhat believed his story. He was too panicky not to be telling the truth and his thoughts were clear. "I'll bring you to them, if you want," he added. I hesitated for a moment.

"Take me," I insisted. "Just understand one thing; your doom still hangs by a thread."

Joe looked at me with a bit of disgust that I didn't trust him the way I once did. However, he was obedient and didn't pursue an argument because he was well aware of what would happen if he did.

As Joe was putting on his shirt and shoes, I pointed to and told Helena and Ava to go and retrieve Dianna from her apartment and bring her back here to the house.

"Just tell her I got caught up in something and I'll meet her back here. She doesn't need to know the details," I ordered.

Helena, of course, nodded and left Joe's room to get dressed. Ava, on the other hand, always has to have some kind of sarcastic remark before doing something she was going to end up doing anyway.

"You finally decide to fuck your girlfriend and act as if you have the right to give orders. What makes you so high and mighty?" She said and folded her arms.

I was calmly leaning up against the wall in Joe's room with my fingers wrapped around my belt loops, waiting for him when I answered her— so matter of fact.

"First of all, don't be resentful towards me because I didn't choose *you* as my mate. Most of all, don't be disrespectful or indignant to Dianna, because that I won't tolerate by anyone. Let's be clear about one thing, the thought of *me*…ever fucking *you*…again, much less mating with *you*, was *never* going to happen—so you need to get over that, and fast. Actually, you should be thrilled that Dianna and I mated because it put me in a generous mood. Could you imagine how atrocious I would be right now if I didn't get the chance to *fuck* my girlfriend?"

That was a dig directly to Joe and he knew it. I saw him nod his head in agreement while he was putting on his shoes. Obviously, he was well aware of his fate if he completed the mission he set out to do to Dianna.

I stared deep into Ava's eyes, "Now go, and do what you're told," I snarled. My stare must have been more intimidating than I realized. She timidly said that she would get dressed and go with Helena to bring Dianna to me then lowered her head and began to cower out of the room.

All of a sudden, Christopher, decided to grow a pair of balls and speak out on Ava's behalf. The guy has been a vampire for only a few months and suddenly he decided to make his presence known by debating me. Although I never actually talked to the guy since he's been here, he was here long enough to know that I wasn't the most patient or tolerant of our clan. However, we were all patient enough with Ava's charade of pretending that Christopher was her mate, when in fact we all knew that he wasn't. That was an attempt by her to try and get a rise out of me, unsuccessfully I might add. Considering there wasn't any harm done we let it go unnoticed, mainly because none of us really cared one way or the other, until right now.

Ava isn't a very good liar, she forgets that she needs permission by her creator to mate, and even if she mated without consent, we would be able to sense his blood throughout her entire being.

"You didn't need to talk like that to Ava. Who are *you* to order anyone around?" Christopher shouted.

He was either incredibly ignorant or very stupid to speak to me as loudly and arrogantly as he did. I looked up at him and smiled crookedly with a small and subtle laugh. Ava didn't have a chance to leave the room before Christopher spoke. I didn't make any eye contact with Christopher. He was on the bottom of the totem pole and wasn't worthy of an explanation. I turned to Ava and spoke evenly and directly to her about the ineptness of Christopher.

"Ava," I said and she spun around and rolled her eyes at me. "I want you to know that everyone here is aware that you and this misguided fool, never mated. There isn't any bond between the two of you. Even a human would be able to see through your charade. We also know that he was nothing more than a mistake on your part. We can't have anyone insignificant living here. There's too many of us as it is. So as far as I'm concerned, he's nothing more than a loner or a stray and if he doesn't learn his place—I'm going to rip him apart," I said, stringently.

"I'll handle it," Ava said in a quiet, nasty tone and pulled Christopher by the arm to leave the room.

"I'm not finished yet," I said just as nasty and pulled her back into the room while I was still leaning against the wall.

"You need to take responsibility for this abomination that you created," I said, pointing at Christopher. "You need to teach him our ways and our rules and quickly! If you don't...I'm going to have Joe rip out *your* fangs because of *your* stupidity for turning someone into one of us and bringing him home. If that wasn't stupid enough—you tried to pose him off as your mate, and I hate when anyone tries to insult my intelligence. Your little game is over, and you've won nothing. You might find that feeding will be difficult without the right equipment. Therefore, you better get your head out of your ass and take care of this."

I paused for a few seconds and smiled as I continued to speak condescendingly to Ava,

"Aren't you glad that I fucked my girlfriend? The two of you might be dead by now if I didn't."

Ava needed to understand in no uncertain terms that Dianna was my mate now and that these teenage games of hers were never going to work. Although, I must admit, I enjoyed rubbing Ava's face into the fact that Dianna and I were together and bound. I wanted to push all her buttons and test her limits. It was also my way of letting Joe know too that if the situation between Dianna and me turned out differently—his death would have been inevitable.

Joe joined in on the lecture between Ava and I, and asked how his name got into the conversation He wanted to know why he would be the one pulling out Ava's fangs if things got out of control.

"That's simple Joe, if I decide to let you live, you'll be indebted to me forever. A lifetime of servitude, so be prepared. You're still not off the hook just because the situation enhanced onto Ava and Christopher. The only difference is that you know when to shut the fuck up and they don't," I answered more sternly than I did the entire evening.

Joe nodded in defeat. Ava and Christopher left the room faintly without hesitation. Sebastian stayed quiet through out the whole ordeal. He just observed in one of the corners in Joe's large bedroom. It was very unlike him not to get involved to try and keep the peace among us. He kept his bounds this time, I was appreciative yet suspicious of him at the same time.

"So, are you ready to go?" Joe asked casually.

I waved my hand towards the door for him to go first and I followed. Sebastian paced himself behind us in his black silk slippers and called to me before we left.

"When you get back from wherever it is you're going, there's something important that we need to discuss."

His speech was getting more feminine with each passing day. He tried to keep his sexual preferences a secret to us, but we all know that Sebastian is gay.

"Sure, no problem," I said and motioned to Joe to lead the way out the main door. I followed behind him. Helena, Richard, Christopher and Ava were departing as well to bring Dianna home to me. Richard shut the door behind us.

"What the fuck is he doing here?" I demanded and pointed to Christopher.

"He's coming with us," Ava confirmed.

"No, he's not..." I shouted to Ava turned to Christopher and commanded, "Go back inside!"

Christopher was about to speak but I saw Ava nervously shake her head at him as a signal for him not to utter a sound. Christopher threw his hands up in the air, muttered some words to himself and went back inside.

All five of us were silent until we got into the elevator. I told Ava to stay home as well and start teaching that monstrosity that she created a few things. I also reminded Ava to consistently inform Christopher just how *lucky* he is to be alive, that I was being charitable because I believed that he was an idiot and I was in a very good mood.

Ava didn't argue with me. Before ascending to the main lobby, she pushed the button for the elevator door to open and stormed back into the apartment. As the elevator door was closing, all I could think to myself was, *I hate rookies.*

Richard and Helena are different. They are anything but rookies. They are well mannered, loyal and respectful. Richard, of course, was quiet through out the tribulation and I extended my hand to him. I thanked him for never questioning, never taking sides, and always being there when needed. I winked at Helena to acknowledge her loyalty as well. I was giving Joe the benefit of the doubt for his actions because Joe shares my blood, even back to the days when we were human. We were cousins, practically brothers. Joe may have acted impulsively most of the time, but he has never acted out intentionally against me. He was more than a kindred brother and I had to give him the chance to prove himself.

We walked through the main lobby and departed through the smoked revolving doors. Helena and Richard made a right turn and Joe and I made a left turn. Each of us en route to our destinations.

2

Ruth and Bea

Not one word passed between Joe and I during our paced walk into Midtown. All I could do was think about Dianna, and how angry and sad she was going to be when she saw Richard and Helena instead of me. I probably should have kept to our plan and picked her up myself but my curiosity got the better of me. I wanted to know where this endless supply of enchanted blood, or the more commonly known street name, "E.B" was. The thought of it was very enticing. Not only for the taste and the euphoria, but as a potential business endeavor also.

The spinster's home was located in one of the many side alleys off of Canal Street. The street was dark, gloomy, and perfect for any vampire who wanted to go unnoticed. There were about five doors along a red brick wall. These were the apartments where tenants dwelled. Most of the apartments were abandoned and dilapidated.

"This is it," Joe said and he stopped in front of the corroded door.

The last rusted steel door in the alley was where the witches lived, apartment number five.

We heard the sound of footsteps coming from inside. There was a small retractable window at the top of the door. It opened without warning and someone yelled from inside,

"Who is it, who's there?"

"Hi, Ruth. It's me, Little Joey."

I looked at Joe as if he was out of his mind. I don't think I've ever called him Joey much less, Little Joey.

"Joey? Since when do you call yourself Joey?" I said, low toned.

"They like to call me Joey, so who am I to argue?" He seemed annoyed and embarrassed.

I laughed at the thought of him actually being called, Little Joey. *He is over a century old and now he's going by a child's nickname.*

"Hello Little Joey, give me a minute and I'll let you right in," said Ruth from beyond the door. Her voice was old and snarled that it cracked in between words. It was typical of what a human would perceive a witch to sound like.

The door opened slowly before the woman who was behind it was in full view.

She was small and old, actually—very old and thin. Her short hair was the color of salt and pepper and had many bald patches of where it was falling out. Her face needed a flat iron to take out all the wrinkles, but her eyes were a sultry jade green with the slightest hint of beauty. Her attire was that of a vagabond. She wore a long white stained night garment with many tears, rips and holes. She was walking bare footed and both her finger and toe nails were yellowed and long. They were thick, calloused and looked like bird beaks.

The moment she cast her eyes upon Joe, or should I say Little Joey, she gleamed brightly. Then she noticed me, and at first, she didn't seem too enthralled that Little Joey brought company,

"Is he a friend of yours?" She asked Joe, harshly.

"Not only is he a friend, but he's my creator as well. If it weren't for him, we never would have met," Joe answered flirtatiously and smiled that pretty smile of his. If a vampire was able to get sick, I would have hurled, right then and there, all over Joe's shirt.

She checked me up and down before letting us in. She turned to Joe and said,

"Well, he is a fine…specimen." Then she smiled at me with her four rotting front teeth and let us in.

She led us down a long dark hallway into a low-lit cluttered room where her sister, Beatrice, was sitting at a worn round table indulging vigorously in what appeared to be a cooked rat. At that point, I was very thankful about a vampire's diet.

Beatrice, of course, was overjoyed to see Joey and scrutinized me up and down with a glimmer of delight.

Beatrice appeared to be slightly younger than Ruth. Her hair was silver and cut evenly around her ears. Unlike Ruth, there weren't any visible bald spots. She was overweight and from the amount of decayed food that was on table, it was easy to see why. She wore an old blue jogging suit and big round glasses.

They both had more than a few vampire bite marks visible on their skin. I can't imagine any vampire biting into these women anywhere; except where it was visible. Regardless how delectable E.B is, some things just aren't worth it.

"So Little Joey, who's your friend?" Beatrice asked, trying to be provocative.

"This is Danny. I've told you both all about him and he just couldn't wait to meet you and spoil himself in your delectable loveliness."

I had to turn my head away to keep from laughing at his suave attempt to be poetic. I couldn't believe the complete bullshit that Joe was dumping on these women. I'm not quite sure if they believed a word he said to them, but one thing for certain was that they loved hearing his luscious words. He is truly a gifted vampire. Other than his incredible speed, his charisma and charm is exceedingly above that of any other vampire. Joe could probably charm the pants off a mannequin.

"Doesn't *he* talk?" Ruth bawled, referring to me.

"He doesn't need to, just look at him, he's delicious," Beatrice infringed, happily.

I forced a weak curved smile on my face in hopes that this humiliation would end soon. I'm not one who likes to be gawked at by any one, much less an old, decrepit, sex starved witch.

"Time to get down to business," Ruth said and sat herself down. "We know why you came here today Little Joey, so let's get the show on the road." It was obvious that she was able to see through Joe's charms, but it gave her pleasure all the same.

"I want Danny to drink from me," Beatrice ordered.

She stared at me and smiled. She was trying to be seductive, but no magic in the world was going to make that happen.

Joe lunged into Ruth's neck and began to feed. The second he bit into her neck, her body began to shake and she was holding onto the arms of the old rickety chair with all her might while her old haggard body was writhing in lucid rapture. Her eyes rolled behind her head and she gasped for air.

Beatrice waved her finger for me to approach her. She cocked her neck and pointed for me to bite into her. I was really hoping just to bite her wrist but I can see that wasn't an option.

I paced toward her slowly, firmly held her jaw line and bit down hard into her dominate blue veins. I heard her gasp. I took a big swallow and the repulsiveness of these women seemed to vanish. The taste was amazingly saccharine. And I was in pure rapture. The feeling a vampire received from drinking E.B was indescribable. It was rejuvenating, satisfying and sent a rush of energy through the veins.

I could have drained this woman within minutes if I was given the chance. Then just as Joe warned me earlier, after about a minute, the taste became bitter. I had no choice but to extract my fangs from Beatrice's neck and spit out the foul blood.

"Not too much," Beatrice said coyly. "We want to make sure you come back for another round. Don't behave like Little Joey where we would have to cut you off."

She smiled at me and blew me a kiss with her hand. I was sickened by this gesture but I didn't want to offend two old cranky witches. I just smiled at her shyly and motioned my head to remove my hair from my face.

"I just love the strong quiet type," Beatrice stated and gawked at me with hunger in her eyes.

It was apparent to Joe that these women were annoying me and he intervened,

"We have to go, but we'll be back," he said and I nodded in agreement.

Ruth got up from the old rickety chair and we started walking down the long hallway.

She escorted us out and thanked us for our company, "Goodnight, gorgeous," Joe said.

Ruth smiled and her eyes glistened at the sound of Joe's kind words. Joe knew how to lay it on thick. Apparently, they welcomed his flirtations, despite how phony they were.

As for me, I couldn't get out of there fast enough. I walked out first and waited for Joe. I just wanted to get back home and see Dianna. I never appreciated her as much as I did at that moment. I wanted to see her and hold her, but E.B is such a strong and rare drug for vampires that we embrace it whenever we can out of fear and desperation; afraid that it won't be accessible ever again. Just like any drug addiction, you tend to forget your priorities and E.B is addicting from the very first swallow. The mere thought of E.B can take control of the reasonable perspective of the mind.

However, the true reason that I wanted to meet these women was to make money. Distributing E.B to other addicted vampires could be a very profitable business.

Once Ruth shut the door in front of us, I told Joe that I wanted to open up a club for vampires much like *Hell on Earth*. With the one exception, having a supply of E.B. I guess Dianna and her bookshop did in fact, inspire to me to run my own business. If Joe could convince these women to come and share the taste of their blood with other vampires, we, as a clan, could gain a lot of power among our kind.

Now that I was bound to Dianna, it was more than likely that my *Hell On Earth* clubbing days were over. I still needed a place to gamble and socialize with my own kind, other than my kindred clan. I wasn't giving up my social life that easily, I still wanted to do the things I liked to do, despite the fact that Dianna is now in my life for eternity. A new business was a winning situation for us both. Dianna will be happy because I'm not at *Hell on Earth*. As for me, it'll be the same as it always was, just a different address. I don't have to sacrifice anything, but she didn't need to know that. It's just another winning hand on my part. Vampires aren't that much different from humans when it comes to partying and being among our own kind, we are just more intense about it.

Joe was indebted to me, he owed me his life for not killing him. I wanted to be repaid, so he had to do all he can to make this plan fly.

Sebastian owned a lot of commercial real estate in the city, so getting the right place wasn't going to be an issue. Every piece of property that Sebastian owned was vampire friendly.

"So Little Joey," I said mockingly while striding down the alley and back into the core of Midtown. "Do you think your girlfriends will go for the idea?"

Joe put on a twisted smile before laughing at himself in a cunning manner,

"I think I can talk them into it," Joe said, without much concern. "There is just one thing that might cause a problem," he insinuated.

"What's that Little Joey?" I asked.

"First of all, stop calling me Little Joey," he sounded embarrassed and continued. "They don't leave the house. They haven't left there in years."

"We can get them a new place within the business. I'll set something up. The last thing I want to see is those two wretched things walking the streets. I commend them for not leaving the house."

"Payment might be more than the price of a orgasmic vampire bite to get them to leave the only place they have ever known," Joe said, seriously.

I was well aware what he was insinuating. However, that wasn't going to be *my* problem.

"I hope you enjoy fucking their brains out then," I directly implied. "Just make it work."

I wasn't joking about my implication. If that's what he had to do to get the project rolling, he was going to do it. He knew me well enough to know—I wasn't kidding.

"Death might be the better option," Joe said in defeat but then laughed at his usual quick wit. He probably wasn't joking about that either.

We continued to walk back to Park Ave at the average human pace. Fortunately, we worked out many of our differences. Joe admitted that he was nervous about seeing Dianna again. He didn't know how she was going to react to his presence when she seen him.

"Do you want me to stay out of her sight and just stay away from home until she leaves?" Joe asked with much apprehension before I answered him.

"Joey, I mean—Little Joey; she's my mate now so she will be living with me. Do you really think I'm going to let her leave now that I got her back? You know better than that. Just come inside and we'll work it out. She'll be alright, she has to be. Just don't ever let me catch you anywhere near her alone, because then I will kill ya."

Joe nodded nervously and fixed his long silken ponytail, "Can you stop calling me Little Joey now?" He asked in order to change the subject and snickered.

I smiled at his awkwardness and said, "I don't know Little Joey, we'll see." Then I paused briefly and asked him sarcastically, "Just how little is your dick that your girlfriends call you Little Joey?"

"Fuck you!" He shouted. He was really getting pissed off and to be honest, it gave me a sense of pleasure.

Despite the fact that we worked our way through our diversity, I was still outraged and infuriated by what he did to Dianna. I was just being refined about it. I needed Joe to get those witches to cooperate so my business could be a success. I had to keep a level head and keep all my outrage and anger caged inside. If Joe fucked up one more time, I would probably be sent over the edge and kill him without question. I hold grudges and I never forget when someone has wronged me. Even though Joe and I were and still are, thick as thieves, my outlook applied to him as well.

Joe was more than positive that he wasn't going to live down the incident with Dianna for a very long time. If not, forever. And he was right in his assumption. If the worse thing I was going to do to him was call him Little Joey, he should consider himself lucky.

We stopped to feed before we went home. The small amount of blood that we received from the spinster witches wasn't a hardly a meal and it wasn't meant to be sustained as food.

3

Passing the Throne

When we finally reached our building, I was actually getting excited and a little anxious about seeing Dianna. I raced inside and down the elevator before Joe stepped one foot through the revolving doors. I only left her a few hours ago but it seemed so much longer. I missed her.

I opened the front door as slowly and quietly as I could. I wanted her to be a little surprised by my arrival. When I looked inside, there she was. She was standing in front of the black leather sectional couch that stood about five or six feet away from the front door. The back of the couch faced the door so she wasn't able to see me. Even though all I had seen was the back of her head, I couldn't help but smile vibrantly. I couldn't wait to hold her in my arms again. We were apart for so long that I wanted to make up for lost time and touch her at every chance I could get.

Everyone was in the living room, even Christopher and Ava. They were playing what appeared to be *Trivial Pursuit* and Dianna was reading a question to Sebastian. As she was reading the trivia question, I jumped over the couch and grabbed her waste and said, "There's my baby."

She turned around swiftly and I was taken in by her smile. It gleamed brighter than a million stars. She leaped up into my arms and securely wrapped her legs around my waist. She wore a knee length black flair lace and gauze dress that was very witch-like. The top of the dress was tight fitting and her breasts were looking very appetizing. She looked more beautiful than she usually did.

I lifted her from her buttocks and pulled her closer to me,

"I like the dress, it makes for easy access. I want you to always wear a dress from now on," I said as I slipped my hands underneath to touch her silky skin. However, I didn't get to touch her silky skin—only her silky underwear.

"I love the way you look, feel and smell—except for one thing. The damn underwear. You really need to get over the underwear fetish and lose them," I discreetly whispered into her ear. I knew how shy she was about being blatantly sexual, even though she took so much pleasure in it when it was actually being executed.

I smiled at her and kissed her devotedly on her voluptuous lips. She responded with just as much force, if not more.

When our lips parted, she hugged me tightly and laid her head gently on my shoulder. I held her close while she played with my hair softly and lovingly with her hands and finger tips. The scent of her hair was so sweet and seductive, the only thing running through my mind at that moment was being intimate with her again. Nothing or nobody else in that room mattered at that moment. We had each other and everything around us seemed to blur or disappear. Whenever we touched or looked at one another it was always magical.

Dianna was so child like, and I admired that quality. Her innocent and naive ways were so captivating and alluring that I wanted to take her at that very moment.

She was resting at ease in my arms, her head was relaxed comfortably on my shoulder when suddenly, I felt her entire body tighten up like a snake strangling it prey.

She quietly slid down from my grip, nestled her head into my chest, and held on forcefully to my Rolling Stones T-shirt. I leaned back to see what it was that disturbed her, only to see that Joe had entered the room. He was courteous enough to sit on the large throne like recliner that was placed in the corner of the room by the front door. I leaned my head down, kissed the top her head, and whispered to her that everything would be fine and she was safe. I caressed her hair gently, brought her back around the couch by the hand, and sat her down next to me. I kept my arms tightly around her as she cuddled into my chest and arms. As much as I adored her child like ways, I hated to see her so genuinely scared. It was times like these that I wished I punished Joe more severely. The moment she saw him, her entire being locked down and I automatically resented Joe for that.

Joe's eyes were ill at ease when he saw how Dianna reacted and the tension in the room grew. It was so thick that you could cut a knife through it. Everyone felt it and we all sat quietly and waited for someone to break the ice. Joe tried by saying, "I gotta get going, I forgot to do something. I'll be back later."

It was obvious that he was leaving for Dianna's sake, and I gave him a little recognition for somehow trying to rectify the awkward and difficult situation that he created.

At that moment, Sebastian decided that he was the one who was going to loosen things up. He got up from his seat quickly and extravagantly and presented himself in the middle of the room. He was still wearing the same silk pajamas that he had on when I left with Joe.

"No, you're not leaving Joseph, now sit down!" Sebastian ordered in a gleeful way. "I have an announcement to make and you need to hear this too, it concerns all of you." He turned his head toward all of us.

Joe did as directed and sat back down in the corner of the room to keep from Dianna's sight.

I was assuming that this was the news that Sebastian was going to share with me earlier. However, he evidently believed that this would be the best time to release some of the pressure in the room, and say it to all of us. There weren't many secrets between us as a clan. So for Sebastian to include everyone was more than normal.

We all stared at him quietly as he took center stage. When I saw Sebastian standing there with so much conviction and presence, I couldn't help but comment,

"Do you want a microphone because you look like you're going to burst into song any second."

Then Joe made a sarcastic yet harmless comment as well, "Could it possibly be *Somewhere Over The Rainbow?*"

Everyone, even Sebastian, snickered lightly at the remark. Dianna even managed to release a small and cute giggle, much like a toddlers laugh. I kissed her forehead and smiled down at her contentedly as she looked up at me and smiled back. She still wouldn't let go of my T-shirt or me for that matter. It was as if she was holding on to the edge of a cliff hoping she won't fall. I must admit that I didn't mind that she was holding me so deeply, I only wished that she wasn't holding me out of fear.

Sebastian was a good sport and actually sang the first line of *Somewhere over the Rainbow,* and shockingly, he sang it well. Then he earnestly told us to settle down because what he wanted to say was important and we all needed to hear it. We all respected him very much and allowed him to speak without interruption. Even Christopher was on his best behavior.

"I've come to a decision, I've been head of this household and making the decisions that apply to all of us for a very long time, and I'm getting tired. Therefore, I decided to step down and pass the torch down to Danato," he paused. "I hope you all respect this decision and honor it."

We were all speechless.

I don't think any of us saw that coming, especially me. Although it was quite an honor to be Sebastian's predecessor, and the power I would have was intriguing, I wasn't sure that I wanted such responsibility.

I subtly let Dianna go and sat her down, before I stood up to face Sebastian and walked over to him. Since nobody was going to say anything, I felt that I should be the one to speak up,

"Why are you doing this?"

Sebastian seemed content in his judgment but gave us the respect and privilege of explaining his reasons for such a drastic action. Once a vampire steps down and passes the torch, they can't go back.

"Honestly, I have been thinking about this for a long time and I wasn't sure if you were ready to handle the responsibility that comes along with being the superior of a clan, until today. You handled the situation with Joseph fairly and sternly. You did well."

"Does this mean that you'll be leaving?" Richard asked with much concern.

"Oh no, I'm not going anywhere. I just want to be the elder vampire who stays in the shadows and gives advice and prophesizes all day. I want to take my monthly weekend excursions and make them weekly. I think almost two-hundred years of worrying about everyone before myself is enough, would you all agree?" He paused briefly, we all nodded in agreement and he continued. "I want time for myself now. I don't like to be alone any more than any of you. I want to find happiness. I've taught you all very well and I know Danato will be a fine leader. This is a day for celebration!"

What was I able to say to that? He always put us before himself. Therefore, I extended my hand to him in gratitude. He smiled and hugged me like a *father to a son.*

Then, out of nowhere, Christopher felt obligated to open his mouth and comment on the transformation, "Why Danny? What makes *him* so worthy?"

He was rude and haughty in his questioning.

Who the fuck does he think he is?

It took everything inside me not to rip him apart. Sebastian intervened swiftly because everyone in that room, even Dianna, believed Christopher was out of line with his comments. If eyes could talk, this would be *The Jerry Springer Show*. The random thoughts they were going through everyone's mind were overwhelming. I sat back down next to Dianna and held her close to me.

"Everyone calm down," Sebastian ordered. "It's a fair question. This is all new to Christopher and he doesn't fully understand our ways yet. I don't mind explaining them to him."

Before he continued with his explanation, he told me to sit down and wanted all of us to listen also. Sebastian loved being the center of attention and right about now—he was eating this up. He turned to face Christopher,

"It's like this Christopher, Danato is the only one here that I created, and he's the eldest, it starts from there and works it way down the line and rightfully so."

Before Sebastian could go on with the family history, Joe decided to put his two cents in,

"I'm curious Sebastian, the day you turned Danny, why did you choose him? I was there also. Why Danny?"

"I heard Danato in that infirmary every night that he was there, begging for life and death at the same time. He was a man who wanted so much to live but didn't want pain in his life and wasn't afraid to die. I was able to save him from the pain and give him the new life that he left Italy for. I gave him both...life and death. As for you...all you did was cry."

Joe was slightly embarrassed but laughed because Sebastian's statement was true. However, Joe being Joe, had to take Sebastian's explanation and turn it into a joke because he didn't come out looking too good in the story.

"Oh, well, we all thought that you wanted Danny in *other ways*, if you know what I mean—"

Everyone chortled a little bit because that thought has gone through everyone's head, at least once.

I interrupted with good intent and said, "Something as good looking as me has to live forever. What a waste it would be if I died."

"I agree," Sebastian said. "You are beautiful, if nothing else."

"I told you Sebastian wanted you and that's why he turned you," Joe teased.

I wasn't going to let Joe's remark go unanswered without some kind of come back,

"Not everyone could be as beautiful as you, *LITTLE JOEY*."

That was all I had to say to shut him up and nobody had any idea what the hell I was talking about.

Dianna just looked at me and rolled her eyes at my arrogance, but she managed to put on a grateful smile that I was still alive to be with her.

Christopher still had some questions. His tone mellowed and we all believed that he asked these questions because he was genuine about learning our ways.

"I want to be sure I have this right, all of you were sick and dying when you changed over?"

"Yeah, weren't you?" I asked.

"No," he answered firmly.

"Were you homeless or something like that?" I asked again with seriousness.

"No," he confirmed again and shook his head. "I had two or three dates with Ava. The last thing I remember in my human life was fooling around with her in the car. Then the next day, I woke up here. I didn't know what the fuck was going on and I wasn't sure about anything. I thought it was all I dream and I'd wake up back in Brooklyn by the morning."

Everyone got very still after Christopher summarized his story. Each individual clan had their own set of rules. We believe that the only time you turn a human is when they are sick and dying or if it's something that they really want. In either case, we don't want them to have any ties to family and friends. We go to large extremes to keep our identities hidden from the human world. The last thing we want is for a vampire to have human loved ones only to find them as one of us.

Christopher shrugged and continued, we were all more than eager to hear the rest of his tale.

"I never wanted this. I had a decent life when I was human. That's why I've been going back to Brooklyn and changing some of my human friends into one of us. I miss them."

Everyone was stunned by that revelation. Helena dropped the television remote. Richard jumped from his chair, and Joe gradually walked closer to Christopher. I removed Dianna's head from my chest, stood up slowly, and glared demonically at Ava before I turned my attention back to Christopher.

"I have just one more question for you, Christopher," I asked. "How did you know how to turn a human into a vampire?"

"Ava told me what to do," he answered quickly.

We all looked at Ava for a reaction. Her head was lowered as she tried to get up from her seat and attempt to slither out of the room without being noticed. I turned to Sebastian,

"Do you want to handle this?" I asked him, in hopes that he would.

"No, I'm retired. You'll do what needs to be done," he answered confidently as he sat quietly back on the couch and began to play a game of solitaire.

I pulled Ava from the back of her hair and threw her across the room and into the fireplace. I reached over and slapped her across the face,

"You stupid bitch!" I shouted.

She sat with her knees up and cowering up against the marble mantle.

Dianna jumped from her seat and ran to Ava.

"Danny, stop!" Dianna said meekly as she bent down towards Ava and extended her hand to help her.

I quickly snapped Dianna back and pulled her out of Ava's reach.

"This doesn't concern you, now go sit down!" I commanded.

"Get off me!" Dianna yelled and went to reach for Ava again.

I pulled her by the arm and held it tightly,

"You're hurting me!" She pleaded.

"I know I am, that's why I want you to go with Sebastian," I said harshly.

Sebastian and I both had advanced telepathic qualities. We were able to communicate with each other through our minds and we were able to control this extraordinary power at will. I mentally informed Sebastian that I had already read Christopher's thoughts and I didn't like what I saw.

Christopher is hateful toward Ava for doing this to him. He is seeking revenge.

He nodded in agreement.

Once it became evident that Christopher's was bitter at Ava, it was necessary to know what he was thinking.

It was apparent that Dianna wasn't going to walk away from this either, therefore, Sebastian approached her humbly and said,

"Come with me Dianna, I don't believe you ever seen this side of the house before," he pointed down the hall. "I have an enormous library that you would just love!"

He put his arm around her shoulders and led her down the hallway. Dianna wouldn't disrespect Sebastian's wishes. However, she made sure to glance at me with narrowed eyes one more time before she reluctantly walked down the hallway with him.

She was angry and the devilish onyx color of her eyes said it all. That was just one more thing on my plate that I would have to deal with on this day of havoc.

At this point, everyone was on the same page. We are all able to read minds, but my abilities are more advanced than the others. I was aware that everyone tuned into Christopher's thoughts. We all have qualities that exceed the others. I have advanced telepathy and I have incredible strength, which was why I usually have the pleasure of doing the dirty work.

As I said before, Joe is extraordinarily fast and is extremely charismatic. No one could resist Little Joey. We all have the ability to hypnotize humans but Richard has the rare power to hypnotize *vampires*, with just one look into his eyes. Helena can allure anyone into her grasp and she is one of the few vampires that can shift change into just about anything, although she didn't like to talk about it that much. As for Ava, other than being incredibly stupid, we still didn't know what great power she possessed.

Christopher and Ava sat nervously with their mouths sealed while I watched Dianna and Sebastian walk down the hallway and fade out of sight before I made my next move.

"Everyone into the kitchen!" I commanded.

"Why the kitchen?" Joe asked in a low whisper.

"Because the rug in here is white and blood stains," I answered under my breath, but loud enough for Joe to hear.

I walked in first through the kitchen doors.

I leaned up against the refrigerator and instructed Joe and Richard to sit Christopher down at the kitchen table. They both stood on each side of him. Helena and Ava stood directly across from me, leaning against the stainless steel stove.

"Do we all know why we're here and what we have to do?" I asked and everyone nodded, except for Ava and Christopher.

"I don't know why we're in here," Christopher asked self-importantly. "What are *you* going to do?"

"Because Christopher," I began to lecture. "Ava obviously never got around to tell you about a vampire's mind reading ability. Everyone in this room can read minds, and since you're so brand new, you don't have any control over your thoughts. We know that you've been turning humans into vampires to seek out and build a clan of your own—to bring wrath and revenge to us. We know it's because Ava did this to you, without warning, and you're angry. I'm aware that your intentions are justifiably so, however, this I can not allow. For the sake of my clan."

I walked behind Christopher and motioned for Joe and Richard to hold down each of his arms. Then unexpectedly, quiet, well obedient, Mr. "Never-Cause-Trouble", Richard—belted a close-fisted punch into Christopher's face and possibly broke his nose in the process. Everyone looked at him stunned and speechless. Christopher was wallowing in pain, Richard stared at all of us and smiled, and Helena looked kind of turned on by his recklessness.

"I never really liked the guy," Richard said before holding down Christopher's right arm.

We all remained hesitant for a few seconds and looked at Richard oddly. Then, just as quickly Joe was standing at Christopher's left side and held down his arm, "Get the fuck off of me!" Christopher yelled while I walked around behind his head. Joe and Richard pushed his arms down harder than before and started to laugh sadistically at him. I placed both my hands on his head. He tried to squirm his way out of my grip.

"Danny! Please, don't do this to him! This is all my fault!" Ava interrupted the moment in his defense. "I should be punished! Not him!" I quickly glanced at Ava, "Don't worry, you will be." I agreed sternly.

"What are—" Christopher started, but before he could finish his sentence, I snapped his neck on both sides before decapitating him. I jumped back quickly to keep the blood from getting all over me. Once you do something like that a couple of times, you learn when to get out of the way. My shirt and neck got a little drenched with blood, but nothing too bad.

I walked over to the sink took off my blood stained shirt and washed my face and neck. I quickly dried my face and ordered Joe and Richard to dismember Christopher and throw all his remains into the furnace that was located in the outside hallway, beyond the front door.

"Why?" Joe questioned once again. He was really starting to get on my nerves.

"So he fits into the furnace asshole!" I yelled. "I'll be right back."

"You're not going to help us?" Joe asked, obviously annoyed.

"I did enough," I said as I stomped out of the kitchen. The reason I left so abruptly was because I sensed Dianna leaving the library and was starting to make her way down the hallway. I ran down the corridor at my top vampire speed to stop her in her tracks. I was in front of her before she realized I was there.

"Where ya going baby?" I said with a smile, trying not to look like I just decapitated someone.

"The kitchen, I'm thirsty," she said as she kept trying to crawl under my arms as I was blocking the entire hallway to keep her from passing.

Then she stared at me peculiarly and asked, "Where is your shirt and why is your hair wet?"

"I was hot," I answered hastily.

"You don't get hot!" She said with a real nasty tone.

"That isn't what you said last night," I smiled at her deviously and tried to kiss her, but she turned her head.

"Don't kiss me," she said and put on her best baby pout and crossed her arms. "I'm not even speaking to you!"

"That's okay, but I need for you to *not speak to me* from the library," I said, very calm yet serious and pointed down the hall. However, that doesn't mean she wasn't still pissed off at me.

She turned around in a huff and stormed down the hallway to go back to the library, but not before she gave me the middle finger to inform me just how pissed off she was.

I'll take care of that with her later, I thought to myself and rushed back into the kitchen to deal with Ava.

When I got back in the kitchen, Joe and Richard were already finished dismembering Christopher, and they were dumping his remains into the furnace. Helena leaned calmly against the stove biting her nails, and fiddling with her rings, while Ava was sitting on the counter shivering and shaking. She looked more like a ghost than a vampire at that moment and she jumped the moment she saw me.

"Don't worry Ava, I'm not going to kill you," I said, able to read her mind. "I just have a few questions for you."

She nodded and I continued to rant.

"You realize that Xavier, who leads in Brooklyn is going to be on my ass now because you and Christopher were in Brooklyn changing humans into vampires and putting a small dent into his food supply. He's also going to wonder why we, as a clan, are turning humans in Brooklyn. He's going to think that I'm trying to invade his territory and build up a clan there. Also he's been trying to find an excuse to cause trouble ever since I took Sergio's fangs for drinking in our territory. Do you understand the seriousness of this?"

Before she could answer, Joe and Richard came back in from the furnace. Richard reported to me that it was all taken care of. I nodded in satisfaction and turned my attention back to Ava.

"Well, do you understand?" I asked more serious than I did the first time and she simply nodded yes.

"Good, then you'll understand why I have to take your fangs."

"No!" She screamed.

"Joe take her fangs," I insisted.

"No!" Ava yelped again. "Please, I'm sorry…"

"Are you really going to do that to her?" Joe questioned me for the last time.

"Joe, you've been questioning me all night and it's really pissing me off, more than you know. Honestly, someone who is walking on as much thin ice as you, shouldn't be questioning a thing unless…you wanna take her place?"

That put an end to the questions and remarks. I wasn't fucking around anymore and they all knew that. Richard walked behind Ava and pulled her head back by the hair.

"I'm sorry about this…" Joe whispered to Ava as he frowned and reluctantly reached into her mouth and pulled out her fangs.

Ava shrieked.

She quickly grabbed a dish towel, covered up her mouth to stop the blood and ran out of the kitchen.

The kitchen was a bloody mess. I told Helena to get the humans that dwelled in the house as donors to clean it up. She did as instructed immediately.

I spoke out to all of them and said,

"I'm done now. I don't want to hear any opinions or strategy right now. We'll talk about it tomorrow. Right now, I just want to take a shower and I don't want to be disturbed until sunset."

I left the kitchen and walked to the library to get Dianna, yet another obstacle.

There she was, sitting in one of the antique wing chairs reading a book. I leaned in the doorway with my arms holding onto the door moldings and asked her, "Are you still pissed at me baby?"

She snubbed me and turned her nose up before she looked away from me.

"Well, I guess you are," I was very calm and more than aware of the little game that she was playing.

"Okay then, I'm going to take a shower. When you're done being pissed off, feel free to join me," I was cocky, but I wasn't giving into her nonsense, not now.

I exited the doorway and walked down the hallway slowly to see if she was going to follow. She didn't. However, I heard her throw whatever book she was reading across the room. That gave me some satisfaction. I smiled to myself knowing that she was never as mad at me as she let on. She took pleasure in adding fuel to the fire. She liked to push my buttons while being delicately flirtatious.

She wanted me to baby her, but that wasn't going to happen, at least not at that moment. As a matter fact, her little hissy fit put me in a better mood. Dianna forgets to realize that I could play head games too. I silently laughed to myself all the way into the private shower that was part of my room. That was part of her charm and why she is the most precious thing in my life.

She never did join me in the shower as I requested, but she was waiting for me in my bed. Before I could join her she stopped me, "Here's your wallet back," she said and handed me back my wallet.

It was lighter than usual.

"You spent some cash I see, what did you get?" I asked cheerfully. I wanted to spoil her rotten.

She leaned over the bed and reached into a shopping bag from Saks Fifth that was laying on the floor, beside the bed.

"I got a new robe!" She exclaimed and held it up for me to see, it was nice, sexy and…pink.

"And I got you this," she handed me a new black alligator wallet. I scrutinized it, it was nice and expensive.

"Thanks for thinking about me," I smirked and laid it down on the desk.

"Well, aren't you going to use it?"

"This one still has some life in it," I said holding up my old battered wallet and placed it down on my desk. I pulled of the towel that I had wrapped around my waist, got into bed with her and laid down.

"You don't like it, do you?" She pouted.

"I do, now stop talking," I said as I kissed her to silence her and she immediately responded, forgetting about our earlier quarrel and the wallet.

Needless to say, we did share another passionate night of intensity together, as we always would when we were in bed together.

4

Trick or Treat

The next two weeks were moving along smoothly and Dianna moved in with me. She was a little uncomfortable at first but slowly tried to fit in. She would have preferred me to move into her place but that was an impossibility. Considering the fact that Sebastian just made me head of the household, I couldn't leave even if I wanted to. Also, Dianna's apartment wasn't vampire friendly, it was much too sunny and it didn't make much sense for me to leave Park Ave just to hide in a dark corner and she understood. However, she still kept her apartment in the village. It was her first taste of independence and she didn't want to let it go. She wanted a place to call her own, something that belonged to her only. She also kept up with her bookshop. She was very proud of her success and I understood why it meant so much to her. She didn't go as often as she did before, but it was something for her to do during the day. Her appearances at her night time Wicca workshops were cut from six days a week to just one or two. To be frank, I didn't really like the idea of Dianna ever being without me but she was lucky enough to enjoy the daylight hours, so who was I to deprive her of that luxury? I wanted to give her anything she wanted, spoil and baby her unmercifully. Her happiness means everything to me and I would do whatever it takes to keep her that way.

She questioned the sudden disappearance of Christopher and the excuse I gave her was that he and Ava lied about being mates so he was asked to leave. How could I tell her what really happened? She wasn't ready to hear things like that yet. She also questioned why Ava's fangs were removed and I was mostly honest about that. I told Dianna that because of Ava's deceit about Christopher, removing her fangs were a necessary course of action. Dianna believed it was a harsh judgment, but she didn't know the whole story or our ways. She felt sorry for Ava, but I reassured her that Ava's fangs would grow back in time and she would be just fine. They were already starting to come back.

I still haven't heard from Xavier from Brooklyn as of yet, but that would manifest within its own time. Sebastian offered one of his many commercial buildings for all of us to be part of this business venture. He vowed to let us run it our way without any interference. His only condition was that our entire clan had to be a part of it and we agreed to those terms. That was never an issue. Despite our arguing and daily brawls, we were a loyal and noble bunch. Everyone was content with the conditions, if for no other reason than to have change in our lives. Eternity is….well…eternal…and we had to have some kind of diversity in our ongoing existence.

Joe needed to do his part and convince the two old decrepit, wart-infested witches to do their part as well; otherwise, this idea probably wouldn't fly. A vampire business needed to have something unique to survive against the rare but few places that were in existence, and an ongoing supply of E.B had just that.

It was Halloween and Dianna told me about a party that she had planned with her book group during her human masquerade. I truly didn't want to go or have any part of a human event, but it meant a lot to her. In my eyes, humans are nothing more than food and pets, so why would I want to spend an evening with them? It was inevitable that my mate would be a witch, a vampire or some other kind of mystical creature, because I disrespected humans that much. Dianna felt indebted to these humans because they helped her to function daily during my absence. I guess a small part of me was thankful to them for being a part of her life and watching over her, like the loyal pets they are meant to be. I hated the idea of Dianna being alone and scared, and I must admit, I suffered with a lot of guilt about that and I still do. The horrible way I treated her and the disgusting things I said to her still haunt me. Dianna has done everything I've asked of her, so I couldn't deny her this one small favor. Therefore, I told her that I would go just for an hour. This little act of kindness on my part excited her to the utmost extreme. That was enough for me. I loved seeing her smile and watching those beautiful stormy gray eyes of hers shine.

We were both in my room. She was getting dressed while I was on the computer playing internet Texas Hold Em' waiting for her.

"I'm ready, let's go," I heard her say.

I turned to get out of my chair and when I saw her, I almost forgotten just how stunning she is. She looked absolutely gorgeous.

She wore an subtle orange,—over the top—,sexy, corseted shirt with see-through tight lace sleeves. She had on a strapless black bra underneath that was visible to the eye, black lace and silk mini skirt that complimented with the flat over the knee leather boots. Her eyes were gleaming brighter than usual and her hair shined brighter than every light on Broadway. I lost control of my senses, she was hypnotic. I stared at her endlessly as I sat in my faded jeans, Jim Morrison T-shirt and steel toe work boots.

"Are you okay?" She asked.

I was hesitant about answering her because at that moment I was in an erotic trance.

"Uhhh…yeah, I'm okay. It's just that you look so…hot."

I got up from the desk chair and took hold of her hands,

"Let me look at you," I said as I twirled her around to see the front and back of her. Then I pulled her in my arms and kissed her deeply. She responded but backed off before things got heated.

"Wouldn't you just rather stay here so I can rip off your clothes? That is the look you're going for, right?" I said while raising an eyebrow. She was still locked in my arms and smiled with a small amount of evilness only because she was flattered.

Her cheeks turned a little red and said, "No," as she broke free of my grasp and put on her slim fitting leather jacket.

"Let's go," she added.

"Okay. We'll go, but I have to ask you one thing, and I can't believe I'm going to ask this…"

She had a puzzled and concerned look on her face as I spoke.

"Please tell me that you're wearing underwear?" I asked.

She laughed cutely and lifted her skirt to show me that she was. I was relieved.

The one thing I didn't want to deal with was a bunch of humans pawing all over her. Witches have an uncontrollable alluring ability around humans. The mere thought of male humans slobbering around her made me more than a little uptight. However, I wasn't going to say anything to her about that. She didn't need to know that I had a fragment of vulnerability and insecurity.

I would try my hardest to let her enjoy her night and get through this one hour of torment with her. Although I couldn't make any promises to myself that my jealous and possessive nature wouldn't get the better of me.

Dianna loved the fall weather and wanted to walk. I was more than willing to accommodate because I wasn't in any rush to get there.

As we walked arm in arm down to her shop we indulged in simple conversation.

"Why do you hate Halloween?" She asked, although I never told her that I hated it, but I guess it was obvious that the day didn't matter to me one way or the other.

"I don't hate it. I just think it's stupid. A bunch of humans dressed as vampires and witches, trying to be something they're not. To be honest, I find their perception of vampires insulting."

"What do you mean?"

"We don't walk around with black capes, black suites and our hair slicked back with blood dripping from our mouths. Don't you get a little offended by the way they perceive witches? Green faces, black pointy hats and warts all over the place?"

"No, not really," she answered. "It's all for fun. As a matter of fact, I think we both should have worn costumes!"

She put on her most pathetic face and batted her eyes to try to look cuter than she already was.

I laughed at her silliness. I then extended my fangs and showed them to her.

"Now I'm dressed as a vampire, are you happy?"

She giggled and said, "You can pull that off with your teeth but what kind of costume can I come up with during a walk?"

I stopped walking and turned her around. I pulled her towards me, tilted her neck, and bit down lightly and delicately, barely breaking the skin. Leaving two small red vampire teeth marks.

"You can be my victim. Now we're in costume."

She smiled bashfully and she was overjoyed by my small amount of participation.

We finally arrived and I must admit I was more than a little apprehensive about being part of this fiasco. I'm not much of a socialist among my own kind, much less humans, UGH. I consider them as food, toys and pets, nothing more. In my opinion, humans were beneath Dianna and I regardless of any friendships or loyalties made to her. I don't think Dianna realized how hard this was going to be for me. However, I promised to see it through for her sake. I put my pride aside and held the door opened for her as she walked in and I followed behind her. All the dread that I had inside of me came to surface.

There were about ten people there and everyone seemed to be in couples. There was the typical and predictable woman dressed as a sexy witch, but no one sexier than my witch. She was there with her partner who ironically was dressed as Dracula. Dianna introduced them to me as Heather and Steven. It was difficult for me to look at them without bursting into laughter.

However, I managed to compose myself and shook their hands like a gentleman. I held on to Dianna. She stood in front of me as I held her around her waist. Dianna was actually my safety net in this particular situation. Holding onto her kept me calm and rational. If I removed my grip from her, I'm not quite sure how I would have behaved in a room full of delicacies.

"How come the two of you aren't in costume?" Steven asked with much enthusiasm.

"We're in costume," Dianna answered and showed him her bite

marks. "Show him your teeth baby," she said as she elbowed me in the stomach.

I did what she asked and flashed my fangs for Steven and Heather to look at.

"Great teeth!" Heather said.

"They look so real," Steven agreed. "Where did you get those?"

Dianna immediately answered, "Party City, where else?"

I faked a smile at this charade and let them ramble on. This was more grueling than I thought possible but I didn't let on to Dianna just how dismal I thought this masquerade was. My fangs were being used and displayed as a party prop.

Within a few minutes, Dianna's arrival became evident and the rest of these insignificant beings found it necessary to hug and kiss her hello. In which she responded hesitantly.

With every meaningless hug and kiss she was receiving, I was finding it harder and harder to excuse this behavior. I turned my head so I couldn't see them touch what rightfully *belonged to me*. The rage inside me was building up and I didn't want to explode and create a scene. I was thankful that there weren't more people there and these inconsequential gestures of affection ended quicker than I thought.

Dianna sensed my uneasiness and we walked over to the large buffet table hand in hand. There wasn't any one standing there so it seemed like a relatively safe place.

"Are you alright?" She whispered sincerely.

"Never better," I whispered sarcastically. "Let's just say you owe me big for this." I said with a smile as I watched her eat a taco.

"We'll see," she said with risen eyebrows and reached for a chocolate cupcake with orange frosting mounted on top.

Things were going well for a small amount of time because it was Dianna and I. We were both in our own realm within the party. She consumed a lot of food. I didn't think it possible that someone as tiny as her could eat so much. It was kind of astonishing. Other than the taco and cupcake she devoured: potato chips, nachos, an apple and a beer.

"You better not get big and fat on me!" I was kidding when I said that but there was a little seriousness in it too. Then I gave her a sweet subtle kiss on the cheek.

"It'll just be more of me to love," she answered sweetly as she took a big bite out of a chocolate chip cookie.

We both smiled and laughed. I was starting to feel a bit more at ease because there wasn't anyone around to annoy me. Until Steven and Heather deemed it obligatory to join us.

"So big guy," Steven said to me and smacked me on the back while I wasn't looking. "Do you want a beer or something?"

I wasn't expecting to be touched. My first reaction was to snap my head back defensively to see who had the audacity to touch me. Apparently my eyes turned red, because Steven complemented them as a great touch to the supposed costume I was wearing. The only thing I could do to keep myself tame was to pull Dianna closer to me. She was my only means of stability at that point. I would never put her in harms way and with her in my arms, I knew I wouldn't attack. I was frustrated and felt like I was being deliberately tormented and tested. Although, I was well aware that it wasn't anything like that. It was just human nature to try and be hospitable.

"No man, I'm good," I answered without making eye contact with him, he was irritating me. This was all new to me and it wasn't what I bargained for. I haven't been at a party with humans in over a century.

"Oh, come on!" He insisted as he reached down into the cooler and handed me a beer. "You have to have a beer or something!"

"No man, really…I'm good," I repeated. "I don't want one!"

I was squeezing Dianna tighter than I wanted to. She knew that this atmosphere was becoming very difficult for me.

"Steven, he's a recovering alcoholic and he can't drink," Dianna interrupted. "He's on the 11th step, he's almost completely recovered!"

I threw my head back to move the hair out of my face and smiled at Dianna's quick cunningness to get Steven off my back.

"I apologize, I didn't know," Steven said embarrassed by his actions.

I gave a slight nod, "It's all good man, don't worry about it," I answered.

Then in a friendly way, he smacked me lightly on the back again, "Do you want a soda?"

This person was really annoying me.

I couldn't understand why he wouldn't just leave us alone.

I whispered into Dianna's ear quietly,

"It's bad enough they were all touching you, but now he's touching me, and I have a real problem with that," Dianna was aware that I was serious and as simple and acceptable as these actions were in the human world, it wasn't for me.

"Really Steven," Dianna said sternly. "We're just fine. In fact, we really need to be going. Danny had promised a friend of his that we would stop by."

She looked up at me and said, "Isn't that right, baby?"

For a second I wasn't sure what she was talking about because I was too busy trying to calm myself down.

"Oh yeah," I said following her lead. "We need to go, I forgot about that, thanks for remembering babe."

"That's what I'm here for," she said as she continued to play her role.

"Well, that's too bad," Steven said.

As Dianna and I headed towards the door, Steven and Heather decided to see us out.

"Good night Dianna, we'll see you at the next meeting!" Steven said and kissed her on the cheek. I didn't let my jealous instincts get the better of me. I knew this calamity was ending—so I just let it go.

He extended his hand out to me and waited for me to shake hands with him. I was hesitant at first but I saw it through.

"It was nice meeting you. Maybe the four of us can hook up one night and double?" He asked.

"That would be great," I answered and eased Dianna closer to the door with her hand in mine.

"Well take care!" Steven said before we left and he lightly smacked me on the back one last time before we exited the building.

Once we were out of sight from the store front I quickly turned to Dianna and asked her,

"How can you stand these people?" I was obviously confused about her association with such inept and bothersome beings.

"I know you were really uncomfortable in there, and I also know that Steven was just inches away from being a late night snack, but *please* don't kill any of them."

She seemed extremely concerned, and of course, she should be.

She was thinking about her friend Janet and rightfully so. I would never do something like that to her again in fear of losing her heart and trust. When Joe set out on his mission to dispose of Janet, it was because she was easy bait. I just happen to be there. I didn't stop him and joined in on the feast. I was satisfied that Janet would be out of Dianna's life. Honestly, I didn't like or trust the girl. I read her thoughts of seduction towards me when I first met her. I also believed that she would get in the way of my time with Dianna. She also took Dianna to a place and put her life in danger and that was something I could never forgive. I still had a lot to learn when it came to tolerance.

"Now we're even," she continued proudly.

"What do you mean, we're even?" I couldn't be sure what she meant.

"You once took me to a place where it was all vampires and humans mingling. In that place, there was one particular person who did more than just hug you hello. It was difficult for me to get through that night, but somehow I did."

Needless to say, she was referring about her first experience with me at *Hell On Earth* and the waitress, Lizzy. Her second experience wasn't any better. There wasn't any way I could argue with that, she was right. Dianna was the only being who had the power to lay a guilt trip on me.

"Is that why you took me there? To get even with me?" I asked with some surprise. I didn't think Dianna could be vengeful just to even the score.

"No," she answered. "I wouldn't do that. If I see you're uneasy then I become uneasy. It's just that the situation was kind of the same thing in reverse, and it forced me to think back in time."

"Well then, touché'. We're even." I answered and removed my hand from hers and put my arm around her shoulders instead.

"Now I don't owe you anything," she said smugly and smiled wide.

"I guess not," I answered and kiss the top of her head.

We walked and talked for a short time. We were trying to agree on going to a place that would suffice us both. In the midst of meaningless conversation and jokes, Dianna stopped walking.

"I'm feeling a little dizzy; I need to sit down a minute," she whimpered.

She was swaying in my arms and had difficulty walking steady. I carried her over to the many benches that were along the curb. She laid her head down on my lap and I began to caress her hair. It was drenched, she was sweating prefusley. She was panting as she was breathing and her skin was becoming pale.

"We're going home," I said nervously. As I gently removed her head from my lap, I noticed that she didn't have any response and her eyes were pulling with gravity. She lay there still and almost lifeless. I leaned over her and lightly tapped her face to wake her up,

"Dianna…"

No response.

"Dianna!"

I swiftly cradled her up into my arms and swooshed home at top speed. It was probably the fastest I ever ran. I was home within seconds.

I was confused, nervous and frantic. This was the first time in my life that I was indisputably afraid. The thought of Dianna dying would put whatever light I had in my life out.

5

Thirst

When I reached the front door, I kicked it open, hard. I didn't have time to fuss around looking for keys.

"Sebastian!" I yelled, my voice echoed throughout the house. "I need you!"

I stormed down the hallway to place Dianna in our bed. Sebastian and everyone else was followed behind me.

I placed Dianna's body securely on the bed and sat down next to her. I ripped off her shirt because her body was so incredibly hot and the beads of sweat were accumulating by the million with each struggling breath she took. Helena ran into the bathroom to get a wet cloth so I could cool Dianna's face and body. Sebastian stood right at my side while everyone stood around waiting to be of any assistance should the moment arise.

"Sebastian, what's wrong with her?" I asked with dread in my voice. I never took my eyes off her as I was cooling her face and neck with the wet cloth that Helena handed me.

"She's…hungry," Sebastian answered calmly, but with dread.

"Hungry?" I answered. "What the fuck do you mean? All she does is constantly eat," I was so baffled by his diagnosis.

He shook his head and looked at me sternly,

"She's hungry for *blood*, not for food."

We all just looked at him strangely as he was holding Dianna's hand.

"Did you turn her, Dan?" Helena asked.

"Of course not, I wouldn't do that to her!" I snapped.

"Are you sure? Because she has a lot of bite marks on her body. You might have taken too much blood from her, and when she drank from you—she turned."

"Don't worry about her bite marks, I know what I'm doing. I didn't take too much blood from her. I know better than that. Besides, I never drank from her without sharing blood," I said, insulted.

"I don't doubt that you know what you're doing but sometimes, even the almighty you can make a mistake," she said, insensitively.

Sebastian immediately interrupted our dispute. He was well aware that I wasn't going to be tolerant with Helena much longer.

"What are you all waiting for, she needs to drink, so can someone please accommodate?" He seemed maddened by our brief debate on Dianna's behalf, and honestly so was I.

I was wasting precious time.

"I still don't know what you're talking about and I don't think it's going to help…but of course, she can have my blood." Without hesitation, I went to bite down on my wrist and Sebastian stopped me before I penetrated my skin.

"Not from you," he said as he pushed my arm down from my mouth. "She's immune to your blood, it won't do anything for her."

"She can drink from me," Joe stepped right up without any indecision and before anyone else had the chance to volunteer.

He bit down into his wrist and his blood began ooze. It was clear that Joe was trying to redeem himself for his previous actions, and if this current gesture of his saved her life, he would well be on his way towards redemption.

He loomed his forearm over Dianna's face and his blood slowly dripped onto her lips. She didn't have any response and I glared at Sebastian. Within a few moments, her lips began to open slowly as Joe's blood seeped its way through the cracks of her mouth. She sluggishly reached for his blood with her tongue, then her mouth latched onto his incision, and she began to drink. She was getting a fragment stronger with each swallow. She managed to grab hold of his arm and pulled it closer to her mouth to get a better grip.

I was shocked and stunned by what I was witnessing. I didn't know what to think of it nor did anyone else. I just sat in admiration and watched her drink with immense enthusiasm, concern and confusion.

"Dan…"

I heard my name but I kept my eyes fixed on Dianna, ignoring the voice without intention.

"Dan!" Joe shouted. "You have to make her stop she's taking too much. I can't get her loose and if I push her, I'm going to hurt her. Hurry up!"

I shook from my trance and immediately took hold of Joseph's arm and pried them apart. After they were separated, Joe walked a few feet away toward Richard who was standing in the back of the room.

"Fuck!" I heard Joe yell as he was holding his arm. "She's strong for such a little thing."

It was evident in Joe's sudden paleness that Dianna had taken too much of his blood and he was slightly deteriorated by the loss. Richard rolled up the sleeve of his shirt and extended his arm out to Joe.

"Bon' Appetite' Joe," he said and Joe bit down into him to regain some of his strength back. Richard didn't have to fear that Joe would over drink from him. We've all been through situations where we had to drink from each other and we all knew how to control it. As I said earlier, we are loyal to one another despite our differences.

Dianna's eyes were open and they were blacker than coal. It was almost frightening. She lay back down on the pillow and tried to force a smile when she saw me. I smiled back and brushed the hair from her face. I took the wet cloth and began to wash her down. It was just about impossible for Dianna to drink blood without getting it all over her face. She has drank from me an uncountable amount of times and she always ended up with blood all over her face. I sometimes wondered if she swallowed any of it. She is truly the sloppiest eater I have ever met, but I loved her for it. Somehow, it gave her a substance of innocence.

Lizzy, the waitress/barmaid, a *human*, didn't spill blood when I allowed her to drink from me. It was very rare and only a few times that she did.

We never shared blood, but every now and then Lizzy wanted the erotic sensation of vampire blood running through her veins, but Dianna didn't need to know any of that.

I leaned down, kissed her forehead, and asked her how she was feeling.

"A little better," she said. "What happened?"

Before I can answer her Sebastian interceded and said,

"This isn't over, she still needs to feed. That was only a quick fix to give her enough strength to be able to actually feed properly."

I stood up from the bed and approached Sebastian. Helena assumed my position and began to help Dianna put on a new shirt, and escort her into the living room.

"What are you talking about? What the fuck is going on here? I want answers!" I insisted as we followed Helena and Dianna into the other room.

"What don't you understand? You need to help her find a human victim so she can bite down on him or her and drain the blood," he was very indignant when he spoke.

"How is she going to feed? She doesn't have fangs. What's happening to her?"

I asked without any disrespect, but Sebastian was getting intolerant towards my questioning. "Sebastian, I have to know."

"Danato," he said. "If you want to save her life she has to do this. She *does* have fangs and they will appear on instinct. She has to be the one to bite the victim. Everyone here knows that the actual bite is half the satisfaction from feeding. Trust me, Danato. I *would not* misguide you, especially now. I promise, when you and Dianna get home and she's recovered, I'll explain everything, but right now time is of the essence and you have to help her through this if you want her to live."

"Of course I want her to live," I said, dreadfully and softly.

"Well that's good. I want you..." He said pointing to me. "Joseph and Ava to go to Central Park. Ava and Dianna will sit alone on a bench appearing to be two unsuspecting women while you and Joseph stay close enough and hide in the shadows. Dianna and Ava will more than likely be approached by men who want to be acquainted with them. After all, it is

Halloween and there will be plenty of ruthless people out there. Those people will be your victims."

The three of us nodded in agreement. It sounded like a good and simple plan.

"Just one more thing Danato," Sebastian said. "You're going to have to push her to do this. She isn't aware of any of these new instincts," I nodded and held on to Dianna as I walked towards the door.

"Danato," Sebastian shouted into the hallway we were waiting for the elevator. "I probably won't see you until the morning, she's going to be a little rambunctious when this is all said and done." Then he stepped back inside and closed the door.

During our speedy journey to Central Park, my mind was a dense storm. Roaring thunder, heavy rain, thick fog, and crackling lightning. This was all just too much too soon. None of us knew what was going on or what was going to happen if anything at all. I felt like the bird that just left its nest. I was lost without any guidance.

Central park has many different areas. Naturally, we wanted to be in the most dangerous area for two young women to be. Therefore, we walked deep into the park beyond the zoo and restaurants. We needed to find a bench where there wasn't too much light and near a wooded area. It didn't take us much time to find the perfect spot to lure in unsuspecting humans.

Although Ava didn't have use of her fangs, she still had her strength. I wished that Sebastian chose Helena to do this but I didn't want to undermine his decision.

Dianna and Ava sat on the bench quietly. Dianna was quiet and disoriented. She didn't have any idea what was happening nor did she question anything. She was just too weak. She was propped up like an ornament and it was ripping me apart inside to see her like that. I hated that I didn't have any control over the situation at hand. I was more than disturbed that I couldn't be by her side through out this entire ordeal.

We waited almost thirty minutes before a group of four gang members approached Ava and Dianna. The waiting was endless. I was growing more anxious as I watched Dianna deteriorate before my eyes. I didn't have any control and there was nothing I could do about it. However, just as Sebastian predicted, the human scumbags approached Dianna and Ava.

Ava was seducing them perfectly to draw them in and I must admit I was actually proud of her at that moment. The four men surrounded them. Two of them were standing directly in front of them and two behind them. Entrapping Ava and Dianna as if they were in a box.

Ava had her head down while one of the men was making obscene gestures with his tongue and crotch.

Suddenly, with forceful speed, Ava reached out and grabbed the necks of the two men that were in front of them. That was mine and Joe's cue to come out of the darkness and grab hold of the two men that were standing behind them.

Ava dug deep into the veins of their necks with her fingernails and began to feed from one of them, and snapped the neck of the other one.

Joe immediately began to feed from the person he grabbed. Joe was still a bit weak from sharing his blood with Dianna and he was hungry. This human didn't have a prayer. Joe devoured him.

The other one that was in my grasp, was still alive and quivering with fear. I sat him next to Dianna and stared deep into his eyes. I needed to put him in a hypnotic trance. The only way Dianna would be able to see this through was if her victim was willing. Once he was under my control and became calm, I let go of him and kneeled in front of Dianna.

"Babe," I said as I tapped her face with my hands to be sure that she was coherent.

She was conscious and just stared at me in a state of bewilderment. Now I just had to think of a delicate way to explain to her what she had to do.

"Will you do something for me?" I said in gentle yet firm tone and looked deep into her red eyes. She nodded yes and I smiled at her.

"Do you see this guy next to you?" I asked nudging my head toward the human. She looked his way to assure me that she was aware of his presence.

"I want you to bite down on his neck as hard as you can and drink from him."

She gave me an appalled look of alarm, disgust and turned her head from me. To be quite honest, I felt the same way. I never wanted any of this for her.

With my hand, I soothingly turned her head back to face me.

"Baby," I said, my voice full of devotion. "If you don't do this you're going to die, and if you die, I'll die, and I don't want to die. Please Dianna, I'm begging you to do this for me, do it for us. I love you, I can't lose you, not now, not again."

She tried to speak but I put my finger over her lips to hush her. I didn't want her to use any of the remaining energy that she had unnecessarily.

She gazed at me, saw the sincerity in my eyes, and struggled to turn towards her soon to be victim. I leaned him closer to her and tilted his neck in her reach. I wanted this to be as easy as possible for her.

"Just bite down baby, he's not going to fight you."

As I watched her lean into his neck to take her very first bite, my curiosity got the better of me. I just had to see with my own eyes if she really did have fangs.

She bit into him unenthusiastically until the first drop of blood dripped out. She *did* have fangs and just as Sebastian had said, they came out on instinct.

As soon as she got her first taste, she became more alive, almost instantly. She was drinking from him firmly trying not to spill a drop, but I knew her face would be a covered with blood when this was over. She drank vigorously, crawled on top of his dying lap, and drank with vast passion and strength. Normally the way she straddled herself around her victim would have made me furious but considering the circumstances, I was able to over look it.

Joe and Ava were done feeding and approached Dianna and me. They were just as curious about her new identity.

"Do you have any idea why this is happening to her?" Joe asked.

"I really don't, Joe. I'm not sure if this is a good thing or a bad thing. I'm just not sure about anything," I answered.

We let her feed for however long she needed to and waited patiently.

I had forgotten how slow new vampires are when they feed the first few times. I hated rookie vampires and now I had one of my very own. Just to add flavor to the pot, she was a rookie with a *conscience*.

She eventually released herself from him and he fell to the floor when she got off his lap. She looked completely rejuvenated, although, just as I foretold, her face was covered in blood. She looked like a baby with food all over its face. I laughed at her inexperience and she just smiled brightly and jumped to her feet. I looked at the four lifeless bodies on the ground and told Joe and Ava to clean up the massacre.

Joe and Ava were more than willing and jumped to their feet to set the clean up in motion. I thanked them before they took the bodies and set off to dispose of them.

"You're feeling better I see," I said happily.

"Yeah, I feel great. Let's go do something, anything," she said as she twirled around cheerfully. She was acting like a child that just had tons of sugar.

I stood up, took her by her hands, and kissed her more lovingly than I ever had before. I was so elated that she was alive and here with me. When I looked at her, I couldn't help but laugh at the amount of blood that was on her face. I took off my shirt, wiped her face clean, and placed it through my belt loop when I was done. She just stood there, pouting, and let me clean her up.

"Okay, okay...I'm clean, let's go somewhere?" She sounded extremely overexcited.

"I think we should go home," I answered, because all I wanted to do was talk to Sebastian about what just happened.

"No! I don't want to go home. I'm sick of home. I want to get crazy. I'm craving for something wild! Can we do that baby? Can we get crazy...please?" She was being cute, jumpy and flirtatious.

How could I deny that?

Sebastian did warn me that she might be slightly rambunctious. Therefore, I conceded and asked where she wanted to go. I was just glad just to have her back and alive. At that moment, I would have done anything for her. Not that I wouldn't anyway.

"Let's go to that stupid place you took me to, the place where you play cards and I get to do absolutely nothing."

I was taken back by her choice of venue but if that's where she wanted to go, then that was where we were going to go. Even though everything in my gut told me she was up to something. There had to be some kind of ulterior motive underneath her cute façade. She never wanted to go to that place. I wasn't going to worry about that now. I just wanted her to be content. Besides, this would be a chance for me to talk with the owner, Adam, about a possible merger with my new business venture.

She climbed up on my back, sat on my shoulders, and kissed the top of my head.

"What are you doing?" I asked, confused.

"I have no idea," she answered, "just keep walking and go fast. I want you to run. I want to feel free!"

I did as she asked, but her words concerned me. I didn't want her to do anything rash.

I wasn't sure what was happening to her or why, but I was certain about one thing, I knew I was going to have to be the one to guide her through this transformation. Something told me that she wasn't going to make it easy for me. I was already seeing the spoiled child that has been unleashed.

6

Rambunctious

When we arrived, she leaped off my shoulders and strutted inside ahead of me filled with sheer confidence. She walked right up to the bar and got herself a beer using her bewitching feminine charms. She definitely wasn't herself, she was peculiar, overbearing and loud. She stood up on the bar stool, leaned over the bar and spoke to the human bartender in an elaborate seductive manner. I grabbed her by the arm rough but not nearly as rough as I would have liked it to be. I pulled her off the bar stool but not before she took her mug of beer off the bar and drank it with just one swig. She smiled provocatively at the bar tender as I was pulling her to walk with me. This was so unlike her and I knew that this was going to lead to trouble before the sunrise.

Big Bald Billy was sitting at his usual spot guarding the descending staircase. He recognized Dianna immediately as she did him.

"I remember you!" She shouted and pointed her finger in his face. "You're the guy who fell down the stairs the last time I was here. Hmmmm…. gee, I wonder how that happened?" She was more than just cocky, she was down right mean.

Billy ignored her and turned to me, "I thought you didn't want her in here anymore?"

Billy was human and more stupid than most.

"Billy, if she's with me, it's okay," I answered, annoyed.

"Oh, okay, Dan. Go ahead in," he said.

I started to walk down the stairs but Dianna didn't follow right away. Dianna was staring at Billy maliciously without saying a word and making him weary. I walked back up the three steps that I just walked to grab hold of her again to guide her down the stairs.

"You know what Billy…" She began. He stared at her waiting for her to finish her statement, and before I could get her down the stairs she turned to him and said, "It must really suck to be you!" And she smiled with such delight with her new found wickedness.

Once we were down the stairs and into the main room of the bar. I pulled her to the side before I mingled with Adam.

"What the fuck is wrong with you?" I asked firmly.

"Nothing, what's wrong with you?" She asked sarcastically and didn't even look at me when she spoke. Her eyes were just scanning the room.

"Dianna!" I yelled as I pulled her face with my hands so she would look at me when I spoke.

"I want you to calm down and behave. We don't need any chaos because you need to be a spoiled brat." She was rolling her eyes as I was speaking to her.

"I'm fucking serious Dianna, don't test me!" I was more than stern, I was commanding and the red in my eyes was enough proof for her.

"Fine, I'll be good. You never let me have any fun," she agreed in a heavy huff. She took hold of my hand and walked with me properly.

I saw Adam standing by one of the pool tables and I approached him and shook his hand. Dianna was at my side being quiet but fidgety, as if she was on a jackhammer. Adam had already heard about the business I wanted to get going and was waiting for me to make contact with him about it.

Adam became a vampire when he was about forty years old in human years. He was a biker type guy. His hair was long, blonde and wavy. He wasn't tall at all, he stood only as high as my chin. He still liked to wear his biker colors even though it has been years since the gang of his existed. He owned a saloon in his human life and that's what inspired him to own one in his eternal life.

We were speaking of plans and ideas. He seemed to be interested in the idea of merging. Adam loved the idea of E.B being readily available. He also seemed to welcome a change to a new area and bigger space. I had the capital and the real estate and he had the clientele. Most of all, I had the witches with the selling product…hopefully.

We were getting deep into conversation and I let go of Dianna's hand without realizing it. As a matter of fact, I didn't realize she was gone until I heard a ruckus upstairs. I looked around and didn't see her. I clenched my fist and bit my lip, I knew that it was *her* making a menace of herself. I was angry that she walked away from me but I at least knew she was still in the club and not out wondering the streets alone. I excused myself from Adam and told that I would be right back because I had to go and tame my toddler mate.

"You have your hands full with that one," he said with amusement.

"Adam, you haven't any idea just how much," I said with much irritation.

I walked up the stairs and before I could ask Billy if she was there he told me that she was and pointed her way.

There she was, loud and in charge of her surroundings. Dancing on top of the pool table, and gyrating every part of her body in a seductive fashion while drinking shots. The human males swarmed around her like bees to honey, watching her move and shake that well rounded apple ass of hers.

She still had on the black mini skirt that she was wearing earlier, but the only thing that was different was that it was covered by the T-shirt Helena put on her. It was one of mine and it hung over her skirt, therefore it looked like she was just wearing that. I don't know what she did with her boots because they were off by the time I got there.

I can't explain the jealous fury that came over me. My temper was steaming and my fury was building intensely.

I stormed over to the pool table and grabbed her by the arm.

"Get down now!" I screamed.

"Hey dude! Take it easy," an unfamiliar voice said, and then he attempted to push me away from Dianna.

"Are you fucking kidding me?" I said as I turned to the body building human and grabbed him by the neck with one hand and sent him flying across the room and into the wall. His body put a large hole in the wall and he laid unconscious on the floor.

All were still and quiet after that and the humans just backed away from me and Dianna. "Why did you do that?" She asked.

"Get down.... now!" I ordered.

Something rational came over Dianna and she realized that this wasn't fun and games anymore. People were going to get hurt because of her actions. She jumped off the pool table and put her arms around my waist.

"I'm sorry," she said in her most childish way. "It's just that I got so bored and you were ignoring me. I didn't think you would mind if I stayed around humans because it would be less trouble than me being around vampires." She went to kiss me but I turned my head. I wasn't amused by her games and that's all this was.

I put her over my shoulder and carried her down stairs and placed her on a bar stool.

"Just sit there and don't fucking move or say a word. Do you understand?" I reprimanded her unsympathetically, because if she wanted to act like a child, I was going to treat her like one.

Adam approached me and asked, "Is everything alright? How much damage do I have upstairs?"

"Not much," I said and we both laughed a little because of the reputation of my temper.

We talked some more and Dianna was on her best behavior. She asked me if she could go to the bathroom instead of just leaving on her own. Under normal circumstances that wouldn't bother me, but in the state of mind that she was in, I had to be more than just a little overbearing.

I told her to go and I watched her walk towards the restroom. As she was walking, Lizzy was walking by with a tray with two pitchers of beer on it for upstairs. Apparently they ran low on their supply. As Dianna walked by her, she didn't make eye contact, but she smacked the tray from under her and laughed when she fell flat on her ass and the beer spilled all over her.

Actually, I thought it was funny too. I was also flattered by Dianna's little fit of jealousy.

"Bitch!" I heard Lizzy shout.

"Are you talking to me?" Dianna turned around and asked casually.

Lizzy went to attack her, but before she could make contact with her, Dianna punched her directly in the face. She took care of herself without the use of magic and I was impressed. As much as I was enjoying this, I had to stop it. Not only do male humans like chick fights, vampires do too. I walked over towards Dianna slowly. I wasn't in that much of a rush to stop it because I found it entertaining.

Dianna was on her guard and ready if Lizzy decided to make a move. Lizzy looked up at me somberly and was hoping that I would give her some sympathy. I looked down at her shrugged my shoulders as I stepped over her. I put my arms around Dianna's waist and kissed her. Dianna took pleasure in my uncaring attitude towards Lizzy. Dianna looked at Lizzy and raised just one of her eyebrows, curved an evil smile, and strutted away with her nose held high in the air. We walked into one of the private rooms and shut the door so I could try and talk her rationally and discreetly.

She leaned against the wall with her arms folded and one bare leg against the wall.

"What's with you?" I was concerned in the way I spoke to her.

"You're with me?" She said in a valley girl sarcastic tone. *Here we go,* I thought to myself.

I walked up to her and stretched out my arms on each side of her making it nearly impossible for her to move away.

"Dianna, baby, I want you to listen to me very carefully," I said decisively as she was turning her face so she wouldn't have to look at me. I banged the wall with my hand only inches away from her face to get her attention. She turned to me with fury in her eyes.

"Can't you just shut up for once and stop lecturing me?"

"Did you just tell me to shut up?" I asked as if I didn't actually hear her say that but I knew she did.

"Yes, I did!" She ranted. "I am so sick and tired of everyone in my life telling me what to do. All my life, I was always told what I have to do. I was told that I had to control my powers; I had to behave. I had to function in a human world. Then I met you and I was told that I had to control my sexual desires and understand your ways. I had to learn how to live without you and control my feelings and now I have to learn how to live with you and I never know if what I'm doing is right or wrong and I'm sick of it. Nobody has ever allowed me just to be me, and now I don't even know who I am anymore."

She was starting to break down. Tears were flooding her eyes and I pulled her close to me and held her tightly.

"What the fuck is happening to me?" She asked and nestled in my chest. "What the hell am I?"

I rocked her back and forth, caressed her hair and just let her speak.

"I'm scared Danato," she said whimpering. "What if you stop loving me?"

"That'll never happen," I tried to reassure her.

"Do you promise?" She asked, innocently.

"I promise," I said. "I don't want you to be scared either, I'll always protect you. So please, just relax."

She started to calm down and the tears began to subside.

"Do you want to go home so we can talk to Sebastian and find out what's going on? Don't get excited, it's not an order, it's a question and I'm *asking* you if that's what you want to do."

She simply nodded yes.

I dried her eyes with my bloody shirt before we walked out the door.

Adam was standing outside and asked if everything was alright. I told him that I had to get Dianna home and I'd be in touch with him in a few days, and we shook hands.

Then I heard an all too familiar dramatic voice.

"Dan…"

It was Xavier.

Just what I need, I thought to myself.

It was apparent that he knew I was there. Xavier had a keen sense of smell within small distances. He approached me quickly as Dianna and I walked out of the room. He started right in with his forged aristocratic voice. Honestly, if he would just talk normal he probably wouldn't irritate me so much because he sounded like an idiot.

"Dan," he began. "It's come to my attention that Sebastian passed his crown of glory over to you and you're the one I need to see."

"What do you want, X?" I asked, obviously not in the mood for small talk.

He ignored me and approached Dianna.

"This must be the lovely Dianna who we've all heard so much about." He reached for her hand but she pulled away before he could touch her. She held on to one of my belt loops and stayed behind me. Which was exactly what I wanted her to do.

I took a good look at him and he looked ridiculous. Xavier had his short black hair slicked back and was wearing all gothic vampire paraphernalia. More than likely from Hot Topic. He was about my height but very thin and lanky. He was with his red headed mate Carla and two of his oversized cronies and three males that I never seen before.

I just had to ask him as well as embarrass him,

"Don't you think you're getting a little carried away with the whole Dracula get up or…is it Phantom of the Opera? I'm not that sure what look you're going for?" I was cocky in my questioning but I was actually curious.

"What's with all the vampire tattoos, are you trying to look intimidating?" He asked mockingly.

"That depends. Am I intimidating?" I answered. He avoided that question and nervously began to speak about the reason why he was here, but I already knew that answer, but I would play it out.

"Okay, enough chit chat. I'm here because you owe me something."

"Do I really? How is that?"

"Do you see these three vampire males behind me?" He asked and pointed to them. "Well, they've been running a muck in Brooklyn. They've been feeding immensely and shortening my food supply. They don't clean up the bodies and now human law enforcement is everywhere. They have been looking for their creator who mysteriously disappeared. Would you know anything about that?"

"Nope. I don't see what Brooklyn vampires have to do with me."

"It seems that one of the females from *your* clan created someone from Brooklyn and caused all this."

"What's your point?" I asked.

"The point is, I am now stuck with three inexperienced vampires and a dead creator. More than likely by your hands. You cannot have your clan come into my city and just take over what is mine. You took Sergio's fangs for the exact same thing. Just because you're the elite clan from Uptown does *not* allow *you* to invade *my* territory."

"Ava was punished, I did take her fangs," I barked back. "No one wants that shit hole that you call home. So what is it that you want from me?"

"So sorry to inconvience you but we can't all be from Uptown."

"No, we can't, so why don't you take your jealous ass the fuck out of here and go back to Brooklyn."

"This can be ended on mutual grounds and without argument if you would just agree to my terms."

"And what would they be?" I asked knowing that it was going to be something ridiculous and unreasonable.

"I want you and your clan to abide by my wishes. I want you and yours to be ready and willing to fight for me should I need it. I want you to jump at my whim and bow at my feet. I want part ownership in the club that you are opening as well."

"Is that all," I asked sarcastically. "Do you want my dick too?"

He dramatically put his hand on his head as if he was about to faint. Again, I wouldn't mind talking to him if he just acted…normal. "I can see we aren't going to be able to reach an agreement tonight. However, some how, some way, your debt will be paid to me."

"Get the fuck out X, you're boring me, and your requests are ludicrous—even for you."

Dianna and Carla have been eyeing each other up and down during this dispute. Both of them standing by their mates and ready to attack if necessary. However, Dianna wasn't going to wait for anything. She wanted to go home. Carla was wearing a ruby ring and Dianna was eyeing it. At first I thought she might have been admiring it, but that would be too easy. Her magical glance burst the ring into flames and Carla jumped back and tossed it on the floor. She was startled and scared and hid behind Xavier.

"Someone doesn't like fire," I said, arrogantly.

"We all have our weaknesses Dan, and you need to control yours," Xavier said as he pointed and glared demonically at Dianna.

"Speaking of weaknesses," I said. "Don't you have to go home? You have less than an hour before sunrise and you know you're not as fortunate as the rest of us when it comes to sunlight. I hope you brought your sun block because you'll never make it back in time."

Xavier anxiously looked at his watch and seen that I wasn't lying. All vampires were weakened in the sunlight and eventually it would kill us, but not right away. It would take an hour or so before that happened. However, Xavier wasn't that fortunate. If just one ray of sunlight touched his skin he would start to deteriorate.

"We'll be in touch," he said before he and his posse erratically ran to the door to depart.

Once Xavier was out of sight and out of the building, Dianna asked me if we could leave. She understood that Xavier's appearance wasn't my doing, and she was more than tolerant and I appreciated that. I wanted to go home just as anxiously as she did so we could both find out what was happening to her.

I wanted to get home and hear Sebastians theory about Dianna, However, I couldn't help but think of Xavier. Now that he has met and seen Dianna, I knew that he would go after her to get to me. That was inevitable. The mere thought of him anywhere near her or just thinking about her infuriated me.

This dispute of ours was far from over and I needed to be on my guard constantly, we all did.

7

Temper

We arrived home seconds before sunrise. Apparently everyone else had just gotten home as well and were all sitting in the living room having a casual conversation. Sebastian was still in a state of slumber and wasn't part of the gathering. This was actually a good thing. I was mentally exhausted from Dianna's behavior and just wanted to rest. I wasn't in the right mind frame to discuss Dianna's transformation. As for Dianna, she was too playful and rebellious to hear important details about her existence and identity to take it seriously.

However, we joined everyone in the living room and sat on the couch. Dianna strolled inside illuminated and vociferous. Her conduct was that of a drunken wench. I sat on the couch while Dianna was saying good morning to everyone obnoxiously. I leaned my head back just waiting for her to shut up. Everyone was trying to smile undercover to hide their laughter. They weren't laughing at Dianna; they were laughing at me. They found my attempt to be patient comical.

After Dianna shared her loud and ear piercing good mornings she found it nessary to leap on my lap. She was bright eyed and smiling brilliantly. All I wanted was for her to go to sleep. Hopefully when she awoke she would be back to herself. If I was capable of getting a headache, I'd have migrane.

Helena made the simple mistake of asking Dianna what happened to her boots.

"I haven't any idea," Dianna screeched. "I took them off to dance on the pool table and I don't know where they went after that."

Helena looked at me and smiled, Ava turned her head to laugh and Joe, who was sitting beside me, had to put his two cents in.

"You were dancing on the pool table?" He asked, shocked. "Damn little girl, you're lucky to still be breathing."

Apparently she wasn't afraid of Joe any longer. She commented playfully to his remark.

"Why am I lucky? What was he going to do, rip my head off?"

Everyone found that hysterical, except me. I was still leaning my head back on the couch and just blurted outloud to anyone who was listening,

"Will this night ever end?" I whined as I covered my face with my hands.

Dianna didn't understand why everyone found that statement laughable so she shrugged her shoulders and kissed me.

Joe just had to keep her talking and give her the attention she was craving. Joe was a child too and loved to stir the pot.

"So what else did you do tonight, princess?" He asked shrewdly. *He just has to keep instigating.*

"Nothing really," she was so child like, like a five year old that just got a new toy when she spoke.

"I met this guy Xavier and he wasn't really that nice. He was making threats and stuff."

All eyes turned to me and no one was laughing any more.

"Okay, that's it," I intervened and leaned my head forward. "We're not gonna talk about Xavier now." I didn't feel that Dianna needed to know why Xavier was a problem. There were certain things that I wanted to keep secret from her. She wasn't a part of that particular situation and it was better left unsaid.

"Why not? What's the big deal?" She persisted.

"This doesn't concern you Dianna, just let it go," I asked as patiently as I could.

"I don't see what the big deal is."

"The big deal is that it's not your concern so please just shut the fuck up already!" My patience was starting to wear thin.

I picked her off my lap and sat her down forcibly on the single chair adjacent from where I was sitting.

"Just sit there and be quiet for five minutes and I'm asking you to please, change the subject," I was as tolerant as I could be and sat back down.

Everyone else was quiet and the tension in the room was growing. The short lived silence was refreshing but Dianna just had to keep chatting and disregard my request.

"So does everyone here know Xavier?" Dianna persisted. Helena was trying to signal to her to shut up by shaking her head back and forth. Helena was certain that I was at my boiling point.

"Dianna!" I shouted. "Stop it now!"

"No, I don't want to stop it! I want to know why Xavier said the things he said," she sounded like a spoiled brat and turned her head from me but not before giving me a cunning smile.

That wicked smile of hers sent me over the edge. I picked up one of the many trinkets that was on the coffee table and threw it across the room.

I walked over to her and leaned down inches from her face. She didn't show any fear she just stared at me with the same intensity.

"It's enough now Dianna, you've been testing me all night and you're really starting to piss me off!"

She turned her head from me and began to speak to Helena. She was ignoring me and my requests and her disrespect was inexcusable. I was hardly amused by her attempt to dismiss me. That kind of behavior I wasn't going to tolerate.

"Hey!" I yelled and turned her head forcefully to face me. "I'm not going to tell you again. Knock it off!"

"And what are you going to do about it?" She mocked.

My first and only reaction was to open handedly slap her across the face. It was hardly gentle and my handprint imprinted on her cheek. Dianna finally shut up and stared at me in bewilderment while holding her stinging face.

Now I was angry at myself for hitting her. The last thing I ever want to do was hit her, but she kept pushing and pushing.

Everyone in the room fell quiet, except for a few silent comments made by Joe and Helena.

"I saw that coming," Joe said under his breath.

"A little over due," Helena answered in the same manner and she began to bite her nails.

Ava ran into her room. She was aware that this conversation wouldn't be happening if it wasn't for her stupidity.

"Fuck!" I shouted. "I didn't want to do that!" Then I punched a hole in the wall right above her head.

Dianna has seen me be mean and uncaring. She has even seen me feed, but she has never felt threatened by me. I was aware of my short fuse and this was a side of me that I didn't want her to see and I never wanted to lose my temper so fiercely with her. This was one of the reasons why I didn't want her to know anything about Xavier. I wasn't ready to let her know all the things I was capable of. We haven't been back together all that long and I wanted to ease her into a vampire's lifestyle, but she had to keep pushing.

I was so aggravated at myself that I kicked the coffee table clear across the room. I then walked into the kitchen to be alone and cool down. In my efforts to calm down, I felt compelled to pick up one of the kitchen chairs and throw that too. Right before I punched a hole or two in the kitchen wall.

After a few moments of solitude, I returned back in the living room with the rest. All were in the same seats and Dianna was in the single chair with her legs curled up and her head on her knees. There was a very loud silence in the air. Sebastian was awakened by my outburst and he didn't look too happy when I walked in the room.

"You have to stop wrecking the house every time you get angry," Sebastian reprimanded.

I nodded my head without really listening to him. I sat quietly and let him rant before he retired back to his room.

I glared at Dianna apologetically. She stared at me babyishly with her sultry gray eyes. It was obvious that she didn't know how to react to my reappearance and was waiting for me to give her some sort of response. I reached my hand out to her and waved her over towards me. She took hold of my hand cautiously. Before she could sit on my lap I stood up and quietly said, "Let's get some rest," and we quietly withdrew to the bedroom. Everyone else followed our lead and went their separate ways to slumber.

We didn't say anything to one another. I leaped into the bed with my jeans and shoes still in tact. I was completely exhausted by her exuberance and my outburst. Dianna was fully dressed as well. She lay on her side not to look at me. I lay on my back, looking at the ceiling.

I couldn't take the silent treatment any longer. I had to have some kind of closure. I began to play with her hair not for any other reason than the fact that I wanted to comfort her.

"I'm sorry I hit you," I whispered sorrowfully.

"It's okay," she answered insensitively. She didn't turn to look at me. She lay there heartless and cold and I didn't like it. This wasn't her. However, I gave her the benefit of the doubt.

"What about you?" I asked.

I believed that I deserved an apology as well. Not that I should have ever hit her, but because she was deliberately pushing my buttons. It was uncalled for.

"What about you?" She was smug and shrill in her response. She wouldn't even give me the courtesy of looking my way. This kind of disrespect I wasn't going to put up with. I wasn't going to feel like a stranger in my own bed.

I moved my hand from her hair and leaped out of bed.

"Fuck this!" I said loudly and walked out the door and sat on the living room couch.

I was a little surprised that she didn't follow me. It was probably a blessing. To be honest, I was glad she didn't pursue me because I probably would have only hit her again. She was a nasty little witch when she wanted to be.

I was too tired to continue playing her mind games. I would deal with her babyish nonsense after some much needed rest. I was awfully fed up with her behavior to let it linger in my mind. I closed my eyes and fell into a deep state of slumber.

I was settled and relaxed for about thirty minutes when I was awakened by Dianna crawling on top of me. I opened my eyes and stared at her blankly.

"I'm sorry," she said sweetly in her baby charm.

"For what?" I asked coldly. I wanted to know if she was sincere and knew why I walked out, or if she was apologizing just for the sake of apologizing.

"I'm sorry for everything. For dancing on the pool table, being mean to that big guy Billy. Trying to undermine you in front of your family and deliberately trying to make you angry. Although, I'm not sorry for puching that sleezy bar maid or for setting that other girl on fire."

The two things that she didn't apologize for made me laugh. She sat straddled on top of me and smiled brightly.

"Give me a kiss," I said and she leaned down and did just that. However, I did cut the kiss short, and she seemed a little disturbed but accepted it. I didn't want this to lead to anything because I really just wanted to rest. Besides, it was as good a time as any for Dianna to learn that she can't always get her way.

"So are you coming back to bed?" She asked.

"Yeah, get up," I answered as I patted her ass in an effort for her to move. I walked ahead of her down the hall and into the bedroom. I flung myself back in the bed. I was still drained from the mental events of the evening. Dianna curled up next to me and put her arms around me and began to kiss my chest and attempted to unbutton my pants and reach inside.

"Babe, I really have to rest or I'll be drained. Vampires need rest too. Stop it," I said as I pulled her hand from between my legs.

I couldn't allow her sexual advances to go any further. She was going to learn that she can't always get her way, and sex is a very big deal to her. Besides, Dianna and I didn't have quickies. We would be romping around for hours and to be quite honest, I just wasn't in the mood.

However, Dianna being Dianna, and not knowing how to take no for answer continued. I was annoyed but calm.

"Your bewitching, seductive charms don't work on me baby, so you're wasting your time. Now turn around and go to sleep."

She turned around and slammed her head on the pillow. She was fidgety. Moving around, kicking my legs—pretending it was accidental and throwing her arm on my face. I was silently laughing to myself at her persistence of trying to get what she wants.

"Dianna," I said casually. "You're not going to get laid so forget about it or I'm going back on the couch."

"Fine!" She said in a loud whisper and narrowed her eyes. She turned around in a huff and fell asleep almost instantly. It was like the child who comes down from a sugar rush. I was so grateful that this nightmare was over and she was finally quiet.

I'm not sure how the tables turned in my favor but I was glad they did, and finally, three hours after sunrise I was able to crash.

8

Untold

I woke up well rested and hungry. Six straight hours for a vampire is well beyond what is necessary. Dianna was still in deep sleep and I let her sleep. After all, she had a rough night also. Everyone was out of bed doing typical things. Sebastian was cleaning the wreckage I caused in the living room and kitchen. Joe was playing the PS3, Ava was reading, and Richard and Helena were cuddling on the couch. I walked straight the room of the human donor, Michelle. She was sleeping also and I preferred it that way. When they didn't see it coming, it wasn't as personal. I reached down as she lay sleeping and bit down into her neck and quenched my thirst temporarily. She jumped up from a dead calm sleep, but relaxed once she was completely awake. I was patiently waiting for sunset so I could feed properly.

I went back inside and sat on the couch, picked up one of the controllers to the PS3 and joined Joe in a racing game. It was a moment of familiarity and I welcomed it.

Sebastian called out to me while he was picking up broken glass and asked me to wake up Dianna. I told him no.

"What do you mean no? She has the right to know whats happening to her, or do you want to hide that from her too?" Sebastian was obviously still upset with me for wrecking the house. However, I was offended by his arrogance.

"I want to know what's happening to her also, but I want her to sleep. When she gets up, you can tell all of us."

"I have things to do today; I would like to get this out of the way."

"What do you have to do?" I asked arrogantly, because Sebastian never had plans and if he did, we were aware of it weeks in advance.

"I have to buy a new coffee table," he said a bit viciously. I laughed subtly to myself because I very rarely seen this side of him.

"It's really very simple Danato, just wake her up and bring her out here. I'm sure she's anxious to understand what she's become and how it happened. It should take you all but five minutes."

"Sebastian!" I said a little less tolerant. "It's not that simple. If I go in there and wake her up, we're going to be a lot longer than five minutes. Trust me."

Sebastian may not have sexually preferred women but he understood the meaning of my statement.

"I'll wait a little longer," he said and nodded as he walked graciously into the kitchen.

Before he entered the kitchen, I quietly asked Joe, "Has he been in there yet?"

"Nope." Joe answered.

We both laughed mischievously knowing that the kitchen was wrecked also and he was going to blow his top. To see Sebastian angry was entertaining. He very rarely lost his cool.

"This is ridiculous!" I heard him shout. He walked out of the kitchen frantically with his hands on hips.

"Danato!" He ranted. "If this continues, you're going to be the one to clean it up. I have had it! Now I have to buy a kitchen chair also. Do you realize how hard its going to be find two new chairs that match the others?"

"Okay, boss," I said while continuing to play the PS3. He has told me that so many times and frankly, I didn't find it to be much of a threat. We go through this argument at least twice a year.

Then I heard her voice.

"Why didn't you wake me up?" She asked groggily. She walked over to me and needless to say, she sat on my lap with the comforter around her petite body.

"You looked so peaceful. If you're still tired go back to sleep," I said while I cradled her in my arms.

"I can't sleep without you there," she answered.

"I think she's a little attached," Joe interrupted.

"Of course she's attached," Sebastian said smiling cheerfully. "Danato isn't just her lover—he's Dianna's creator also."

I gazed at him baffled by his allegation and Dianna seemed confused, we all were. She didn't say anything, she eyeballed me warily yet disbelieving what she just heard.

"Ha! I told you so!" Helena said confidently.

"I would know if I turned her. He doesn't know what he's saying!" I was angry by his accusations.

"Helena is right, you did turn her but not when she thinks you did," Sebastian confirmed.

"Sebastian," I said without much tolerance. "Stop beating around the bush and being so theatrical and tell us what the fuck is going on. I did not turn her!"

Sebastian turned to Dianna and asked,

"Dianna, the marking on your right wrist, is it fading?" She looked at him cautiously then glanced down at her arm.

With much surprise she answered, "Yes, it is. I didn't notice that until now. Why is that?"

"That's not the mark of a witch, it's a vampire bite. To be more specific, Danato's vampire bite."

This was getting to unreal and bizarre. I moved Dianna off my lap and stood up.

"What are you talking about Sebastian? I wouldn't do that!"

"You wouldn't do that now, but you did. It was about twenty or thirty years ago. Don't you remember anything at all?"

"Enlighten me," I answered arrogantly, sat back down forcefully, and kicked the footstool. My temper was starting to boil. I couldn't believe that I was being accused of turning the only thing I loved into a fiend.

"Danato," he said calmly. "I want you to sit back and listen without speaking. Don't lose your cool and destroy the house. I just started to clean up. Don't ask questions, I just want you and Dianna to listen. Do I make myself clear?"

Sebastian was demanding and serious and Dianna and I both agreed to his terms. The entire clan was just as curious and we all sat quietly while Sebastian spoke.

"Around twenty or thirty years ago…" He began, his attention toward Dianna. "Danato accompanied me on a trip to Vermont, paying a visit to your parents. Most witches and warlocks that dwelled in America knew each other and were a close knit before the witch trials," he paused.

"When we arrived to the home of Jerry and Sarah," he continued. "I asked Danato to wait outside, in the shadows. I know Dianna's mother, Sarah, all to well. Chances were that Danato wouldn't be invited in so easily by a mistrusting, nervous, shrewd witch like Sarah."

Suddenly, flash backs of twenty or thirty years ago at Dianna's home came barreling in like fists of fury. I sat up more intrigued by Sebastian's story of the past. *That was so long ago, I can't believe I put it behind me.*

"I remember now…" I said ashamed and I began to explain my exact feelings and the events of that faithful day. The day I met the love of my life for the very first time. "I followed my sense of something sweet. I ended up in a small clearing of the many acres of wooded area that Jerry and Sarah owned. There were wildflowers, trees of all kind, winds of tranquility and Dianna encompassed in the clearing.

When I laid eyes on Dianna, it was relevant to me what she was. A witch that enveloped enchanted blood. She immediately became my prey, I just had to have a taste. I stalked her. She was practicing her spells, picking wildflowers and watching the sun set, completely unaware of my presence. I lunged at her from behind. Her reflexes were fast, faster than a human but not faster than mine. I grabbed her by the arm and bit down without hesitation and drank from her with flames of passion. I was in awe as I drank her thirst quenching sweet blood. I looked up into her eyes and I saw that she was almost drained. Her spicy red lips turned bland and her gray eyes were swallowed with tears. She turned her head faintly and she gazed deeply into my eyes. It was hypnotizing. I released my mouth from her wrist and bit into my own and let my own blood drip into her mouth. I couldn't drain her. She had an incredible hold on me and I didn't want her to die. There was something about her that had me lured.

I already had Dianna in my sight before Sebastian made it to the front door. Sebastian senses were sharp and he instantly knew of my troubling intent. He and Dianna's parents sprinted to the clearing to stop me, but it was too late. At that moment, I wanted to take her back home with me. I was her creator and I wanted her to be with me the second that the single drop of my blood lined Dianna's lips.

I slipped back into the shrubbery and watched as her parents panicked. She swallowed the drop of blood, and a rash appeared instantly. I watched as her parents and a sudden stranger carried her away.

I resented Dianna for being the only being I ever felt comapassion and mercy for. I'm a killer, a predator and such feelings were incomprehensible. The gift of my mind control is so overwhelming that I was able to block out that moment through out my lingering life and I never looked back."

"So, you did turn me into a vampire?" She asked sadly.

"I'm so sorry. I didn't know. Do you remember anything at all?" I asked.

"I have had dreams, but I thought they were only dreams. How can my parents not tell me this?" She asked and turned to Sebastian.

"They probably just wanted to protect you. They did what they thought was best for you." Sebastian answered.

"What...am I...Sebastian?"

"Dianna you are first and last of your kind, a hybrid," Sebastian explained. "You have the magic of a witch and the blood thirst of a vampire. There have been many prophecies that foretold this coming of a new breed in both our cultures. Perhaps, these prophecies are true and you are gifted more than any of us were aware of."

I was speechless and so was everyone else.

"I won't expand on the prophecy right now, it would be too much to handle all at once. I will save it all for another time in the future. Should I see any signs of the prophecy arise before then, I'll explain further."

I took a collective sigh of relief, this was more than enough to endure.

It's natural for a witch to turn into a vampire immediately following their final breath. They are called Creators in our world. They were able to eat food, walk in the sun without consequences and feeding wasn't essential.

It only became necessary when they drank often and became immune to its taste. When Creators drink blood, it is only for the prime purpose of creating others.

However, witches would lose the use of their magical ways. It was like trading in one gift for another, but this was natural and accepted between both our kinds.

Dianna didn't die. There hasn't been a witch in history that has ever been turned over. The enchanted blood of a witch was just too tasty for a vampire *not* to drain and kill the witch. Therefore, no one knew for certain what Dianna actually is or what her gifts are. The only things we knew for sure was that she still had the use of her magic and new vampire gifts surfacing. We didn't know if any of her other gifts decreased or increased; only time would tell.

The vampire in Dianna laid dormant for all those years because she never fed. When she first met me at her bookshop, her eyes kept fading to black. The vampire in her was wanting, begging to come out. When we mated and she drank my blood, all her vampire gifts began to take over her witch ways. It was like an ongoing battle between good and evil. When she released her killer instincts and took her first deadly bite from a human was when the mark on her wrist started to fade. She was unleashed and untamed. It now made perfect sense why Dianna wasn't repulsed by drinking blood and welcomed drinking with so much enthusiasim. Dianna wasn't only drinking from her mate and lover she was drinking from her creator and guardian as well. Nothing is more binding than that. This would also clarify her instant and extreme closeness to me and mine to her as well. I often wondered why we were immediately connected from the first time I saw her at the bookstore.

Now that Dianna actually fed as a vampire, she would need it more often. According to Sebastian, she would more than likely need to feed every few days before she became deathly ill again. Her instincts have been exposed and her aging process came to a halt during the transformation.

Dianna's witch instincts forbad her to kill. Dianna would always be fighting for a sense of balance—life and death, good and evil. I suddenly became her teacher as well, and it was going to be a hard road for us to travel. However, I would guide her through it and train her thoroughly. I would vow to do all I could to keep her out of harms way. There were so many diffrences in our cultures and somehow Dianna had to find a gray area suitable to her needs. She had to feed and kill and that was going to be the hardest thing for her to learn and accept. She also had to learn how to be neat and not be such a sloppy eater.

Dianna was now a killer by my hands. Being a vampire was normal and natural to me. I never had any misgivings about my existence and the role I played. I was comfortable in my skin. I always believed my transformation was my destiny, not an accidental twist of fate. Dianna also loved what she was, as did I, but now, somehow, I felt like I took away part of her identity.

As I said, I was speechless and so was everyone else. Everyone except Dianna. I had to laugh at the first question she asked.

"If Danny is my creator, is it even legal for us to be together?" Everyone was amused by her innocence and sincerity. Although, I think a part of her was still stunned by the news.

"Of course it's legal," Sebastian said cheerfully. "To be intimate with you're creator is quite natural in our world. Just look at Helena and Richard."

She felt a little embarrassed. Therefore, I intervened to make her feel at ease,

"If you think about it long enough it's really the only thing in our world that makes sense. It's normal for any species to stalk a mate and breed. We're not human, but we're not animals either. We are somewhere in-between and being intimate with one's creator kinda fits into both those worlds."

While everyone else was making small talk among each other. It was the perfect time for Dianna and I to disappear. We went to the corner of the room for a brief moment of privacy. I asked her how she felt about our history. She seemed more than acceptable about the situation, in fact, she seemed delighted, but she still didn't have much recollection of the events that occurred. As for me, the memories of that faithful night resurfaced again. I remembered the look in her eyes, her face and how feeble she seemed when she gazed into my eyes. The image that I tucked away for so long was now embedded into my memory like rust to metal. I had a sense of guilt that would last for an eternity. *I almost killed the only thing I will ever love.* I hugged her and held her tight and apologized over and over again.

"Don't be sorry. It was so long ago. It's the reason we're together. I'm glad it happened. If it didn't, who knows where you and I would be right now. I can't imagine ever being without you and now I know why. You didn't kill me because we are meant to be together. You gave me life, because of you...I was reborn," Dianna said.

I smiled, "I love you so much, Dianna," I said and kissed her. She was so optimistic and positive about everything. She took my guilt ridden feelings and made me realize that it was all fate and destiny. This happened because it was the only way we could be together.

As Dianna and I were clasped in each others arms I heard Joe's cell phone ring. He answered it and walked over to me and tapped me on the shoulder.

I turned to face him. I was annoyed for him interrupting mine and Dianna's moment.

"It's for you," he said and handed it to me, it was Adam. I walked into the kitchen and away from Dianna's hearing distance. This was a phone call I wasn't ready for her to hear yet. There was also too much conversation going on for me to hear Adam properly, so my reasons for walking away from her appeared to be on the level.

The first thing Adam told me was to get out of the 1800's and get my own cell phone. Then we immediately talked business. He wanted to meet Ruth and Beatrice and see the new home of *Hell on Earth*. I wanted to get the ball rolling on this venture and obliged to what he asked. Adam wasn't pushy or arrogant. He had time tonight to spare so I had to take advantage of his schedule.

I called Joe into the kitchen and asked him if he spoke to Ruth and Beatrice about the part they would playing in this escapade. He said that he did and they were just waiting for us to go to them and put an offer on the table. Beatrice especially wanted to see me again. That was something I couldn't fathom. We had an open invitation. That was something that came in very handy when you're a vampire. We had to meet Adam and his boys at his place within the hour before we set off to see Beatrice and Ruth.

The only hurdle I had to jump over was Dianna. We just had a terrible fight that morning and we still didn't make up suitably. I owed her that. I turned her down in our bed and I know she was really hurt by that. I also needed to spend time with her and prepare her how to use her newly found gifts as well and help her along with accepting the fact that she is a vampire. It probably wasn't the best time for me to be selfish and take care of business, but I had to take care of business when the time called for it, and now was that time. Bea and Ruth were ready to talk business and so was Adam. I had to do this while they were hot for the idea. It's just like buying a new car, I couldn't give them too much time to think about it.

Dianna came barreling into the kitchen before I had time to think about what to tell her.

"What's going on? What's with all the secrecy?" She asked adamantly.

"We have to go feed," I answered quickly. Joe agreed just as quickly.

"And what else?" She asked and folded her arms.

"I won't be long babe, there's just something I have to do," I answered.

"You never tell me anything! I'm sick of this. You always have to do something and you never tell me what it is. Just tell me why you don't want me to go with you?" She was very commanding. I hesitated and I told her bits and pieces of the truth, leaving out the little details.

"Joe and I are starting a business so we need to meet a few people about it, and…."

"Yeah, I know it doesn't concern me. Nothing does," she said abruptly and stormed out of the room.

I heard our bedroom door slam shut. I looked at Joe and told him I had to take care of Dianna first. He nodded and asked me to make it quick because we had less than an hour.

I turned the knob to the bedroom door and it was locked. I laughed. As if a locked door could keep me out.

"Dianna, open the door or I'll break it down," I ordered.

She opened it well aware that I would follow through with my threat and walked over to the desk and picked up a book.

Her head was hidden behind the pages. She asked what I wanted and why I hadn't left yet.

"Come on baby, don't be mad. I'll make it up to you I promise. I won't be long," I paused for only a second. "I don't like seeing you like this."

"Apparently you do, so just go already," she said viciously and waved her hand.

"I really do need to feed. It isn't just about business.".

"Whatever. Just go," then she waved me off again without looking at me.

I couldn't believe she was throwing me out of my own home and the more shocking thing was that I did as she said. Mostly because I was self indulged at the moment, and took the opportunity to leave when it became suitable. I thought about how hard things must be for her right now. I thought about it all night, torturing myself with my own self indulgence. I realized again and again that I should have been by her side that night to help her cope with her newly found identity. The shocking news of our history also concerned me as well. There wasn't a reasonable excuse for me not to stay with her. I was wrong, but despite that the only thing I was sure of was that I was going to meet Adam regardless of Dianna's well deserved temper tantrum. It was the wrong decision, that much I was certain, but it wouldn't be the first wrong decision I've made over my many lingering years and probably wouldn't be my last.

I walked into the living room and Joe had already told the others about our meeting. That was fine. I didn't mind, after all this was their venture as well. So we all decided to go as a clan and feed on the way. One thing that pierced through my mind was the fact that I didn't include Dianna, but I included everyone else. Without realizing it, I was making her feel like an outsider. Although that wasn't my intent. I wanted to keep her out of harms way and not be part of any kind of brutality or shadiness. I wanted her to stay innocent.

When she was exposed to Xavier the only thing I was concerned about was her safety. I didn't trust him. I read his thoughts and when he makes a move he will use Dianna as his ace in the hole. I wouldn't be able to keep an eye on her and talk business at the same time. Also I didn't think it appropriate for Dianna to meet Ruth and Beatrice. I believed that it would be fair to say that Dianna wouldn't be supportive of my idea of selling E.B at the cost of her own kind. She wouldn't be too happy about that. It was with great sincerity that I believed the less she knew, the better off we both would be. Perhaps, I was being sneaky to protect my own ass. Maybe, just maybe, I was actually afraid that Dianna wouldn't love me for the creature that I really am. I have never been afraid of anything in this never ending existence of mine, but that terrified me. I never wanted her to see that side of who I am. At least not now. She wasn't ready for that part of my life and I wasn't ready either.

I realized that I've been keeping Dianna in the dark in more ways than one. I'm not sure if I was right or wrong but she was an angel among demons and I was one of the demons.

I would put up with her baby antics when I came back. I'll give her whatever she wants and let her think she's calling the shots. It was a small price to pay.

Sometimes I wish that she just let me go the night I saved her from Joe. For her sake—not mine. I never believed that my world was good enough for her, or that I was good enough. That's why I left her in the first place. I tried my best to make her loathe me. At the time we didn't know the truth about what I really was to her, her creator. That would explain why she was and is so loyal to me considering the terrible way I've treated her.

I wondered if that was the only reason why she was with me at all, because of the instinctive connection between creator and descendant. Although when Dianna looked at me, there was nothing but pure, unconditional love and when I looked at her there was nothing but serenity and peace in a world full of monsters.

9

Midtown

I put the ordeal with Dianna in the back of my mind. I had to have a clear head. Although, tonight, it was actually easy to do that. This has been the first time in a long time that we were out as a clan. Things always worked a little differently when clans traveled as a whole. Nothing severe, just different.

Vampire clans weren't that much different from human gangs and the armed forces. When my kind travels in packs, it is customary to show our pride, loyalty and supremacy by wearing our insignia. Human gangs would call them *colors,* and the military would refer to it as *uniforms.* We refered to our insignia as a *coat of arms.* It set us apart from other clans. For most clans a coat of arms was usually just that, a coat or a jacket. While a few of the smaller clans would change it up by wearing things like red sneakers, identical shirts and other things like that so they could stand out in the crowd. I'm talking about someone like Xavier. The coats of arms that they represented themselves in were long black vampire capes that tied at the neck. Garments that were obviously purchased at a costume outlet or Hot Topic.

We on the other hand, were simple and typical. We wore long black leather trench coats that hung just below the knee and flared out slightly. The only difference was a small red crest of the Egyptian symbol, *Amenta.* It was sewn into the collar and its meaning is the land of the dead or the underworld and the horizon of the sunset. Sebastian chose this symbol many years ago and appropriately enough. Adam and his clan would more than likely show up wearing there denim biker jackets from back in the day. Displaying a large skull and cross bones plastered on the back of the jacket.

Although we were allies with Adam, we didn't share the same blood, and blood is blood. We would always defend our own to the death regardless if they were right or wrong. It's a matter of loyalty. There was always a fine line between allies in the world of a vampire. The reason we became allies in the first place was that we both had the largest clans in Manhattan. He controlled Downtown while we ran Uptown. The Midtown vampires were small and weak. There wasn't anyone running things in Midtown. Midtown was neutral territory between Adam and I. And Midtown was something Xavier wanted, although he never actually admitted to it. He would imply that he could maintain things in Midtown. Xavier was a theatrical snob and wanted to be among the privileged Manhattan circuit, but Adam and I would never let him be a part of it. Xavier was power hungry, dense and inept. In addition, he was just a little too clever and cunning to be trusted. To be honest, Xavier and his clan were beneath us. We didn't want anything uncontrollable, undisciplined and untrustworthy in our city.

Adam and I scheduled our meeting in neutral territory, meeting at Times Square. The new club would also be located in Midtown as well. Everything had to stay neutral to keep the peace between our two clans. Both Adam and I were civilized enough to accept the terms without insult. Ruth and Beatrice's residence was only a few blocks away. As luck would have it, they dwelled in neutral territory as well.

It was early November and the sun would set about 5 P.M. We had some time to spare before Adams arrival, and took the opportunity to feed on the many vagrants who wallowed on the closed railroad tracks of Penn Station.

Adam, his clan and his mate Lidia, arrived prompt as usual. As predicted they were wearing their coat of arms. Adam and I shook hands and he handed me a Verizon cell phone. I looked at him oddly.

"That's for you. I know you'll never get one on your own, you cheap fuck," he said humorously.

"Probably not. I don't always wanna be found," I answered. However, I accepted his gift and put it in my pocket.

"I can't keep calling Joe. He talks way too much. Besides, when I do call you on his phone you're always with the little woman," he paused and looked around. "Speaking of Dianna, where is she?"

"She's home. I don't think she'd appreciate this idea too much, knowing I want to use two witches for profit. Then we would get into a fight it and we're already in one argument that's pending," I answered.

"You're pussy whipped," Adam replied. "Who would ever think a little thing like Dianna could wrap you around her fingers?"

"You're calling me pussy whipped? Dianna is home, your woman is here. So who's really pussy whipped?" I asked jesting.

"It's definitely me. I can admit it," Adam answered. "Lidia can be cruel. I don't wanna ruffle her feathers."

Lidia rolled her eyes and let him ramble as she talked with Helena and Ava.

"You don't live with Dianna. She doesn't just ruffle feathers…she plucks them," I answered.

While we were engaging in meaningless conversation, we were walking to the home of Beatrice and Ruth. We arrived at the front door of their low grade home. Joe took out a key and opened the front door.

"I don't even wanna know what you had to do to get that key," I said disgusted.

"It's not what you think," Joe said arrogantly and opened the door.

Both clans stepped inside while Joe led the way. The place was dark and lit by many candles, the perfect setting if you're a vampire. The hallway seemed narrower than I remembered. Beatrice and Ruth were in the cluttered living room talking to one another while eating something unrecognizable. Adam stared at me with concern and revolt in his face.

"Trust me," I said. "Looks are deceiving, the taste of their blood is sweeter than a threesome of young freshly plucked virgins in a pool of blood."

Adam smiled sadistically and laughed wickedly.

Ruth looked up to see who entered their domain.

"Look who it is. It's Little Joey," Ruth said with excitement.

"And he brought friends," added Beatrice who seemed overjoyed.

Joe introduced the witches to Adam. "Ruth, Bea, this is Adam, and of course you both remember Dan."

"I remember him," Beatrice said. "He's the quiet one." I simply nodded, folded my arms and tightened my lips and continued to stay quiet.

Ruth was the smarter of the two and she intervened immediately.

"Let's get down to business. I know why you are all here." Then she narrowed her eyes and scanned all of us. "So what's in it for me and my sister?" She was shrewd if nothing else.

Joe was about to answer but I cut him off before he could speak. That would be over the line. When it came to business matters that involved our entire clan, I would be doing the negotiating. It was an honest mistake on his part considering he was the only one who actually knew Bea and Ruth. He accepted my intervention and backed down without hesitation. Adam and I both stepped up to Ruth and asked her if we could talk privately. It was apparent that Ruth called the shots.

We adjourned into the kitchen and she sat on a chair beside the smelly, corroded and broken kitchen table. Adam and I both decided to stand instead.

"Little Joey told me about this business venture of yours and that you want me and my sister to be a banquet."

Adam leaned to me and whispered, "Little Joey?"

I shrugged my shoulders, "I don't know why."

Adam didn't seem too concerned about Ruth's discord.

"More like a star attraction with benefits." I replied. The word benefits seemed to spark an interest with Ruth.

"What do you mean benefits?" She seemed a little warily but was curious just the same.

"First of all, you can have a whole new place within the club. A beautiful home. You can pick, choose and allow who you want to drink from you. Possibly something else can flourish with all the types of humans and vampires that you'll be meeting."

"Are you insinuating that I or my sister is interested in a relationship?"

"We all get lonely."

She lowered her eyes and thought about it. It was evident that she was pained by her appearance and didn't want to spend eternity alone. I gave her food for thought.

"That's an improbability," she said firmly.

"The point is you'll be getting a lot of attention. Something you've always desired but never had. Vampires will be coming just to drink from you and your sister. The ecstasy that you'll give and receive will be worth it. And maybe there's one being out there who just might want you and your blood for themselves. You won't be a slave and should you decide to leave you would be free to go, no strings attached."

She lingered in thought. The idea was becoming an interest to her.

"So you can get us out of this rat hole? And you will allow us our freedom to pick and choose or leave if that's what we wanted?" She asked as she pondered her options.

I kneeled in front of her. "Of course we can get you out of this place. That's our first priority. Once you tell us it's a go, we'll start to set up and have you out of here in three or four days. We'll get you whatever you want. And like I said, we don't want slaves, we wanna make money and you and your sister want attention and passion. This idea benefits all our needs."

Adam also kneeled beside me to talk to Ruth. After all, this was his project too.

"Ruth, may I call you Ruth?" He said politely. "I came here with my family just to meet you and your sister. I'd be lying if I said I didn't want to taste your blood, but honestly, this venture can pay off for all of us. Quite possibly bring our two kinds together."

"That would be bit too much to ask for, don't you think?"

"Not at all. You haven't been outside these walls in a long time. Things have changed. The prejudice isn't what it once was. As a matter of fact, Danny's mate is a witch."

I snapped my head quickly and gave him a look of discontent. There wasn't any reason to bring Dianna into this.

"It'll be alright. Trust me," Adam whispered to Ruth.

"Is that true?" Ruth asked. "Your mate is a witch?"

'Yeah, it's true," I answered with annoyance in my tone.

"I'll bet she's beautiful," Ruth said and remembering herself at a younger age.

"Yeah, she is," I didn't like this conversation and my answers were short and cold.

"Can we meet her before we agree to anything?" Ruth asked.

I stood up from my kneeling position, looked down at her and without any emotion as I answered,

"No. I won't bring her here. I'm sorry, but I just won't. This conversation is over."

Adam looked at me with confusion as I started to walk away.

"Where are you going?" Adam asked.

"Dianna isn't negotiable," I was firm and unwavering.

"I apologize," Adam answered. "It was a slip of the tongue, I assure you. Now come back inside and let's get down to business."

Ruth smiled at me, got up from the chair and took hold of my hand. She led me back into the room. She still had questions. She sat back down in the chair and began to speak.

"Tell me one thing. The reason that you won't bring her here, is it because we're witches and she might not like what you're doing, or is it because of the environment?"

"Both."

"You really must love your little witch. It makes me happy to know that even a vampire can open his heart outside of his own kind. You're a maverick, you like to take chances, and it's because of that jesture I will agree to your terms. Beatrice and I will be ready to move out in three or four days."

"Sounds good," Adam immediately answered.

"I would still like to meet her when we are all settled. It's been so long since I've been among my own kind, but how will you explain the presence of Beatrice and me? She's bound to find out eventually," said Ruth.

"I won't have to explain anything. She'll know on her own, and accept it in due time," I said sternly.

Then to move forward and get off the subject of Dianna, I asked if we had a deal.

"Yes, we have a deal. In addition, I'm still looking forward to meeting your mate. What's her name?" She asked.

"When I introduce you to her, you'll know her name, but until that time it's not necessary."

I wasn't flexible about my decision to keep Dianna anonymous. After all, I didn't know these women all that well, only that they were shrewd and untrustworthy. They didn't have any loyalty to anyone other than themselves, that much was I was able to see in their thoughts. I didn't know what their true intentions to Dianna was, if any at all. I didn't trust anyone when it came to Dianna. She was rare, beautiful and *she belonged to me*. She was much too tempting as an individual to wonder free and curious.

"I'm very impressed by you're protectiveness over her. You take passion in everything you possess. I won't have any qualms about being in business with such a loyal and noble being."

"Then we have a deal. Let's bind it in blood," I said and Adam was overjoyed that he was finally going to taste what his thirst has been quenching for since we walked in the door.

Ruth smiled and extended out both her wrists for Adam and myself to drink. Needless to say, we anxiously sunk our teeth deep into her skin and drank in bliss for that very brief moment.

After a moment, the taste became bitter and Adam wasn't aware of that side affect. He did just as I did when I drank for the first time. I explained to him that they had charmed their own blood so they couldn't be drained. Adam thought it was clever of them and understood. *However, now that I think about it, how can only these two witches charm their own blood?*

"Would it be alright if our brothers and sisters tasted as well?" Adam asked.

"Of course," she answered and walked into the living room and whispered to Beatrice. Beatrice got very excited.

We let Ruth lead the way into the other room. I held Adam back and let her walk out before we stepped into the living room

"What's up?" Adam asked

"Business is business. I trust you completely, but don't ever use Dianna as a tool in a business deal again," I was uncompromising. Besides, Adam needed to know who was really running things.

He was more than courteous and apologized. He admitted that he wouldn't tolerate those actions if it were the other way around. We shook hands and never spoke of it again.

When we stepped into the living room, both our clans were already drinking. Beatrice and Ruth were both in generous moods, they allowed us to drink more than once. I indulged three or four times. I can't explain the rush that E.B provides except that you feel God-like.

However, we didn't want to be greedy and stay all night. Also the more E.B that we would drink the more addicting it became. So addicting that any condition that Bea and Ruth set would become acceptable just for another taste, and that was a scary thought. There was a fear that if we stayed and continued to drink that it might lead to things that I shutter to mention. Things that I can't even think about. These were sex starved women, and I was certain that sex would be the only payment they would accept once the free supply wasn't available. Just like any drug dealer, get your victims addicted and take what you want in return. I trembled just thinking about it and it actually frightened me. We satisfied ourselves before things got out of hand and left humbly.

Adam was impressed with the taste. Ruth was impressed with both Adam and me by our mutual respect for one another and our ethics.

My clan of course wanted to stay and drink more but I insisted that we leave and be grateful for what we had. I also tuned into their thoughts to let them know that payment would eventually have to be paid, and the price was high, the price of dignity. Bea and Ruth weren't working for us yet, so nothing was for free. It was only a matter of time before we had an unlimited supply. Adam was thinking the same way as I was and we all parted at the same time.

We walked to 42nd Street and 8th Ave. That was where the new home of *Hell on Earth* would be. It was a two-story building. There was a basement that had its own back entrance. There would be a human section of the club for appearances only. That would be through the front door, up the stairs and on the second floor. While the main floor would belong to Beatrice and Ruth, the first floor also connected right to the basement. It worked for everyone involved. Adam was impressed and like the place. We would schedule another day to set up Bea and Ruth and get things rolling. We didn't want to give them too much time to think things through. We wanted them to be out of there current surroundings as soon as possible.

As tasty as E.B is, the taste didn't linger for long. Once the feeling was gone the craving for blood was steadily more intense. Preferably enchanted blood, but in a pinch human blood would do. When you came down on E.B, the desire to drink and the actual bite was intensely overwhelming.

Adam and his clan, as well as mine, wanted to feed. Since we were now merged in business together, it wasn't so inappropriate to venture out and feed together in Midtown. We roamed the streets together for a while before going to the present home of *Hell On Earth*.

I played a few hands of cards and talked a little business with Adam. He announced the news of relocating and a new partnership to his customers and associates. Most of them seemed elated and applauded, but not Lizzy.

Things were going to be different now that I was going to be her boss. She was pissed off at me for ignoring her and stepping over her when Dianna pushed her to the ground. However, it didn't take much for Lizzy to forgive me. A wink of the eye and a seductive smile was pretty much all I had to do to gain back her trust and loyalty. However, this is where Dianna was going to be a problem. Dianna wouldn't want her there or anywhere near me for that matter. Part of the agreement between Adam and me was that he could bring his staff, and Lizzy was part of his staff. There would be an inevitable meeting between the two of them and it wasn't going to be pretty. Lizzy didn't stand a chance against Dianna, Lizzy is only human after all. There has been talk that Lizzy wanted a vampire to turn her. If that happened, things could get messy. Adam informed me that a transformation for Lizzy would eventually happen but not for a very long time. He still needed her to be human. She was willing to allow the vampire clientele to feed from her anytime and she was a good server and kept the humans happy as well. Not only as a barmaid but also as a sexual toy for both humans and vampires. To be blunt, Adam made a lot of profit keeping Lizzy around. She was more valuable to him as a human. Lizzy was basically a prostitute with some pre-conditions and Adam was her pimp. There wasn't any urgency for Adam to have her turned just yet.

It was early, just about ten o'clock and I decided to go home. Everyone else was staying out and wanted me to stay too, but they didn't have to tend to Dianna. I believed it was best for me to go home and get the *Dianna argument* over with while the house was unoccupied by the others. All that aside, I missed her and wanted to be with her.

10

Predators

I arrived home and walked in as quietly as I could, hoping to find Dianna sleeping. That would be too much to ask for. She was sitting with her back towards me on the couch watching television. My attempt to go unnoticed was a waste of time. She snapped her head at me the second I walked through the door and gave me an evil look before she launched a large decorative crystal orb at me. There was a good amount of force behind her throwing ability but I caught it instantly and placed it down.

"You throw like a girl," I said playfully.

I vowed to myself not to get angry with her. She narrowed her eyes and hissed at me. I was taken back by that and laughed.

"So what are you going to do, *go all vampire me?*" I was still playful pretending to be shaking in fear. I crouched down in a false attack position and she narrowed her eyes.

"Okay, I'll play. Let's see what you got. Bring it on, babe," I told her as I motioned my hands back and forth for her to come and get me.

She got up and began to circle the room obviously trying to stalk me. I began to circle her as well.

"I'll tell you what, if you can catch me...I'll do whatever you want," I teased her confidently.

This was actually a good way for me to see her strengths and weaknesses. It was a good tool to teach Dianna her new vampire skills, and more importantly to prevent an argument.

"Anything?" She asked in a cunning approach and crouched down to stalk me.

"Whatever you want, babe. You just have to catch me. The only rule is no magic, just your vampire skills and senses," I crouched down again and waited for her to make a move.

"Agreed," she answered.

This was actually working out better than I expected. She was willing to play instead of fight, and I was grateful. If I had believed that God actually listened, I would have thanked him.

I was weaving around to test her senses. Her eyes were following my every move before she made her first attempt to attack. She ran impressively fast to catch me. However, I was out of reach before she could make contact.

"Amateur," I said mockingly but in a good-natured way and began to circle the room again.

"You're an asshole," she was being playful as well.

I quickly ran to the other side of the room. Too fast for her eyes to see. She looked around and she lost her concentration by my speed. Eventually she got her bearings straight and focused in on me.

"So why are the reflexes slow? Is it because you didn't get laid and you're a little edgy?" I said sarcastically and waved her on to try and attack me.

"Don't flatter yourself," she ran towards me again but I slipped away and ran behind her and tapped her on the shoulder.

"I'm over here," I said. She turned to face me but I vanished out of her reach to the archway of the corridor.

I was trying to provoke her. I really did want her to catch me. I wanted her to unleash her fury. As of that moment, I wasn't too comfortable or impressed by what I was seeing. She could never take care of herself against a more experienced vampire.

We were playing cat and mouse for a few minutes before she would take her next attempt to attack. She was getting frustrated.

"Can you just stay still?" She asked, discouraged.

"Is that your defense? Come on Dianna, you can get me, just concentrate."

She took a deep breath and took her stance. I let her lunge at me, she almost grabbed me. I wasn't going to make this easy just to appease her. She needed to learn.

"I ran into Lizzy tonight, she says hello," I believed that would get her fire burning and she would let loose. However, that backfired. Her eyes gleamed red and she ran straight towards me and stopped in front of my face.

"That's not funny." She reached over to the shelf on the wall, threw, and broke one of Sebastian's many Waterford crystal vases into a thousand tiny pieces before storming down the hallway and into the bedroom.

I guess that was over the line but I honestly didn't mean any harm. I was mad at myself for making that remark.

I followed behind her and walked in the room.

"Come on babe; don't be like that, I didn't mean to upset you."

She gave me a sneaky look and smiled, "If you want me come and get me." Then she leaped onto the desk and crouched down like a wild cat. This was a good thing, Dianna still wanted to play. I was also impressed by her cunningness to lure me into the room. This was getting better and better.

"Dianna," I said cleverly. "This room is so much smaller, you don't have a chance against me. I'll make it easier for ya, you don't have to grab me you, just have to touch me."

I pretended to take a leap at her but backed off. Her reflexes got better and she leaped from the desk to the top of the bookcase. She looked like a panther perched high on her plateau. Her eyes were gleaming red through her long silken black mane. She looked incredibly sexy and appetizing. I stared her and smiled seductively. I was really being turned on by her animal instincts.

I extended my arms out from below her,

"Come and get me babe because you're making me crazy."

She smiled with victory as she leaped down and landed on all fours. She stayed in a cat like postion waiting to attack at the right moment. I crouched down in the same postion as well. Both our eyes were fixed on one another like two predators waiting for the right moment to attack their prey.

She leaped on me unexpectedly, however I quickly took hold of her and pinned her down. Only as a reminder that the male was the more dominate of our species. We were laying face to face and both of us were sexually turned on by this game.

I had her in a tight but harmless grip. She wasn't able to escape my clutches.

"So, now what are you going to do?" I asked softly.

"Surrender," she whispered.

I reached down, bit her neck, and began to drink. I forgot briefly that Dianna had fangs of her own and she did the same to me. That was the first time anyone has ever bitten me in a sexual situation. I must admit that Dianna was right. There wasn't a feeling like it. E.B couldn't compare to the satisfaction and pleasure. It was an ongoing orgasmic rush of pure pleasure.

I'm not going to get into many details but let's just say that this made our mating look boring. I mounted her from behind and held her tight with my legs so she couldn't escape. I tore her clothes off and mine as well. I penetrated her wet sex from behind forcefully, causing her to screech. I held her down the way wild animals hold down their female mate. Each thrust of my wide shaft was harder than the one before, and she yelped and screamed with every push. Tears of passion came to her eyes. For a moment I believed I was hurting her and I asked her if she wanted me to stop and slow down, and she begged me not to stop as she screamed my name and other things as well. She begged for more as I teased her by slowing down, stopping and pulling out. She couldn't get enough of my nine inch cock and she took it all in, roughly, hard and pleasurably. She held her womanly muscles tight as I penetrated her, making sex more intense and erotic with every deep plunge I rammed inside her. I growled and moaned just as loud as she did from the agonizing pleasure of it all. There was a lot more activities, and sexual experiments that we endured that night, but I'm just gonna end it at that, and leave the rest to your imagination. We were more like two predators in heat as opposed to two lovers being intimate. We were reckless and untamed. During that time, our true animal instincts surfaced. We were howling and writhing in ecstasy. There wasn't one part of our bodies that went undiscovered or unexplored. The destruction in the room was immense. Things were falling and breaking all over the place. Everything except the bed had damage and that was only because we never made it to the bed. Our sexual frenzy lingered at least two hours but it didn't seem that long. This night was better than I expected and I was more than pleased with the choice I made to come home when I did. I learned that Dianna loves rough sex, just as I do, and this made for better nights of passion. I didn't have to be so careful and gentle during love making any more, she isn't as fragile as she looks. Her tiny little body could handle all of me and everything I could offer, I was elated by this new discovery. I was also thankful that the house was empty because I was certain that things wouldn't have turned out the way it did had anyone been home.

We were lying on the floor together. I was on my back, naked with my hands clasped behind my head, and Dianna straddled her sweaty bare body on top of me. She threw her head back to get her long luscious mane of hair out of her face. I instantly laughed and smiled when I saw her face.

"What's so funny?" She asked.

"Exactly how do you drink blood? Do you swallow any of it? It's all over your face."

She shrugged her shoulders, "I don't know. We all have our weaknesses and maybe this is mine."

"That's not a weakness; you're just a sloppy eater." I reached over to grab whatever I could find lying on the floor to wipe her face. Her eyes were still vibrantly red. That is a sign of hunger.

"You're hungry for blood. You have to feed," I smacked her on the ass for her to move.

"Can't we just eat from one of the humans here?"

"No. You need to bite for yourself and drink until you're satisfied. You have to learn to feed the right way, as a hunter. Things, such as blood, don't always come easy and you have to learn how to survive and hunting is the first step. Besides, a small drink isn't going to satisfy your thirst and you'll just be hungry again in a couple of hours. You're a part of a whole new world now and you have to learn things the right way. I know it sucks, but you're like a newborn baby. You're brand new and as your creator I have to be sure you're capable to survive in this world. It's my responsibility."

"And what's your responsibility to me as my lover and mate?"

"As your mate I have to make sure you're safe, unharmed and well cared for. So as you're mate I'm telling you that you have to feed because it's in your best interest. And as your lover, I have to make sure your sexual hunger is satisfied, but I think I have we have that part covered. I have to make sure your hunger is content in both areas," I said and stood up.

She put down her head and frowned while sitting on the floor with her knees up to her chest in her bare skin.

"I don't want to kill anyone," she said sincerely.

"I don't know how to break it to you babe, but you are a killer," I answered as I was getting dressed.

"No, I'm not. The only reason I was able to go through with it last time was because I was incoherent and I don't even remember it," she rebutted.

"Get dressed and let's go. We'll debate this on the way." She did as directed without argument and we ascended to the streets of Manhattan.

When we stepped outside, I handed her a pair of dark sunglasses.

"What are these for, it's the middle of the night?"

"You can't walk around the streets of New York City with glowing red eyes."

She nodded in agreement and put them on. They weren't going to interfere with her vision; after all, she is nocturnal.

"If you're hungry too, how come you eyes aren't red?"

"I can control it. You'll learn in time. You're still an amateur."

"Stop calling me that," she pouted.

"You are an amateur. I'm not trying to insult you but that's the reason why your eyes are red."

I took her hand and we walked the city streets. I had a general idea of where I was going to take her to make this as easy as possible for her. She needed an element of surprise to make this happen. She is a vampire with a conscience. If anything, that is her weakness. I had to ease her into this. I couldn't let her just stalk and prey the first person we saw, but she had to learn how to eat correctly on her own to survive.

As we walked we passed an all night convenience store, I had a minor brainstorm and we went inside. She wondered to the candy section because she was hungry for real food as well. Dianna was always hungry. I walked to the paper goods section to get a small travel pack of wet clothes. There wasn't any doubt in my mind that her face would be covered with blood after she fed and she would have to wash up.

Dianna was waiting for me by the counter with her Snickers bar in her hand and the clerk was gawking at her chest. I thought it to be a little funny considering Dianna wasn't the most voluptuous woman, but then again she is a witch and they have that affect on humans. I walked up behind her and put down the pack of wet clothes and her Snickers on the counter. The clerk was still mesmerized. I banged my hand down on the counter to get his attention.

"Hey, buddy! Eyes forward. Do you see something you like?" I shouted.

Dianna was smiling flirtatiously at both of us and I smiled back and winked. The clerk jumped out of his trance.

"Oh, so sorry, will that be all?" He asked.

"Yeah, that'll be it, just ring the shit up," I said with annoyance.

"Jealous?" Dianna asked.

"Not jealous…. possessive."

We left the store and continued to walk at a fast steady pace. I knew just where I was going to take her.

"Why did you buy those things?" She asked and pointed to the wash clothes as I put the small travel pack into my back pocket.

"Because I'm running out of shirts to clean your face," she narrowed her eyes at me playfully. "After you drink, I'll take you to get something to good to eat. I still owe you a nice dinner since our first date."

"Yes, you do."

We walked to Mulberry Street. There were a lot of dark alleys along there and small time gangs would wallow within them to sell and do drugs. It would be easier for her to attack a human if she felt threatened, although she wouldn't be in any real danger.

We entered one of the alley ways and it took all but five minutes before we were stalked by the true savages of humanity.

We were being followed by three thugs in their late teens. I put my arm around Dianna and whispered to her,

'Don't get nervous, just follow my lead. Keep in mind that I'll be with you the entire time."

"You're really going to make do this on my own, aren't you?"

"Yep," I said and smiled. "You'll do fine, and you'll also be doing society a favor, these guys are the scum of the earth. They prey for pleasure and dominance, we prey to survive."

As sure as the day turned to night they began to walk faster behind us and eventually circling us. One of them told me to get lost *if I wanted to live*. I put my arms up in false defeat and did as directed. Dianna stared at me puzzled by actions. I winked at her and walked about six or seven feet away and hid in the shadows. I wanted Dianna to give into her instincts and do this on her own. She wasn't in any danger. These guys didn't have a chance against her. Her instincts would kick in at the right moment, I wasn't worried.

One of the thugs started walking my way to *do me in* so to speak. He stood directly in front of me looking around confused as to where I had gone. At lightning speed I was behind him. I tapped him on the shoulder and he turned around. I smiled at him just before I snapped his neck with one hand and he fell dead to the ground. The others assumed the thump they heard was me.

"So much for your boyfriend. Now it's your turn, but not before we get to know you better," one of them said to Dianna.

They were standing in front of her and she was scanning them perfectly and smiled slickly as they made their comments. She was waiting for the right moment to attack and she didn't seem afraid. I was happy about that.

One of them, the leader, I assumed, reached for Dianna forcefully. Dianna, more quickly than I expected grabbed him and his comrade by their throats. She had one hand on each of their necks and they were gasping for air.

She shouted out to me, "Babe," I was behind her with my arms around her waist before she finished saying the next word.

She leaned her head back to look at me while tightly holding on to her victims and asked, "Are you hungry? I have extra," her smile was devilishly delightful.

I looked at the two thugs and gazed my red eyes upon them just to give them a scare before dying.

"Sorry boys," I said. "You picked the wrong couple tonight." They tried to scream but the grip Dianna had on them wouldn't allow it. It gave me pleasure to see scumbags like that shiver in fear. Dianna loosened her grip so we could hear them scream. When the first scream was heard Dianna and I both looked at one another and smiled before we feasted upon our meals without haste or regret.

I was done before her but not too much before both bodies fell dead to the ground.

"Did I do good?" She asked childishly.

"Yeah, you did good," I answered as I pulled out the package of wet clothes out of my pocket and cleaned her face. We were both laughing at her sloppiness. I removed her sunglasses from her face to find that her eyes were normal once again.

I picked up the three corpses and threw them into one of the many dumpsters that were along the ally wall. I covered up the bodies with a lot of old newspapers before lighting a match and throwing it into the trash.

"Why do you have to dispose of the bodies? I know it's not because you're afraid of the law."

"It's because if they are found by humans it'll be apparent that they were drained of their blood. Our bite marks remain on their bodies. We don't want any evidence of our existence. We don't want to be exposed or exploited."

We were already in China Town and we started to walk to one of the many all night Chinese restaurants as I promised. She ordered sesame chicken with rice and I ordered the same for the sake of appearances. I didn't have any doubt that Dianna would eat what was on my plate as well.

The waiter placed the plates of food in front of us and Dianna dove right in. I still couldn't understand how something so small can eat so much. She didn't have much to say at first because she was to busy devouring her food.

When she was almost done with her dish she asked, "What would happen if you eat that?".

"I'd get sick. Food repulses me."

"That's a shame, because it's really good. Do you ever miss human food?" She asked as she switched her empty plate with mine and began to eat that too. I placed a napkin on top of the empty dish not to look at it.

"No, I don't even think about it. Like I said, it sickens me just to look at it."

"What do you mean get sick, like deathly sick or vomit sick?"

"Vomit sick," I answered without looking at her. Watching her engage in food that nauseated me.

"I'll change the subject," she said.

"Good." I answered, and she began to ramble.

"Remember earlier when you said you would do anything I wanted if I was able to grab you?"

"Yeah, I remember, what do you want?" I answered, hoping it wasn't another meal.

"I want to go back home to Vermont for a visit. I need to see my family."

"That's not a problem, but what's the sudden change of heart?"

"Closure. I'm not what I was when I left. I want to know more about the day I met you for the first time and why I wasn't told about it. I know I have to leave my old life behind me so I just want to let it go properly and say good bye to the world I once knew."

"Dianna, you don't have to let go of the things you love just because you've changed. Your still who you always were, you're just...this too now."

"You don't know my mother. She's very controlling and she isn't going to like what I've become or you for that matter, so to keep peace I have to let go. I still want my family in my life but under my terms. They have to accept me for what I am now, no matter how much they will be in denial about it. I think it's best just to let that world go and start over. Like you said, I'm a new born and it's time to start taking steps," she seemed stern about her decision.

"If that's what you want, then we'll go together. When do you want to do this?"

"Thanksgiving."

"Just what I need, to be surrounded by food, but it's alright, I'll muddle through it. We'll drive up for Thanksgiving."

"You drive?" She seemed really taken back.

"Of course I drive. I also have a car. Why are you so shocked?"

She dropped her fork and pushed away her half eaten plate, "You mean to tell me we've been walking around all this time and you have a car?"

"Yeah, I have a car. It's in the building garage. I don't like driving in the city. That's the one thing I have in common with humans. The traffic here sucks. It's faster to walk. I only drive on those rare and few occasions I leave town."

"So what kind of car do you have?" She asked eagerly and the waiter walked over and placed the check on the table.

"I'll show you when we get home," she smiled happily. I left the money for the bill and a hefty tip on the table and we headed home.

We went straight to the garage to show her my car. She didn't seem too surprised when she saw that I drove a black Dodge Viper Venom Hennessy 1000 with chrome wheels and the blackest tinted windows one has ever seen. She asked me to open the doors, and I did and she sat herself down in the passenger seat. I leaned on the door while she was touching everything. It was like a shiny new toy for her.

"Teach me to drive," she insisted.

"Not now. I'm still teaching you how to eat. Besides, you can use your magic to make any car drive, you don't need to actually know how to do it to get it done."

"I know, but I want to learn the real way. Show me."

"Not now, another time…maybe…I'll teach you to drive when you can eat with out getting blood all over your face."

She curled up her lip and raised one eyebrow and admitted that she would probably never learn to drive the real way. Dianna got out of the car, and we headed upstairs to our domain.

There still wasn't anyone home even Sebastian was out. I couldn't even begin to wonder where he was or what he was doing. We went into the rec room and played pool. I put on music, The Rolling Stones to be precise. Dianna was actually pretty good at shooting pool. Although, she found it necessary to cheat every time it was my turn to shoot. She would wave her finger to make the ball I was aiming at move.

"Are you going to let me play or not?" I asked good-naturedly.

"I don't know what you're talking about," she answered cleverly.

Then she turned around not to face me. "I won't look at you when you take your shot and then you can't blame me because you suck at pool," she said teasing and proud that she was in control of this situation.

However, I did take my shot and I did sink the balls that I wanted to into the appropriate pockets. She turned around quickly. Her eyes were wide and she looked nervous.

"Did you just sink those balls?"

"Yeah, why?"

It took her a second to admit she was cheating and she couldn't understand why her magic didn't work when she wasn't looking.

"This is just great!" She exclaimed. "Now I have to actually see things for my magic to work. The gifts I've gained in one area seemed to take away from the others."

I put down the pool stick, picked her up and sat her on top of the table.

"Don't let this upset you," I said as I kissed her face.

She through herself back on the table and screamed "Ugh! This sucks!"

I leaned over her and kissed her. We were engaged in passionate kiss until I heard a voice,

"Do you two have a thing for pool tables?"

It was Joe and Richard. Dianna quickly jumped up and fixed her shirt.

She was still very shy when it came to anyone seeing her in an intimate situation. She was very private about her sexuality and inhibited by the thought of anyone seeing her bare body, even me at times, but she has gotten a lot better with that.

"Do the two of you want to shoot another game? You and Dianna against me and Richard?" Joe asked.

"No, we've been playing for a while," I answered while Dianna was nestled in my chest. She was embarrassed that they walked in on us and there really wasn't anything going on. She was also still uneasy around Joe.

"We can all see that you've been playing for a while but do you want to shoot some pool?" Joe said in his sarcastic condescending way.

"You're a dick," was all I had to say to him and Dianna and I left the room and called it a night.

Sebastian returned home as well and he was in the living room picking up pieces of broken glass that shattered when Dianna threw the vase at me.

"Did you do this?" Sebastian shouted at me.

"Wasn't me," I said and pointed to Dianna. Sebastian looked Dianna's way.

"Yes Sebastian, I threw your vase, and I'm sorry," Dianna apologized.

"Did you see how fast he gave you up?" Sebastian was being really unruffled about it and teasing Dianna.

"When you threw the vase, did you hit him with it?" Sebastian asked.

"No, I missed," Dianna answered.

"Next time…be sure to hit him, okay?" Sebastian was really taking this well, he must have met somebody. Dianna was relieved that Sebastian wasn't angry with her.

We retired to our bedroom. Upon entering we remembered the destruction that went on earlier that evening and we both just stepped over broken things and ignored it. Dianna lit some candles with her magic and I closed the door behind us and she hugged me. What goes on behind closed doors should usually stay there. That would put an end to a perfect evening. It was perfect because Dianna had my undivided attention, and that was the way she liked it and I liked giving it to her.

11

Bets

As promised, we had Ruth and Beatrice set up in there new place within the club in four days. They had all new furnishings, modern conveniences and a new wardrobe. Now that they were comfortable and settled, we had to fix some things up to get this project moving. Everyone pitched in. Even Adam's clan cliental and associates helped. I also decided to include Dianna. I couldn't shut her out any longer. She had to start to slowly learn exactly who I am, and what it is she is in love with. There was so much to me than she realized. She knew me at my best, but even I have faults—go figure—and I wasn't as perfect as she thinks.

She questioned why everyone was wearing the same coats and thought it was strange. I explained our tradition to her and she laughed.

"Do you want a coat too?" I asked.

"No, I think they are ugly and stupid," she said obstinately.

"Well," I said. "I'm getting you one any way."

"I won't wear it," she said as she walked over to the newly built stage and helped the others set it up.

The stage is meant for underground vampire bands to perform. Vampires enjoy music. A lot of us were born in times when music was in its infancy and truly appreciated and admired. The era of Mozart, Brahms, Bach and Beethoven inspired us greatly. A lot of vampires can play instruments as well. When you've been around for centuries it was necessary to find something to do to break up the monotony. I played guitar but it didn't amuse me for long. Joe, on the other hand, is an excellent drummer, probably because he is always banging something or someone.

While everyone was helping set up the stage, Adam and I were talking things over and hoping to be open within the next day or two. Adam also brought in a tattoo artist. Adam was a biker in his human existence so it made sense why he was attracted to tattoos. Vampires indulge in tattoos also, especially Ava, who wears them proudly and carries herself well with them. She has full sleeves and she would probably be getting more elsewhere now that an artist was in cahoots with us. It was a good idea considering we could profit from it with the humans also. I looked up to see that Dianna had stopped working and was studying something intensely. She took the red bandanna off her head and started to walk through the doorway that was behind the stage where Ruth and Beatrice resided. I rushed over behind her, put my arms around her waist before she could walk through the door.

"Where are you going?" I asked very matter of fact.

"What's through those doors and up the steps?" She asked as she tried to sneak pass me to take a look.

I didn't want to lie to her. I didn't want to deceive her any more. She had a right to know, but I wanted to tell her delicately and hopefully, she wouldn't pressure me for too much information. *That would never happen, Dianna questions everything.*

"Two witches live there," I answered very straight forward. *So much for delicate.*

"Like me?" She asked with a widened smile.

"No, nothing like you," I answered humorously. She didn't find that funny.

"What's that supposed to mean? What's so funny? More importantly, why do you have witches here?" She was demanding and pushed her way pass me and walked through the door.

I followed behind and let her pursue her quest. It would be an inevitable discovery on her part anyway. It might as well be now more than later when we were opened for business for her to throw a tantrum and cause a scene.

The place was clean and updated. Other than Ruth and Beatrice, there wasn't anything appalling about the place. She walked into the newly decorated living room where Ruth and Beatrice were sitting and playing gin rummy.

"Hello," Dianna said to get their attention.

Ruth turned away from her cards and smiled brightly but Beatrice didn't seem too happy when she saw that Dianna was with me and focused back on her cards.

"Come in child, please sit down. You must the young witch we've heard about. You're also more beautiful than I thought," Ruth said.

"You've heard about me?" Dianna asked and shot me a look that pierced through me like a million daggers.

"Dianna," I said. "This is Ruth and Bea." I reluctantly introduced them and entered the living room.

"We heard that a witch and a vampire were mates and we were quite surprised. During our youth that was unheard of," Ruth said.

"Why are you here?" Dianna pressed, ignoring Ruth's attempt at small conversation.

Ruth looked my way for approval before answering Dianna truthfully. I nodded yes.

Bea interrupted by yelling at Dianna and telling her she was too skinny. She was trying to intimidate her and unleash her jealousy of Dianna's youth and beauty.

Dianna ignored Bea and turned to Ruth.

"Don't look at him, why are you here? Is it because of him that you are here?" She was interrogating and would have made a great lawyer in a human life.

"Only partially," Ruth answered. "He gave us a better purpose for our long and lingering existence."

"What purpose is that? Is it for your blood?" Dianna snapped.

Ruth again looked at me for some kind of guidance. I was gracious to her for not wanting to do anything without my consent. She was loyal to me.

Dianna turned to me and said, "Go away, you're making her nervous."

"No...he's not, dear. Even though he's a vampire, he's a good man and loves you very much."

Dianna stared at me with disgust because in her heart she knew why Ruth and Bea were here.

"Then don't just stand there like a big dope, come in and sit down," she ordered and I nervously listened to her and I sat down quietly. That was a first. Ruth and Bea found her authority amusing.

"Big tough vampire being bullied by a tiny witch," Ruth said to Bea hysterically.

"Okay enough, it's not that funny," I infringed with frustration.

"It is funny," Bea antagonized while putting her cards in order.

Dianna was getting annoyed by the unsubtle attempt not to answer her question.

"Are you here because of your blood?" She asked again, much bolder than the first time.

"It's a business arrangement dear, and my sister and I are both fine with it. Dan and the others didn't force us to do this. It benefits all of us. So don't be angry with him," Ruth pleaded on my behalf.

Dianna was speechless for long moment lost in thought. I put my around her and she pushed me away.

"Thanks for your time; it was nice to meet you," she said to Ruth and Bea and began to walk away.

"Dianna..." Ruth shouted. Dianna stopped and turned to face her.

"Darkness will allow an infliction of six scars upon his skin to expose the light to death itself." Ruth riddled.

Dianna and I both looked at her baffled.

"What the fuck are you talking about?" I said quizzically to Ruth.

"Whatever," said Dianna and stormed out.

Of course, I went after her not thinking about Ruth's riddle. I raced to catch up to her and took hold of her arms before she walked threw the doorway between the stage and the apartment.

"Dianna, stop. You heard with your own ears, they want this too," I said.

"This was your idea wasn't it?"

"Does that really matter?"

"Would you sell my blood for a profit or for a quick fix?"

"You know I wouldn't do that."

"What's the difference? Is it because you don't fuck them and that makes it okay?" She was angry and appalled, but I was starting to get a little pissed off at the way she was speaking to me.

"You know what Dianna, that's it exactly, because fucking you is the only thing we have together. Is that how you feel?" I was sarcastic and arrogant in my tone as I continued on. "If I never fucked you again I still would never do that to you. How could you even think that?"

"Then why them and not me?"

"Because I love you and you belong to me."

"Everyone else who has interest in this place doesn't love me, so what keeps them from putting my blood up for sale?"

"That would never happen. Loyalty runs deep with my kind and it would never happen."

"What about your enemies? Are they loyal to you too?"

"Dianna you're stretching this a little deep, don't you think?" I was getting more than frustrated by this conversation. We were exploring too many avenues.

She paused and let that part of her interrogating end.

"Do you drink from them too or is it purely business?"

I didn't have to answer; the expression on my face said it all.

"Take me home!" She insisted.

Just as she was about to rush trough the exit doors, Xavier and his clan walked in uninvited and unwelcome. Dianna took a step back and nervously searched for me. I was at her side instantly.

"I'm right here," I whispered and she held on to my belt loop and stepped back. Xavier frightened her very much. I didn't really know why she feared him the way she did. I only knew that there was something about him that didn't sit well with her.

Adam rushed to my side and both our clans stood behind us ready to take any action should anything occur.

"What do you want, X?" I asked.

"Nothing, I just wanted to see the new place. Are you ready to settle your debt with me and make me part of this…. escapade?" He asked in his usual theatrical wit. He attempted to push me aside and waltz right in.

I grabbed him by the throat and tossed him against the wall. I raced towards him and grabbed him again, this time I slammed him against the wall. I noticed that Helena, Ava and Lidia quickly got Dianna out of the way to keep her out of harms way. Her fear of Xavier wasn't only obvious to me, everyone sensed it.

Adam's boys and mine had Xavier's clan circled. If they made one move towards Xavier it would have been a blood bath.

"Let's make this perfectly clear X," I yelled. "I don't have a debt to pay to you. The sooner you get that through your thick head the better off you'll be. I don't want to see you and your clan here again. Go back to fucking Coney Island and understand this, you'll never have any part of Manhattan."

The last thing I wanted was an all out war among the vampire world. Therefore I loosened my grip on him.

"You do owe me, and somehow you will pay up," he said as he stretched his neck around to loosen it. Then he looked at Dianna and smiled at her wickedly.

"Don't test me X," I threatened and turned his head from her sight and pinned him tightly to the wall once again. "You will regret it, I promise."

I kept him pinned not taking my eyes off him. I wanted him to make a sudden move just so I could rip him apart.

Adam intercepted the conversation because he knew that I was reaching my boiling point, "X, if he puts you down will you and your clan go?" Adam asked politely, trying to be the voice of reason.

"Yes, we'll go," Xavier said dramatically.

I let him down slowly and watched as he walked towards the door.

"This isn't over; you will settle your debt to me," Xavier said in the hallway with his clan behind him.

"What a pussy!" Adam laughed. "I hate that guy."

"I'm going to end up killing him, Adam," I said seriously.

"I know that, we all know that. All bets are on. Just be sure when you do, it's in your right to do so. We're all behind ya. Now go to Dianna, she looks a little troubled." Adam said and patted me on the back.

I walked over to the back of the room where Dianna was with the other girls and hugged her. They walked away and left us alone. The only thing good that came out of Xavier's visit was that Dianna suddenly was over the Ruth and Bea dispute. At least for now, I'm sure that would resurface in its own time.

Everyone else went back to fixing things up for the grand opening. It was pretty much done; vampires didn't need to many things in a club like this to keep us occupied. As far as the human side of the club, we had human contractors working on that because humans like ambiance. We didn't pay to much attention to that side of the bar and we let Sebastian run the show with that.

Dianna was sitting on a chair in the far back of the room. I kneeled down in front of her and asked her if she was alright.

"Yeah, I'm fine, I really just want to go home," she answered softly.

"I'll take you home, but I just want to know one thing, why are you so scared of X? What do you see or feel when he's around?" I was deeply concerned.

"I don't know," she answered, her voice coarse. "There's just something in his eyes when he looks at me. It's like he's plotting something and I don't trust him."

"I'm glad that you're on your guard and listening to your instincts. I want you to know that the only way X could ever get to you would be in the day and that won't happen because he's too afraid of sunlight."

"He might be, but maybe his clan isn't," Dianna speculated.

"Dianna, I hover you at night because that's when my kind is out and we are at our strongest. You're large wager in this world and a lot of my enemies would like to get their hands on you. That's why I'm so protective of you. I will keep you safe from Xavier, I don't trust him either. If you begin to feel threatened during the day then I would have to insist that you stay home and be with me constantly, but I honestly don't want to take the sunlight from you. That gift is too precious for me to insist upon. I only want you to be sure when you are out in the day alone that you go out three hours after sunrsie and come home three hours before sunset."

"Why three hours?"

"The sun starts to peak in between that time; there isn't a vampire who would venture between those times," I answered and moved the hair from her face. "Are you ready to go home?"

Dianna nodded, and we set off for home while the others stayed and finished up before tomorrow's opening.

I got her home safely and she settled on the couch, turned on the television and I sat with her. Before I could speak she answered the question I was going to ask her.

"I know you need to go back over there tonight and it's okay, I really don't mind. I know you have a lot to do," she said. "Just one thing I need to say before you leave."

"What's that?"

"Please don't drink from those women any more. It bothers me. I find it degrading and offensive. Please don't act like some kind of human junky on the streets," she pleaded.

"I won't. I promise," then as I kissed her lightly on the lips and my cell phone rang.

"What the hell is that?" She asked with surprise.

"My phone," I said as I answered it and told Adam that I'd see him in a few minutes.

"You have a cell phone too? When did that happen?" She seemed confused.

"Adam gave me this the other day," I said. "I hate it."

"You drive, you have a car, a cellphone and you drink from old withces and sell their blood. Is there anything else that I don't know?" She questioned with insistence.

I thought about her question, raised my eyes, and scratched my head and confessed to her that there was one more thing that she wasn't aware of. I didn't want any more lies or surprises between us.

"I'm going to tell you something and I want you to promise not to get pissed off at me because it's not my idea. It's something I don't have any control over, and it means nothing to me," I said before I confessed more secrets.

"Yeah, I promise. What is it?" She agreed in haste.

"It's Lizzy, she will be working there." Before I could finish speaking I could see in her eyes that she was getting flustered and furious.

"Dianna," I said calmly. "You promised not to get angry. This is part of my agreement with Adam. There isn't anything between Lizzy and me, there never was. She was just one of those things. You're the only one babe."

She thought about it for a second and calmed down.

"I'm glad you told me. I really can't take anymore surprises. Just keep her away from me when I'm there, and you stay away from her too, especially when I'm not there."

I smiled and hugged her tightly. She took that way better than I expected.

"Do you want me to stay home with you? I don't have to go back."

"No, it's alright. Really. You go and do what you have to do. I'll have Sebastian here to keep me company and I'm just going to watch a movie."

"Are you sure about that? Because I will stay." I just wanted her to reconfirm my offer so she wouldn't use it against me in the future. She nodded and kissed me. "I love you," I said and walked out the door and to the garage.

I drove back to the club to get there faster. There wasn't traffic at 1:00 A.M. in Manhattan. When I walked in everyone started passing money around. It looked like they were taking bets.

"What's going on?" I asked aloud.

"Oh, we were taking bets on whether you would actually come back or not," Adam answered.

"What were the odds?" I asked as if it were no big deal.

"Ten to one that you would show up, two to one if you didn't. Thanks for coming back, I won a fortune. I was the only one who played against the odds." Adam answered and smiled as he counted his money.

I thought it was pretty funny. I looked at Joe and asked him how much he lost.

"Two hundred," he answered.

"You bet two hundred against me? You're my right hand man, my brother, and that's what you do?"

"Well, you know how it is. I didn't think for a minute you would be back, especially this soon. You and Dianna usually fool around before you go anywhere and that can last for hours upon hours. So I figured by the time the two of you were done messing around, it would be sunrise and you wouldn't make it back anyway."

"What do you do, time us? How do you know what we're doing?" I asked. Honestly, I was a little disturbed by his accuracy.

"The whole apartment building knows. You're really not that discreet or quiet about it, even if your door is closed," he answered.

"Alright, that's enough, and don't ever let her know that because she'll get all bent, freak out and be embarrassed. I really don't want to deal with that. Then I'll be pissed and cranky and you'll bear the brunt of it if my sex life suffers."

"Speaking of a sex life, is there anyone here who could accommodate?" Joe said and scanned the room for a female victim for his sexual hunger.

"It's really time that you find yourself a woman," I said and walked away as he was prowling the females in Adam's clan.

"If he wasn't a vampire, he would be the poster child for STD's," Adam said.

Lizzy showed up and was standing on the stage and gazing my way. *Here we go*, I thought to myself. I acknowledged her by nodding my head and I did smile a bit flirtatiously. She jumped off the stage and walked my way.

"Hey gorgeous," she said. "Where's the little woman?"

"She's home," I answered. Lizzy put her arms around my neck and tried to kiss me.

I gently pushed her away. "It's not gonna happen, Lizzy."

"Why not? You know what they say, *when the cats away, the mice will play.*" She tried to kiss me again. I pushed her away, a little rougher this time. I didn't want any trouble.

"First of all Lizzy, the whole seduction thing doesn't work on me, just back off. It's not going to happen, go find Joe he's ready to pop."

"Why would I want Joe when I can have you?" She instigated as she pressed her body against mine. She was starting to irritate me.

"You can't have me, now go," I said and pushed her again. She was definitely insulted and humiliated but persistent to say the least.

"What can your little girlfriend give you that I can't? I won't tell her.

Do it for me, it's been such a long time since you and I have been together."

It was apparent that she wasn't going to stop until she got what she wanted, or I was going to have to get violent. I didn't like either of those choices. I called to Adam and he looked my way.

"Can you do something with this?" I said and pointed to Lizzy, who was technically his property.

Adam seemed annoyed by her persistence and told her to get off of me and go home. When Adam spoke to her she didn't question him she did as she was told.

I scanned the room and saw that Joe was leaving. He apparently got lucky and disappeared into the night with one of the humans that worked for Adam. She was one of his daywalkers. All clans had them. We were one of the luckier clans because Sebastian was able to walk in the day without consequence, and Dianna too. We didn't have to rely on mortals and their weaknesses.

I only stayed at the club for about an hour. There wasn't much to do. Grand opening would take off on time. Before departing, everyone went to Ruth and Bea for a drink but I stayed true to my word and went home instead. It just wasn't worth upsetting Dianna, because somehow, someway Dianna would know if I broke my word to her. We are connected to each other; there weren't too many secrets we could keep from one another.

When I got home, I found Dianna sleeping on the couch. I carried her into our room quietly. She woke up and smiled at me.

"I'm glad you're home, I hate sleeping without you," she whispered with her eyes half closed.

I laid her on the bed and made her comfortable and she instantly fell back to sleep. After what Joe had told me about our inability to maintain a respectful and tactful sexual encounter, I was glad that she slept. I laid beside her, closed my eyes and rested peacefully until I heard noises travel throughout the apartment.

Thud... Squeak.... Squeak... Scream.... Moan.... Bang... Moan... Scream... Squeak... Thud... Squeak...

Apparently, Joe got lucky with the day walker he picked up at the club. He had her in his room, and as it would turn out, Joe wasn't very discreet either.

12

Grand Opening

Dianna was up and about before any of us. She and Sebastian were in the kitchen eating breakfast, laughing and conversing with one another. I walked in and they stopped talking and began to laugh quietly to one another. It was apparent that I was the brunt of a joke.

"What's so funny?" I asked.

"Nothing," Sebastian answered. "Dianna and I were just discussing how her mother's reaction is going to be when she meets you."

I forgot all about that. I have to take her back home in a week. Shit.

"Should be interesting," I rebutted.

"You forgot, didn't you?" Dianna said with a smile.

"Uhh, no I didn't," My lack of enthusiasm was apparent. "I can't wait."

"You are so full of it," she said, humorously.

"I tried," I said and kissed her on the head. She and Sebastian both found my upcoming introduction to Dianna's family entertaining.

"I'll just leave you two alone so you can have a good laugh at my expense," I said wittily and departed into the living room while the two of them stayed in the kitchen a little longer and conversed.

Helena, Richard and Ava were up and playing Nintendo Wii Bowling. I walked over to the televison, switched the input, and put the television on instead, just to aggravate them.

"What the hell are you doing?" Richard yelled.

"You're such an asshole!" Helena shouted and I vaguely nodded.

Ava didn't say anything. She was still frightened of me. Her fangs finally grew in and she didn't take any chances to upset me. She sat down and watched television.

Helena turned the game system back on.

"Come on Helena, I don't wanna watch you play games, put the tube on," I said.

"There's about six other TV sets in this house, go find one and watch it," Richard said, obviously pissed off.

It always stuns me when Richard speaks up. He may be quiet for most of the time and a lot of my kind would underestimate him, and that was a mistake on their part, but when he speaks up, he is very direct and ruthless.

"There's also an entire game room with every game system imaginable, can't you go in there and bowl without a ball?"

"You're being a dick," Richard said and turned the game system back on and threw his imaginary ball.

Sebastian had candy in dishes throughout the house for Dianna. I threw a couple of hard candies that were in one of the dishes at Richard just to irritate him. He immediately thew the entire dish at me.

"Why do you always have to start shit?" Helena shouted and pushed me, barely.

Richard smiled at her, they both lunged at me good-humouredly, and the three of us started romping around. It's been a while since we had one of our living room rumbles.

Joe walked out of his room with his one night stand who was wearing his U2 T-shirt. Joe gently pushed her aside and joined us. Joe's woman sat on the couch next to Ava and introduced herself. Sebastian and Dianna came from the kitchen and walked into the chaos.

We stopped for a brief minute and looked at Sebastian to get his reaction.

"It's a losing battle, I give up," Sebastian said defeated and walked into his bedroom throwing his arms up in the air as if he was surrendering.

We started up again and I noticed that Dianna sat next to

Joe's...uh...whatever she was and introduced herself. The girl introduced herself back as Crissy. Dianna, Ava and Crissy sat on the couch conversing to one another as if nothing was happening. Joe's new interest has been a part of our world for a long time and was used to behavior like this. As for Ava and Dianna, this was just a typical day even though it's been a while and overdue.

Joe accidentally pushed Helena a little bit too hard and Richard got angry. His eyes turned red and he went into a true attack mode.

I held him back and talked to him, "Come on Rick, it was an accident, we're just playing around. She's alright." I didn't need any rivalry among my own.

Helena butted in and put her arms around Richard. "I'm just fine honey, watch this," Helena said and plunged her knee right into Joe's groin.

Richard pulled back and laughed. We all did. Dianna didn't laugh; she widened her teeth and seemed more than delighted that Helena did to Joe what she always wanted to do.

Joe crouched down and threw himself on the floor. Crissy ran over to him to help him up. Joe was laughing as well, and accepted defeat. When you're a vampire, the pain didn't last very long. Males could shake that off within seconds.

Needless to say, when we sat down we turned on the televison and not the game system. I got my way, as usual.

We were all talking, joking around and bonding. All except Ava. She seemed a little laid back and distant. Probably because everyone was paired off but her and I actually felt bad for her, this had to be a hard, uncomfortable situation for her. It was a shame that Christopher was untrustworthy. Ava and I didn't see eye to eye on much, but she did share my blood and that was all that mattered.

Joe seemed to take an unusual interest in Crissy. He was attentive and physical with her. Usually when Joe would bring someone home he would just show them to the door when they woke up and we never saw her again, or he turned them into a mid morning snack. Crissy isn't the blonde bombshell that Joe would usually take an interest in. She is small and slender yet her bosom was well beyond that of a woman her size. It was apparent they aren't what God had given her. She is a natural brunette with blonde highlights thru out her hair. Her eyes were a sage green and she had brilliant, perfectly aligned white teeth.

Dianna was quiet; she usually was when we were all together. I wasn't blind and I could see that she was never really at ease when we all together. Dianna wanted my attention focused on her only. She didn't want to share me in any way. That was something that she would have to learn to accept. Preferably the sooner the better. We would all try to include her in conversation and situations but she always shyed away from that. She would sit real close to me and nestle her head on my chest and to be honest, I hated it. Dianna's unconfortability made me uncomfortable. I was able to understand why she would shy away from Joe but not anyone else. Although, even Joe went out of his way at times to joke with her in his way and try to lighten her up. Joe did save her life by sharing his blood with her, in hopes that it would mend some of the damage that he has done. I'm not sure that Dianna was even aware of that, because if she was, she would probably be more gracious, or maybe appalled. All I know is that time was ticking slowly and I just wanted to get out of the house and feed, preferably as a group and then go to the grand opening.

I whispered into Dianna's ear and asked her to come with me in the other room because I wanted to talk to her privately. I was concerned about how withdrawn she was. She got up and follwed me into the library.

I closed the door behind her and softly asked her, "Are you alright? Why are you so quiet?"

She shrugged her shoulders.

"Dianna, why are you so uncomfortable here? I hate seeing you like this," I was gentle and concerned in my tone of voice and I caressed her cheek softly.

"I don't know. I guess I just do better in small groups," she responded.

"That explains why you get quiet, but not why you shut yourself out. Not just today but all the time."

"The last time when I made myself comfortable, you hit me and I don't want you to do that again."

"That was different you were drinking and you fed for the first time.

You weren't yourself that day," I said attentively. It hurt me when she brought that day up, although I deserved it.

"I just don't feel like I belong. I don't feel like I belong anywhere really. It sucks to be different from everyone else. Except when I'm with you, then everything is okay."

"Baby, you belong here and I am here with you. Don't feel like that. So you're different, that's not a bad thing. That's what I love about you most."

She smiled at my comment and then she began to get teary eyed.

"Why are you crying?" I asked and pulled her close to me.

"I don't really know why," she attempted to laugh through her tears. "I'll try to be more sociable, but please don't push me into it. You have to understand one thing; I don't have the allegence that you have when it comes to everyone else in this house. My only allegiance is to you, but I will try. I promise."

"That's all I can ask for, but I want to know something else…is anyone in this house giving you a hard time or being mean to you anyway?" I asked with concern.

"No, it's nothing like that," she whispered.

"Are you sure? Just tell me and I'll take care of it right now." I didn't think that was the case but I wanted to cover all possibilities.

"No, really, everyone is great. It's me. You don't know what it's like to sit in a room and have nothing in common with anyone."

"What do you mean?" I asked.

"I'm not even of the same species of anyone here. I'm half vampire, half witch and I still don't know everything about that. All of you were human once and I never was. I'm just a little out of my league. So I feel it's better to stay quiet than to make a fool out of myself and discuss things that I don't know anything about."

I put my arms around her and kissed her.

"Things will get better. I'll make sure of it. Don't ever feel like you don't belong here, this is your home, and you will always belong to me. Now kiss me again." She gave me a small and gentle kiss on the lips and smiled before we went back inside and rejoined with everyone else.

At this point, we were just waiting for the sunset so we can feed.

Crissy had left while Dianna and I were in the other room. Joe seemed smitten with her and made arragements to meet with her tonight.

Sunset finally approached and we all set out to feed. Dianna and I went our separate ways. The way she was feeling the last thing I wanted her to do was have her feed with everyone else around. I knew she would be embarrassed to do that in front of everyone, she wasn't comfortable among us and with the whole feeding process yet. Dianna would rather stay hungry than put herself in a position where she felt inadequate.

We walked to the Midtown Tunnel where many homeless drunks resided. I had to force Dianna to eat. She wouldn't be aggressive with these people and take the first bite. I had to do it for her. I was patient, but her conscience was driving me crazy. She would rather go hungry than take a life that didn't hold any threat to her. Feeding was going to be Dianna's biggest hurdle, and the most important. Somehow, someway she had to overcome this. She had no choice. She was weak when it came to killing. This wasn't good and it would be a long time before I could trust her to feed on her own. I had to tend to her like a baby and make sure she was fed. Relying on me just to help her feed was a way she could never survive on her own. She needed to understand that she couldn't always be in a compromising position just to eat. She still couldn't grasp the fact that she had to drink blood to function and live. It was hard for her to accept what she is now. And that's understandable. However, feeding is essential, she may not have to drink as often as the rest of us but it still needs to be done.

We arrived at *Hell on Earth* and everyone was already there. It made sense that they arrived earlier than we did, they didn't have to force each other to eat and they just did what they needed to do and moved on.

Dianna was a little more vibrant than she was earlier. Something happens after we feed and we all become more vivacious. I took bets on Joe and Crissy, and how long this fling would last. Dianna played pool and made some money without cheating. I warned her that cheating in pool in this place wouldn't be a good idea because there are a lot of testy vampires who take the game extremely seriously. She agreed without argument.

Adam was high-spirited and was happy about the ways things were going. Xavier didn't have the nerve to show up on this night. He knew that it would be much too crowded and filled with most of the Manhattan clans to cause any chaos.

Lizzy was wondering around playing hostess making sure everyone was comfortable and setting up herself and the other donors in case anyone wanted to drink. She and Dianna made eye contact while Dianna was leaning over the pool table ready to break the balls, but nothing came more of it. I was relieved that both Lizzy and Dianna were able to compose themselves. A loud crackle shot through the club when Dianna broke up the balls. I looked at her at smiled at her crookedly; she smiled just as slick back at me. The night was going smoothly. For once, Dianna and I didn't fight or argue. She was being sociable and she wasn't hanging all over me. However, I never let her out of my sight.

Dianna and Ava were bonding. The two of them teamed up on the tables, ran them for a few hours, and hustled a lot of money. *Dianna had a sneaky dark side after all, who knew?* Although, it isn't about the money, it's about competition, victory and being the more superior vampire in a game of wits.

Dianna wasn't a witch tonight. All of her vampire traits and personality were surfacing. Her instincts didn't control her as it did the first time. She was in control of who she was. I was ecstatic to see that side of her emerge. She didn't make a fuss over the amounts of vampires that were going in and out of the witches place to drink E.B. I stayed true to my word and never attempted to sneak in for a taste.

Joe and Crissy were cozy in the corner among themselves, so I lowered the odds that Joe would be done with her by the end of the night. Crissy just might be the one.

All and all, it was good night and a success. It was a proud moment for me.

13

Vermont

It was the last Wednesday in November, Thanksgiving Eve. Come sunset I would be driving Dianna and myself to visit her family in Vermont. Something I wasn't looking forward to.

A vampire in a house full of witches, this should be interesting.

The very moment the sun set, Dianna was ready to go. She was very excited about the four-hour trip we were going to take. I didn't let on to my dread about this trip. I didn't want to get her upset. Therefore, I sucked it up and we were on our way. I was hardly the boy next door that a girl takes home to meet the family, but it wasn't about that. Dianna wanted to settle things with her family regardless of the result. She was looking for closure in one way or another. Either they would accept her for what she has become or they wouldn't, and I would be there to pick up the pieces.

Halfway through our ride I had to stop at a rest area to feed. Let's face it, Dianna's hometown has a population of about five hundred. It wasn't likely that I'd be able to feed in such a small town. Dianna claimed she wasn't hungry that she fed just the night before and she was alright, and I believed her. That was my first mistake.

Dianna loved the car. She was playing with the radio, the CD player and the Bluetooth, mp3 features that came factory on the car. She kept pressing the button to make the roof open and close. She was like a kid in the candy store. I let her play; after all, it was only a car. However, it wasn't the typical car that you would find in a small town in Vermont. We were going to stick out like a sore thumb. So much for discretion among vampires.

We arrived at 9 P.M., just as predicted. Her small Cape Cod type house stood alone among many acres of land. When I got out of the car, I saw the small clearing in the distance where Dianna and I had our first meeting of chance. The memories came rushing in like a great wind. She didn't remember anything at all. Perhaps, it was better that way.

She grabbed my hand and started pulling me towards the front door. I stopped short before she knocked, "Dianna, this is still your home, you have to invite me or I won't go, and for some reason I don't think you're parents are going to be to willing to let a vampire in their home willingly."

"You're so hung up on that inviting stuff, what's the big deal? No one here will try to hurt you," she said.

"I won't allow myself to be powerless for anything, not even you, so just invite me in, okay?"

"If that's what makes you happy then I will," she said as she knocked on the door.

Both her parents answered the door. When they saw Dianna, they had smiles on their faces that stretched for miles. They hugged each other and Dianna seemed so incredibly happy to be back home. She took my hand and said the magic words, "Come in," and introduced me to her parents, Jerry and Sarah and their pup, Merlin. Her father was gracious and hospitable and shook my hand and showed me around the small old house. It was clean and neat. There weren't many updated appliances or electronic games and computers. They still had an old fashion record player that was still used to listen to records. The kitchen was just off the living room and the dining area was shared with the living room as well. There was one bedroom downstairs and Dianna's old room was upstairs in a converted attic. Vampires were definitely more materialistic than witches and warlocks. The proof was within these walls and the walls of Ruth and Beatrice. Witches prefer natural ways and things. The tools of nature. Vampires are much flashier. We liked our fancy stuff, our trophies and luxury as a whole. We liked our men and women to be attractive and sexy. Where witches were more accustomed for their men and women to be natural. Lucky for me, Dianna was all of the above. We like to progress with the times, witches and warlocks don't. They prefer things to be simple. This place was exactly that…simple. It was like the story of the city mouse and the country mouse.

I adjourned to the couch, sat quietly, and watched a football game. Dianna and her parents sat at the dining table that was just behind me to have their reunion. This night was for her and if she wanted me there I would join them, but for right now I was content with the arrangements.

As I said, her father was gracious, but her mother seemed bitter. She didn't acknowledge me when I walked in. She took hold of Dianna and used all her power to keep her out of my reach. However, it was her mother and they had a lot of catching up to do. When I took the time to think about the situation, I would have to assume that I wouldn't be that happy if my witch daughter came home with the being who tried to kill her. So I just let them be and watched the clock tick slowly.

After about an hour of them reminiscing, Dianna and her mother adjourned to the small kitchen to bake cookies. Her father joined me on the couch to watch the game.

"That's a real nice car you have out there," Jerry commented while petting Merlin. He seemed a little envious but in a good way.

"Thanks," I answered. "Tomorrow morning, why don't the three of you go out for breakfast and take it into town and enjoy your day?" I handed him the keys.

He smiled as he took them from my hand. Dianna had her father's smile. I don't think her mother was capable of smiling. We were watching the game and making small talk about bad calls and bad plays. It was typical human guy stuff but what else could I do. He was going out of his way to make me comfortable and I appreciated it.

We were able to overhear the conversation between Dianna and her mother in the kitchen. At first, it was harmless enough. They were gathering ingredients and making small talk about New York. Dianna told her about her bookshop, and how she still had her apartment in the village, but was probably going to let the lease run out because she lives with me.

"I don't know what you're doing with him, Dianna. That kind is so beneath you. You don't belong with the likes of them," Sarah scolded.

"Mom, please. I am one of them now or at least half of one and you never even told me about what happened to me all those years ago," Dianna answered.

"So now it's my fault?" Her mother shouted.

"No, Mom, I'm not blaming you. He makes me happy, he's good to me and he's helping me through all these changes that I'm going through. Maybe if you told me about this I wouldn't be so dependant on him."

The conversation seized briefly and I was getting more than angry at the way Dianna's mother was talking to her.

Within minutes, Sarah started up again, "Dianna, I just don't understand, how you can belong to a world that is so against everything you believe in?"

"It's not that much different than our world, Mom," Dianna answered meekly.

"You belong among your own kind Dianna, not with a bunch of vampires, and they're not even vampires that were transformed from our kind. They are cold blooded monsters and you don't belong there," Sarah insisted.

"I do, Mom. Whether you think so or not. I don't even know what *my kind* is, because you never told me that I was different!" She began to yell.

"You're a witch, Dianna! End of story!" Sarah shouted back.

"No, I'm not. I'm the only one of my kind and I don't have anyone to guide me except Danny, because you're in too much denial about the fact that I'm part VAMPIRE!" Dianna screamed.

Sarah slammed something on the counter and whatever it was smashed.

"Dianna, you're my daughter and if you didn't get mixed up with vampires this conversation wouldn't even be happening right now. You would have stayed a witch. You didn't need to know what he did to you all those years ago, because you were safe here," Sarah yelled and slammed something else down.

"I still had the right to know, you and Dad should have told me." Dianna spoke softly and her voice was beginning to crack, she would be crying soon.

Sarah kept rambling on, and basically degrading Dianna for what she has become.

I was getting angry and Jerry saw it in my face. I was staying calm and cool and this would all be over soon. I just wanted to take her back home to New York, where she did belong.

"Maybe we should have told you, but we don't have to like it," Sarah said sternly.

"Mom! Could you just leave me alone and deal with it!" I heard Dianna shout.

"I'm sorry Dianna, but I don't like the choices you've made and I'm very disappointed. I expected so much more from you. You couldn't even come visit us alone, why did you bring this predator into our home?"

"Because I want him with me…always!"

"Where are you going?" Her mother shouted before Dianna stormed out the back door.

"I'm going to play with the dog because it's better company than you!" And I heard her begin to cry before she slammed the door.

That was enough for me. Now that Dianna was out of the room, Sarah was going to get a piece of my mind. No sooner than Dianna was out of the door, I stomped into the kitchen and Jerry followed.

I slammed my hand on the counter and said firmly, "I want you to back off and leave Dianna alone and get off her case!"

"I beg your pardon!"

"You heard me, back off and leave her alone! She came here to see you and make some kind of peace with you. She's going through a lot and your support would have been a good thing for her."

"How dare you come into my home and tell me how to raise my daughter!"

"You've already raised her. She's grown. I don't want you upsetting her any more."

"She never should have gone to New York," Sarah scowled.

"You're right, she never should have gone to New York, but she did. What kind of parent ships their sheltered daughter to New York City, without a clue as to how the world works? Not only was she sheltered, she went there thinking she's a witch and turns out that she isn't even that. She was blind to everything around her and no one here gave a fuck. To send her to place with so many walks of life was just cruel."

"It was her idea to go there, not ours," Sarah said in her own defense.

"If you're so concerned why didn't you try to stop her from leaving home? Especially, with the secret you've kept from her for so many years. And now that it's all out in the open you think you can start controlling things and calling the shots because I'm not human or the species of choice? I don't fuckin' think so!"

"If it weren't for you, none of this would be happening! You attacked and wanted to kill my child!" Sarah yelled and slammed the cabinet door shut.

"NO! I wanted to take her away from this place on that very day, and I wish I did. She would have been so much better off, at least she would know what she is and I would have taken care of her the right way. She went to grab my hand to come with me but someone snatched her up before she could take hold of me!"

"Sometimes the truth is better left unsaid, and this was one of those times," Sarah rebutted.

"You believe if you don't talk about the things that happened, that will disappear, just because you chose to hide them away. Things don't go away because you say so. This is who she is and you're an ignorant fool! Now you're gonna pretend that you're concerned and tell Dianna a bunch of bullshit about me and my kind, as if you know anything about my kind, in hopes that she leaves me. She belongs to me now, and I'll take care of her!"

"Are you afraid she might take my advice and leave you?" Sarah asked wickedly.

"That's hardly the case. Let me be perfectly clear about something, I didn't come here to seek your approval or acceptance. I came because for some bizarre reason this is where Dianna wanted to be. Now I'm starting to regret it as I'm sure she is too. I hope that the one thing we agree is Dianna's happiness and right now you're making her miserable and I don't fuckin' like it!"

Sarah and I remained silent for a second before Jerry intervened.

"He's right, Sarah, just leave the child alone. What's done is done. Let's give her our love and support and wish her the best. I don't want to lose my daughter because of your snobbish predjudice."

Sarah was shocked by Jerry's interference and frankly, so was I.

"He's a decent man Sarah, despite the fact that he's a vampire and she's happy. He's obviously good to her, Dianna looks wonderful. Let's just enjoy her brief visit. She came here to make peace and ask us for our acceptance and support of what she has become, and we have to do that for her. No matter what has happened in the past she is our daughter and we can't turn our backs on her. None of this is her fault. We should have told her."

Sarah became very quiet and so did I. It was just in time because Dianna walked back in. She looked around and seen all three of us standing there not saying a word to one another. It looked a little strange.

"What's going on?" She questioned.

"Nothing babe, everything is fine," I said staring at Sarah fiercly.

"Your mother and I were just getting ready for bed, weren't we Sarah?" Jerry said.

"I suppose," Sarah said snobbishly. "Dianna you're room is just how you left it, I know you'll feel right at home. And where will Dan be sleeping?" She was such a controlling woman and I would have loved to have smacked her. She didn't like that I spoke up to her because I don't think that anyone ever has. I think she was even more shocked when Dianna spoke up for herself, that's probably what pissed her off the most. It was plain to see that Sarah was in charge of all that happened within this family. Despite it all, Sarah decided to try to call the shots in other ways. In ways that she thought she had control over. However, Sarah didn't know me at all and how controlling I am.

"He sleeps with me Mom, now stop it or I'll just go home now," Dianna answered.

"It's fine," Jerry said. "You know the way Dianna, now go and get a good nights rest." He gave her a fatherly kiss on the cheek, and Dianna hugged him tightly before he retired to his bedroom.

Sarah watched me and Dianna go up the stairs and into her old room. I turned my head to face Sarah and smiled cunningly at her. *That's right bitch, you lost again and I got my way. I'm sleeping with your daughter.*

I threw myself on Dianna's bed and screamed into the pillow, "Ahhhh!!! What time is it?"

"Midnight," she said with a giggle.

"Only about fifteen hours to go," I answered with my head still in the pillow.

I turned around and took off my shirt only to make myself comfortable. Dianna sat on top of me fully dressed. We were talking about her mother and how her room hasn't been changed since she's been gone. It was the first time we were in bed together...innocently.

Her mother came bursting into the room with a roll away bed.

"Get off of him, Dianna!" She ordered.

"Mom! Stop it!"

"It's okay, get up," I said quietly and she did. I wasn't up to an argument.

I got up from her bed and began to put my shirt back on.

"What the heck is that stuff all over your body, they are disgusting!" Sarah said to me in disgust referring to my tattoos.

"Dianna likes them, that's all that matters, isn't it? I'm thinking about getting another one with Dianna's name, what do you think?"

I wasn't really considering another tattoo but Dianna smiled radiantly and her eyes widened when I said it. I was sure that Dianna would probably hold me to that promise.

Sarah didn't like having her authority challenged. Sarah changed the subject and said, "I brought up this cot for you but I guess that was a silly idea because doesn't your kind sleep in coffins?"

"Mine is in the shop," I barked back. "Besides, I prefer to hang from the rafters and what better place to do that than in an attic." I leaped to the rafters along the ceiling and hung from my legs on the beam just to irritate the woman. Dianna laughed at my disobedience towards her mother.

Sarah looked at Dianna and sighed heavily, "This is what makes you happy?" She asked as she pointed to me.

"Yep," Dianna answered defiantly as she was looking up at me hanging from the rafters with a lavishly brilliant smile.

Sarah walked out of the room in defeat and humilation.

It wasn't any wonder why Dianna felt like she didn't belong anywhere. That was all her mother ever told her. I just wanted to get Dianna out of here and go back to the life we have been building together. This fiasco wasn't part of any dreams that Dianna and I shared.

I jumped down seconds after her mother left the room and went back into the bed. It was only midnight and that was early in the life of a vampire. Dianna assumed the same postion as before but now she was being seductive.

"No way Dianna, not here, your mother will come flying in here on a broom or something and boil us in oil. No way."

Dianna thought about it, "You're right. I'll stop. Besides, the bed would probably fall right through the floor, they are so old," she said and we both laughed.

We talked a lot that night. Nothing special, just little things. We talked for about two hours when Dianna announced she was hungry for blood.

"I told you to feed before we left! There isn't any blood in this town, the population is like 500 and when you left, it was 499. Who are you going to feed from especially at two in the morning?"

"I don't know, but I'm hungry," she pouted.

"Go downstairs and drain your mother," I said in jest, but not really.

"That's so mean," Dianna said but laughed.

"If I get in the car we're going home, besides your father has my keys."

"Why does he have the keys?"

"He's taking you for breakfast and he wants to drive it. I like your father, he's alright."

"That was really nice of you," she seemed pleased by my gesture.

"I try," I answered.

"Can I drink animal blood? We have a lot of deer here," Dianna asked.

"Yeah, you can, but you're not going to like it," I said.

"But...I'm hungry," she pouted again and nudged her head toward the one and only window in her room. "We can sneak out the window, this way they won't know anything."

"Sneak? How old are we that we have to sneak?" I asked sarcastically.

"Please," she whined. "I'm so hungry," she pouted again, raised her eyes and batted them.

"Okay fine, but I'm telling ya, you're not gonna like animal blood," I answered.

She smiled cutely, got up from on top of me and she opened her window.

I reluctantly agreed and we sneaked out her little attic window. I couldn't believe the extents that I was going through just so she can drink from a deer.

"Ya know, I wouldn't do this for anyone but you," I whispered as I squeezed myself through the small window and helped her out as well. *I'm over a hundred years old and I'm sneaking out windows. Ridiculous.*

We leaped from the roof to the ground and walked through the woods where there were plenty of deer. The woods were infested with them.

"Go get one, I'll wait here," I said and sat down on the ground.

"Can you get me one? You're so much faster than I am and if I do it, we'll be here all night," she asked me like a baby. "Please?"

How could I resist?

So I did.

I brought her back a big buck and held it for her because the buck was getting a little crazed and out of control.

"Go for it," I said as I held the buck down for her to drink.

"Aren't you going to drink too?" She asked.

"Fuck no, I'm not eating that."

"How bad can it be?"

"What are you waiting for, try it and see for yourself," I said knowingly.

She did exactly that. She took one sip and spit the blood out.

"That's disgusting!"

"I told ya so," I said justifiably so.

She went to drink from the buck again and this time she held her nose to try to hide the taste.

"That doesn't work, just drink it fast and get it over with," I laughed at how naive she really was.

She drank quickly and spit a lot. Dianna had more blood on her face than she ever has before. I cleaned her up, luckily I remembered my face cloths.

We stayed in the woods for a long time. We talked some more and shared a lot of thoughts and ideas about our future. We also talked a lot about our past, before we knew each other, and we learned how lonely we both were until we found each other again. We didn't meet by chance, we are destined to be together, we just kept missing each other along the way and through the years. There was a reason why I didn't marry that woman in my human days, because even then I was meant to be with Dianna and meant to become a vampire.

It was more private and peaceful outside of her home. Dianna was asking many questions about turning people into vampires. I guess they were normal questions, but I warned her never to do that. Especially because she was so different and no one would know what she would create. She was very curious about transformation; however, she vowed never to do that. I couldn't explain enough to her how our existence depends souly on our discretion. Only a few are welcomed into our world.

We fooled around in the woods before we went back to her room. Dianna is actually more sexual than I am. I could get through the night without sex, but not her. She wanted to get laid whenever we were in bed together. However, since that wasn't going to happen here, the woods were the next reasonable option and our needs were satisfied.

When we got back to her room I covered up the window to block the morning sun, and we both laid down arm in arm to rest. Dianna would be joining her family for breakfast while I stayed in. I liked the idea of not being near her mother. Besides, it would give me a chance to be nosy and snoop through her room while she was gone.

After a much needed rest, Dianna got up, kissed me tenderly on the lips, and went down stairs. I waited a while before I began to look through her things. There wasn't any yelling coming from downstairs, hopefully her mother has accepted things and would leave Dianna alone.

I heard the front door close and the engine of my car roar, they were on their way out for breakfast. I got up from the bed and began to pry through her personal things. The only things that I found of interest were photos of Dianna. There were many old pictures from when Dianna was little. I was amused when I saw pictures of her as a baby, about two or three years old with food smeared all over her face. *She's just a slob.* That was the only reasonable answer for her poor eating habits.

There was one particular picture of Dianna where she looked absolutely stunning. It was like the one missing star in a constellation. Her smile, her eyes and her face could light up the night sky. That picture went right into my wallet. It was a black and white head shot and her beauty was mystifying. Everything else was just typical things as she grew up with the years. She had letters, spell books with weird incantations, old journals that were boring to read and a lot of pictures and post cards of New York.

Time went by quickly and I heard Dianna and her family walk in, but I stayed upstairs. I didn't want to see her mother or be surrounded by tons of food. Dianna came upstairs to see me before she helped her mother prepare for Thanksgiving dinner. Apparently, Dianna and her mother made peace and she wanted to spend the remainder of the day with her family. I didn't have a problem with that. My only condition was for her to be ready to leave at exactly 5:08 P.M., sunset. I would be downstairs and ready to go. She agreed, kissed me and gave me back my car keys before she left her room and joined her family.

14

Conscience

After many grueling hours of anticipation, the sun finally had set. I was up, ready to go, and hurried down the stairs. When her parents saw me, a look of sadness fell upon their faces. They realized that there little girl was going home.

I walked over, shook her father's hand, and thanked him for standing by Dianna. I assured him that I wouldn't hesitate to take Dianna back to see them whenever she wanted. As for Dianna's mother, I didn't have anything to say to her, nor did she have anything to say to me. I told Dianna that I'd be waiting in the car whenever she was ready to leave. I let her say her goodbye's privately, the way it should be.

Dianna wasn't as long as I thought she would be. She was a little teary eyed but nothing tragic.

"Are you alright?" I asked.

"I'm good," she said. "I'm glad I came here. I got to say many things, had a lot of questions answered over breakfast and tied up loose ends. Things are better now and I know that I don't have to lose my family if I don't want to. Thanks so much for taking me here, but now I'm ready to go home with you."

I leaned over and kissed her. Those were the words I wanted to hear. I started the car and we were on our way back home to the frantic city.

Dianna was still hungry. Her eyes were beginning to turn red as we were driving. I had to find somewhere in the middle of nowhere for her to drink. I wasn't going to take a chance of her getting sick again. We were too far from home to let that happen. Hunting season was open and there were a lot of hunters out. Thanksgiving dinner was over for most of them and now they hunted for tomorrow's meal. There was a place in Lamoille County called Bear Swamp. A wooded area opened for hunters with mucky waters, the perfect place. There were humans that could be hunted by Dianna and myself as opposed to them being the hunters. A mucky lake or swamp so full of thick mire and full of vial living organisms and bacteria would surely dispose of the bodies, perfectly.

I told Dianna of my plan and she seemed anxious to put it into action. I wanted be as close to the swampy area as possible. I drove as far as the roads would allow. The swamp was about 100 feet away from my car and I saw a few orange jackets, so did Dianna.

There were two male hunters perched in a tree waiting for an unsuspecting deer to walk into range. They were in their late twenties or early thirties. Leaping into a tree was easy for me and Dianna. It was also a place where our prey couldn't run.

Dianna and I both leaped and took hold of our prey. I stayed on the branch that the hunters were on while Dianna pushed her victim to the ground to feed from him there. I wasn't watching Dianna as I was feeding because I was just as hungry as she was. When I was done, I noticed that Dianna's victim was lying on the frozen Vermont ground bitten and still alive. Dianna was standing along side of him, crying.

"What the hell are you doing?" I asked frantically.

"I can't do this. I can't go through with this," she panicked and ran to the car.

I was left alone with one corpse, a live human who seen us for what we really were and a basket case for a mate in the car.

I looked at Dianna's victim and finished him off. She didn't leave me any other choice. I disposed of the bodies as planned and threw them into the swampy water. Their bodies sank deep within the swamp as if the mud that lingered there swallowed them whole. It was so thick that it wasn't even frozen over. Whatever creatures dwelled there would surely devour them. Eventually, within a few days their bodies would decompose.

I rushed over to the car. I was a little more than pissed off. I slammed my door shut, pressed my foot on the clutch and started the car.

"What the fuck was that about!" I yelled, while shifting from first to second gear.

She was curled up on the seat with her knees up, head down and crying.

"I couldn't do it," she sobbed. "He was too innocent. I felt his living energy. He was a good man out hunting to feed his family. It wasn't right. He wasn't going to hurt me and he pleaded for mercy. I just couldn't do it."

I was driving fast in sixth gear, and I hated her excuse.

"Don't ever fucking do that again! What the hell are you thinking? Letting him see you for what you are, a killer—I might add, and then leave him there?" I was yelling loudly.

"Don't call me that! I hate that!" She shouted back.

I pulled over sharply and put the shifter into neutral and pulled up the e-brake.

"Now what the fuck are you going to do. Look at your eyes, you're starving. I can't pull over every mile just for you to try and eat. This is fucking ridiculous!" I screamed. I was furious.

"Don't yell at me! Killing those others in the city was easy. They would have killed me or you if they had the chance. I'll wait till we get home I'll just do it that way again. I can't do it any other way!"

"Dianna!" I began. "It can't always be that way. You have to eat when your instincts tell you to. Here we are, far from civilization, and you're going to be fuckin' picky?"

"I can't do it!"

"If I wasn't with you just now, you would have left that poor bastard there, alive. He wasn't even near dead and he would have survived knowing of our existence. Do you know how much you jeopadize by doing something like that?"

"No, I don't, but I'm sure you're going to tell me," she was condescending and loud. She was getting annoyed at me for reprimanding her and that was the way I wanted it. I wanted to do something harmless to get my point across and let her get aggravated at me the same way I was with her.

"No, Dianna, I'm not going to sit here and teach you Vampires 101. You really have to start using your fuckin' brain and your wits. It's time you start thinking for yourself. I am getting so sick of this shit. Forcing you to feed all the time is making me fucking nuts and it has to stop."

"Then I just won't feed," she said to spite me.

"Then don't fucking feed. Drink here and there from the donors at home and see how long that lasts before you lose control and kill them because it won't satisfy your thirst."

She narrowed her eyes at me and gave me an evil look. I pressed on the clutch hard and started the car and pulled out fast. I made it to sixth gear with no problem. I was driving at least 100mph. I just wanted to get back to New York.

After about twenty minutes of silence, I had one thing to say to her,

"When we get back to New York, we're just going home. If you want to feed you're on your own."

I was so angry at her. Angry for not eating, for leaving the hunter alive and angry at her for having a conscience. She turned her head from me and we didn't speak for the rest of our four hour journey.

We finally arrived in New York. I drove through the Midtown tunnel and saw my city. I never appreciated it as much as I did at that moment. Dianna was sleeping in the passenger seat. She was sweating and she looked weak.

Needless to say, after four hours in the car my mood mellowed and I wasn't going to let Dianna go hungry. Of course I was going to give in and do this her way.

We weren't speaking as I drove down eighth avenue and double parked. She looked up groggy eyed and yawning to see why I stopped. I got out of the car, walked around and pulled her out. I was a little rough but she could handle it. I walked her down the street and grabbed a crack hooker off the street while walking. I was much too fast for human eye to see. I wisped the three of us into one of the alleys along 42nd street.

I leaned the stoned hooker against the wall. She was so intoxicated she didn't even know what was happening. She was sliding down along the wall and I held her up and bit into her wrist. I wasn't going to wait for Dianna to decide if her conscience would allow her to take the first initial bite that would do the whore in.

"Drink," I ordered, annoyed to Dianna.

Dianna looked up at me with gratitude before she drained the woman within seconds. That was the fastest she has ever drank before. She was extremely hungry and I felt guily for letting her wait so long.

I took off my shirt and threw it at her to clean her face as I picked up the corpse that *she* fed on to dispose of it. I was tired of cleaning up her messes and fixing her mistakes. The fact that she would have left that hunter alive really pissed me off. Although I felt guilty, I was still angry and annoyed with her. I walked over to the dumpster threw the body inside and did what I do. I lit a match tossed it inside and watched the dumpster and the crack whore burn.

We went back to the car and drove straight home. We still didn't say one word to each other. When we walked inside Sebastian was on the couch watching some musical on television with Ava. Dianna walked straight into the bedroom and slammed the door and I joined Ava and Sebastian.

"Trouble in paradise?" Sebastian asked jokingly. I snickered at his remark, but I didn't have anything to say so he continued to speak.

"How did the visit go? What did you think of Dianna's' family and home?"

"It was the best time I ever had," I said sarcastically. "How the fuck do you think it went?"

"Is that why the two of you aren't speaking?" He was trying to be a detective. I don't know why he didn't just ask me what the problem was.

"No, Sebastian, that isn't the reason. It's other things that I really don't feel like talking about right now," I answered.

"You know," Sebastian said. "Everything you and Dianna are going through right now is part of prophecy that has been foretold ages ago."

"I can't really do prophecies and other ancient bullshit right now. I'll deal with it as it comes," I said.

"Whenever you're ready to listen, I'll be here, but you really do need to take the time to listen and learn."

"Is there anything else that you want to lay on my shoulders while I'm here because I just don't have enough shit on my plate right now," I said loudly and patronizing.

Before Sebastian could answer Dianna came out of the room, walked pass me with her head held high, nose in the air and proceeded into the kitchen.

"Fuck this. I'm going out," I said outloud but to myself.

"Don't you think you should tell her before you go?" Sebastian asked but it was more of a command.

"If it'll get you off my back," I said and walked towards the kitchen opened the door and stood in the doorway.

Dianna was sitting at the table and eating a bowl of cereal. She glanced at me when I opened the door then turned her head.

"I'm going out, are you coming?" I asked indirectly and hardly meaningful. She ignored me and kept eating. I really didn't want to be with her right now so I welcomed her silent treatment as a tool to go out alone.

"I'll take that as a no," I said and walked out of the kitchen and apartment before Sebastian could say anything else.

I went to *Hell on Earth*. I was in a good mood despite the fact that Dianna and I weren't speaking. It was a relief not to be babysitting her constantly. I was able to let loose and be rebellious. The first thing I did was go to Bea and Ruth to drink from them. It was wonderful. I felt energetic, rejuvenated and a little wired. To ease the addiction, I seeked out Lizzy to drink from her as well. However, if I was to drink from Lizzy there was a condition that I had to meet, and...I did. I gave her a little and she gave me a little. I met the requirements, nothing to intimate or prolonged, only the basics. I should have felt guilty for being sneaky and unfaithful but honestly, I felt free, and youthful for the first time in a long time. I didn't feel like a guardian or a teacher and I liked it. Once my hunger for rebellion was quenched, all I wanted to do was play poker. Everyone was watching me and my strange behavior in bewilderment, but nobody would dare question my antics. Joe was sitting at a card table and Crissy was standing behind him playing with his hair. He had to of really like this girl. He didn't kick her out of the bedroom after the first date and now he was letting her play with his hair. Joe didn't like anyone touching or playing with his hair. People and some vampires too, have died for less. *She was the one.*

I joined the card table and dominated the game. I was playing for a few hours before my cell phone rang. I looked on the caller ID, and it was Dianna calling. I stood up from the table and walked away to a quiet corner before answering her call.

"What's wrong?" I answered.

"Nothing is wrong. I just want to know, when will you be home?" She asked.

"It depends," I said coldly.

"Depends on what?" She was getting aggravated by my short an unemotional answers.

"If I come home now, are we going to fight and argue? Because if we do, I'll turn around and leave again. The fighting is really starting to get on my nerves," I was very reprimanding in my tone of voice.

"No, I don't want to fight with you either. There's just something I want to talk about and I don't want to discuss it on the phone. So please come home." Her voice was sincere and apologetic and I hung up the phone.

I finished my hand in cards before I went home to hear Dianna's whining. I was home within the hour.

She was sitting in her favorite spot on the couch watching a movie. I sat on the chair directly across from her. I kept my coat on and my guard up in case this turned into a dispute.

"What do you want to talk about?" I asked uncaringly.

"I want to know if you have any regrets about me," she was very direct and that was a good thing.

I threw my head back and rolled my eyes. It was attention time for Dianna and she was probably going to test my patience. I had to play this right and try not to say anything that would make her over dramatize.

"No Dianna, I don't have any regrets about having you in my life. I'm stuck with ya," I said trying to lighten up the moment. I was only kidding but Dianna takes things so seriously and the drama began.

"Oh, you're stuck with me. How can I *un-stick* you? I wouldn't want to be a burden to you." She was getting a little loud but maintained a level that kept this as a discussion and not an argument. I was overwhelmed that she didn't go to the next level.

"I'm just joking with ya babe. Lighten up. I don't have one single regret about you or your learning disabilities. I wouldn't change a thing," I said sincerely.

I got up from my chair and pulled her towards me and hugged her close to my chest. I didn't want her to talk anymore, because somehow she would have turned this into a long winded argument. She liked and needed physical attention and that's why I held her before she could speak another word.

She nestled her head into my chest deeply, then looked up and kissed me, but when she did she bit my lip.

"I'm sorry, it was an accident," her eyes were black and the tone in her voice was anything but soothing.

"I think you meant that, but it's okay," I said and kissed her again.

"Just one more thing," she said in a very controlling manner and held me by the throat. That took me by surprise.

"The next time you need to walk out on me to relieve your stress, make sure you keep your fucking pants on. If your near that bitch again, I'll kill you both. I can smell her all over you. Go take a shower because you stink!" she was firm and commanding before she pushed me into the wall.

Dianna strutted towards our bedroom like a proud peacock with her feathers exposed. She was pleased with herself and actually I was pleased how she enhanced her sense of smell. She had this whole discussion under her control and me at my knees. I was like the kid in the cookie jar until I heard her whisper under her breath, *pay back is a bitch.*

I rushed to the bedroom door faster than should could see to block her from entering.

"It's a funny thing about pay backs," I said with shrewd smile and half of a fake laugh. "Should the day come and you want to *pay me back* and get even with me, keep in mind that I'm not as patient as you, I don't have a conscience, nor do I have a forgiving nature and unlike you I won't just threaten to kill you I *will* kill you both…on sight! There won't be any second chances. Are we clear?"

I had her blocked and she seemed a little nervous.

"Yes, we're clear. I hope you're clear on things as well."

"Crystal clear. I fucked up and it won't happen again," I said and continued. "Come in the shower with me and let's kiss and make up. Let's put this behind us."

She turned her head from me, she was playing games…. again. You see, I was supposed to beg her for her company and plead to touch her. That wasn't going to happen.

I didn't give her time or the chance to make a decision. I pulled her into the shower with me, clothes and all, hoping for the best, and went for it. Things turned out better than I expected. As much as Dianna put on the facade that she wanted to be equal in decision making, she liked the fact that I was controlling and took over all our situations.

We never spoke of the evenings events again. We both were aware of the consequences should either of us decide to be unfaithful to one another from this point on. Although the prospect of Dianna actually killing me was laughable, but I wouldn't put her in that predicament again to worry about it. We both were still a little mad at each other without admitting it and we had a lot of tension and stress that we had to release. We left it at that and had another great, rough, and disorderly night.

15

Christmas

The Holidays were approaching and Dianna was spending more days at her shop. It was the busy season and her business was doing very well. People were buying a lot of mystical, occult and witch perihelia as Christmas gifts. I thought that was strange considering such items are so against the meaning of Christmas, but then again humans are a messed up breed. Dianna really enjoyed the holiday season. She was raised by parents who did all they could to blend into a human world, and Christmas was part of that tradition and Dianna celebrated the day, to a point. However, I did not. I'm sure I did at one time during my human existence but I hardly remember those days. In any event, the holiday season seemed silly and useless to me. The one thing that was good about it from a vampire perspective was that it brought in many tourists, which meant there was more on the menu.

Dianna wanted a Christmas tree in the house. If that's what made her happy then I was all for it. It didn't matter to anyone else one way or another and Sebastian loved the idea. He would have something new to decorate. Dianna wanted all of us to exchange gifts with one another and wrap presents. We never did things like that before. Ava, Helena and Sebastian thought it was a good idea; it was something new and exciting for them. Joe and Richard and I, well, we just didn't get it.

I would buy Dianna whatever she wanted, whenever she wanted. I couldn't understand why these gifts had to be wrapped and be a surprise. I would have rather just took her shopping. Richard and Joe felt the same way. Dianna informed Joe that since he's been seeing Crissy a lot lately that it would only be right to buy her something as well and include her in the festivities.

Dianna and Sebastian went out in the morning and came home with an artificial nine-foot tree with tons of décor from Macy's, Tiffany's, Bloomingdales and Saks. Nothing but the best for Sebastian. The females of my clan and Sebastian couldn't wait to put the rare and expensive ornaments on the tree. However, they didn't want to the hard part, put the tree together. Joe, Richard and I were somehow were nominated for that job. The tree was pre lit, and it was like the blind leading the blind to try to find the right cords and put this monstrosity of a tree together.

"What's wrong with Rockerfella Center, can't we just go there and look at a huge tree with lights?" I asked.

If looks could kill, I would have been dead instantly. Not just from Dianna, but from Ava, Helena and Sebastian as well. They were very excited about this calamity and you would think that I just insulted them personally. I knew when I was beat and I shut up and helped Joe and Richard put the tree together.

After an hour, we got the tree standing and every branch was lit. The lights were quite bright and it was straining on the eyes. We looked absolutely ridiculous sitting on the couch with sunglasses looking at this thing. What was even more ridiculous was watching Ava and Helena hang ornaments with dark shades on as well. Sebastian and Dianna weren't affected by the brightness of the one thousand miniature lights. Joe, Richard and myself still didn't get the concept and decided to play the Wii world series of poker game. The others were so involved with what they were doing they didn't realize that we left the room.

They were at it for three hours at least. Together the four of them had a brainstorm. Tonight was the night that they decided we should all go Christmas shopping together, as a family. We on the other hand were involved with our game and didn't want to go.

Helena is bossy and she was being extremely pushy. She turned the game system off.

"We're going out as a family and we are going to this thing right. First, we'll feed. Then we will pick out gifts for one another without any one knowing what we bought for each other. Then, like it or not, you'll wait on line and get the gifts wrapped. To make it easy we'll go to one store to buy everything. We'll separate and set a time to meet after our shopping is done," Helena instructed. "Now let's go!"

I wasn't too happy about the way Helena took over and tried to be in charge. I realize this was new and exciting for her; however, it wasn't her place to make that call.

"Helena," I said calmly. "Let's be clear about a few things. Primarily when it comes to us doing anything as a clan you don't make that decision, I do. Even if it's as menial as this. Should **I** decide that we are going to do this as a clan or a family then I'll let you know how, when and where it will be. And last, but certainly not least, Dianna doesn't get seperated from me when we're out. Don't turn this into a matter of urgency or I'll put an end the whole thing now and throw that fucking tree into the furnace. You're over the line and don't let it happen again. Do we understand each other?"

Helena recognized when I was serious and didn't question my authority. She was aware that she pushed her limits, went one-step too far, and submitted to my wishes. Richard didn't defend her; he knew she was out of line. Richard, Joe and I continued to play our game.

All was quiet and Dianna tapped me on the shoulder. I turned to acknowledge her.

"I want to go shopping," she asked childishly.

"Not now babe, I want to finish this game. We'll go tomorrow. I promise."

"Please," she pouted. "You need to go out to feed anyway. Just one store, please," she said hoping up and down like a kid who has to go to the bathroom.

I couldn't resist when she behaved so innocently and I conceded to her request.

"We're going too, Richard." Helena ordered and she wasn't going to take no for an answer.

"Of course, we are," he said reluctantly under his breath.

"I'm going to shoot pool and play real cards," Joe said. "Now everyone knows why I don't have a mate. It's just way too much commitment. Are you coming, Ava?"

"No, Sebastian and I are going shopping as well," Ava said.

"I'll see everyone later. I'm going out. I'll just have Crissy shop for me."

"What makes you so sure that she will?" I asked.

Joe grinned. "Look at me, who can deny this?" Joe said admirably as he was pointing to himself. "Any woman would want the chance to serve me at my beck and call. Just to be seen with me is a privilege, much less shop for me. Crissy will do whatever I want her to, in hopes that she'll get to spend another night with me. It's not like I'd have to rape her to get what I wanted. She'll do what I tell and she'll like it too," Joe was self-satisfied with himself and to prove it, he would turn his head in a certain style to make his hair flow evenly in an even stream of silken elegance. Dianna didn't like the rape statement that he made and walked out of the room. She remembered when she denied him and how he reacted and so did I.

"That's enough Joe," I said. "Shut the fuck up." He seemed confused at first and then realized what he had said.

"I'm sorry; I didn't mean anything by it," his tone mellowed and his cocky attitude subsided. Joe headed towards the door and I followed and grabbed him by his arm and took him into the hallway.

"Joe, you say a lot of shit without thinking constantly, but when Dianna is around you need to really get your shit together and think before you speak. You've said a lot of little comments in the past and I overlooked them all. This time you stirred up a lot of memories for me and for her and I don't like it. Don't make me regret the decisions I made."

"I apologized. I don't know what else you want me to do. I didn't mean to offend anyone. I wasn't thinking about that night," Joe answered.

"That's the problem you never think, but it's time that you start because I'm not going to tolerate it." I was angry and he knew it.

"Do you want me to apologize to Dianna personally? I would have a long time ago but I never know how you're going to react."

Joe was genuine about his offer. I understood why he did what he did at the time, but I believed that the best thing for Dianna was to forgive Joe in her own way in her own time. I didn't want to push that on her.

"The only thing I want you to do is think before you speak," I said firmly.

"Now go and I'll see you later, Little Joey." That comment was made to lighten things up between us.

Joe simply nodded at my request. It was apparent by the expression on his face that he regretted what he said. He pushed the elevator button and was on his way.

I walked back inside to find Dianna in the kitchen, eating as usual.

"If only you can drink blood the way you eat your cereal," I joked and she smiled.

"Come on, do you want to go shopping?" I offered. After Joe's remark, I felt compelled to take her. If I have to spend an entire evening in a crowded store with human beings, Joe will owe me in a big way.

"No, we can go another time. It's not that big a deal," Dianna answered.

"Let's go down to the club, I'll tattoo your name on my arm," I would have done anything to make her smile and forget the memories that Joe stirred up. Fortunately, Dianna lit up like a million stars, she jumped from her stool and we were on our way out the door. Helena and Richard were in the elevator with us, they were on their way shopping. Richard seemed to be pissed off that he was the only one who was suckered into Christmas shopping. When we stepped outside of the building I turned to Richard and said, "See ya later, buddy."

I smiled crookedly as I spoke in a smug tone.

"Blow me," Richard said in his direct, monotone way. Helena shot him a look and he took hold of her hand as she led the way.

The streets were packed with tourists. It was easier than usual to get a bite to eat, in which case I did. Dianna specifically told me that she and

Sebastian fed while they were out shopping earlier in the day. She was lying, that was a fact. Not only could I sense her hunger but also it's hard to believe that there were gangs and thugs stirring up trouble during those hours just to intimidate Dianna. Everything else aside, Dianna wouldn't feed unless I was there to accompany her. Her feeding skills were weak, she wasn't comfortable about feeding with anyone besides me, and that was questionable. Dianna still had trouble preying on the innocent. Although, at this moment I wasn't going to press the issue. She was still upset about Joe's inept ability to ramble without thinking. I wasn't going to give her a hard time about feeding, but it still aggravated me that she wouldn't drink unless I forced it on her.

I called Adam before we arrived. I wanted him to move Lizzy to the human side of the club. This wasn't the night for Dianna to come face to face with her nemesis.

When we arrived the place was hoping and Bea and Ruth actually made a short appearance out of there place of recluse. Ruth immediately walked towards Dianna as I sat to get some kind of tattoo imprinted on my arm. I was clueless as to what I was going to put there. I really hadn't thought about it. I eventually came to a decision and told the tattoo artist to write the name Dianna in Old English lettering.

Ruth began to talk to Dianna about ancient prophecies within both our cultures. I heard Ruth say that Dianna held the fate of the mystical world in her hands, because she was a new breed and the only one of her kind, like the Goddess herself. That some of Dianna's gifts were intensely strong and others were extremely weak. There wasn't a gray area.

I told Ruth stop talking and not to bother Dianna with such nonsense. Ruth did as I asked and adjourned back into recluse. Dianna looked confused and didn't know what to think of Ruth's prediction. I, on the other hand, didn't take it too seriously until I took a good look at what was happening at that precise moment. The free lance tattoo artist was scripting Dianna's name vertically along my entire left arm. Each letter of her name working its way down individually from my shoulder to my wrist.

The tattoo artist reached an "N" and asked, "Two N's or one N?"

"Two. Total of six letters."

As those words we're coming through my teeth, I immediately thought of Ruth's prophetic riddle,

Darkness will allow an infliction of six scars upon his skin to expose the light to death itself.

Dianna's name bared six letters that were individualized and scared on my skin with my consent. This was getting a little to surreal for me to think about. I was starting to reconsider my ignorance when it came to ancient prophecies. However, I still believed that some things might be better left unsaid and I would deal with things as they come or perhaps I was hopeful that these foretold events would pass. Funny, I preached to Dianna's mother about the same thing. I was acting like a hypocrite.

Dianna was standing behind me while I was being tattooed. Joe walked over and approached Dianna.

He asked, "Can I talk to you privately for a minute, Dianna?"

Dianna was just about to walk away with him until I grabbed her arm with my free hand and stopped her. I told Joe that whatever he wanted to say could be done right where we were standing. I was certain that he wasn't going to hurt her but I still didn't want him anywhere near her if I wasn't there.

He nodded in agreement.

"Dianna," he said. "I never actually apologized to you for our past...umm...encounter. I'd like to do so now and say, I'm sorry about what happened and if I could take it back, I would. I'm also sorry for the things I said tonight. I don't expect you to forgive me but I just wanted you to know that I do deeply regret what I did."

Dianna was composed and a little surprised by Joe's long awaited apology.

"What's done is done. I know you weren't yourself that night. Besides, if it wasn't for you being a dick, I wouldn't be with Dan," she said as she pointed my way. I was so proud of her when she called him a dick. That was her little dig and Joe accepted it graciously.

"Nah...don't give me any credit for the two of you being together," he shook his head.

"That was inevitable. I just wanted you to know that I am sorry. You're my sister now and if you need me in your corner, I'll be there for you, princess. Can I still call you princess?"

Dianna smiled at Joe's cocky humor and hugged him as a gesture of forgiveness. It was a bold move on Joe's part to apologize to Dianna when just hours earlier I told him not to. However, it seemed to work out for the better and I pushed that under the rug.

"Speaking of princess, look who's here Joe," I said and motioned my head beyond him.

Crissy showed up and approached Joe immediately and still wearing his T-shirt. She cut off the sleeves and the bottom of it to show off her belly and made it more girly looking.

"What did you do to my shirt?" Joe asked with a sultry grin.

"Oh, you're not getting this back, it's my shirt now," she answered with a huge smile.

Joe put his arm around her and pulled her close to him by the neck. He kissed her on the cheek and they both sashayed away.

"Do you wanna go shopping for me?" Joe asked Crissy as they were departing.

"Sure," she said in a very bubbly way. "Can I buy myself something too?"

"I don't care," Joe lightly laughed, smacked her on the ass and they went into the dwelling of Ruth and Bea. Joe would no doubt, drink from both of them and Crissy would be bitten to relieve his addiction.

"Done," said the tattoo artist as he wiped my newly fresh tattoo clean.

My tattoo was done and Dianna was happy about it the outcome. I was weary about it after replaying Ruth's riddle.

"How does it look?" I asked her.

"Great!" She exclaimed. "Can I get one too?"

"No, I like your body clean and unmarked. I don't want anyone's hands on your body except mine. So the answer is no," I answered firmly.

"But—" She attempted to debate me as usual but I cut her off mid-sentence.

"What part of no, don't you understand? No is no." I said self-importantly and got up from the tattoo chair.

"You're so damn bossy," she said slightly irritated.

"You just figured that out?" I was condescending with my answer. "Nothing gets by you."

She rolled her eyes and yielded to a battle that she wasn't going to win.

We stayed for a short while because Dianna was hungry and needed to feed. As I said, she was lying when she told me she fed earlier in the day, but I didn't persist. She still couldn't grasp that she was a part of me and I could feel what she feels. There wasn't much of anything that she could hide from me.

Through out the next two weeks, Dianna me dragged to a hundred stores and shopped for gifts. I stopped counting after a while. She insisted that I go shopping without her to buy her gifts. I really didn't know what to get her or anyone else for that matter. Joe, Richard and myself didn't want to go shopping and buy gifts. It was a hassle and we honestly didn't know what to do or know what to buy.

Vampires like luxury in excess and we already possessed everything we needed and wanted in excess, so I didn't get the point of doing any of this. It didn't make any sense. The only surprise gift I have ever bought for someone else was a necklace for Dianna and she ended up throwing it at me.

We did however, try to shop the next day. As Helena suggested, we decided on one store to go and buy everything else that was on our lists. We went to Bloomingdales. It was seven floors of madness. We looked absolutely ridiculous. All of us, except Dianna, were wearing our coats and three hundred dollar Gucci sunglasses at night and inside the store. False light couldn't hurt us it was just hard on the eyes. During the holiday season I believe that humans were more vicious than my kind. This place was chaotic. People pushing and shoving just to buy an overly priced sweater.

When we stepped inside all eyes were on us. The wealthy humans that shopped here were looking down at us, as if they were better than us. That was a joke in itself. Not only were they the lesser species, but if they wanted to compare lives dollar for dollar I guarantee that they couldn't live up to the wealth that all of us have consumed over the years. They were nothing but peasants among royalty.

"Oh yeah, we blend," Joe said humorously.

"Let's just do this," I said drolly and put my arm around Dianna and we walked in perfect sequence through the store.

A security guard noticed us immediately, *who didn't,* I thought to myself. He picked up his cheap radio and was talking to the others about our arrival. Apparently we were going to be watched. This should be interesting and we all found it amusing. Something like this was playtime for Joe. He would use his speed to sneak up behind the guards and consumers and tap them on the shoulder. By the time they turned their heads he was gone. Joe's hair made him more conspicuous than the rest of us. It was his very prominent appearance than put women shoppers in awe of him the minute they laid their eyes on him. Joe, being the flirt that he is, smiled seductively at everyone of them and quite possibly was looking for his next meal. Joe is a picky eater and feeds on females. Joe's alluring powers are superior and he has a physical and mental affect on human women.

There was one brave security guard who stopped Joe and asked him straight out why he was wearing sunglasses. The rest of us were starting to scatter but stayed close enough to see and hear what was going on. If our kind was to approach Joe without warning we would have been right beside him, but these were humans, and he wasn't in any danger among such insignificant beings.

"Are you talking to me?" Joe asked in his catty wit to the security guard.

"Yeah, I'm talking to you," he said with authority. "On behalf of Bloomingdales, we would appreciate it if you and your friends would remove your sunglasses. It seems to make our other customers uneasy and they are complaining."

"Oh, you want me to remove my glasses," Joe patronized. "Are you sure about that?"

"Yes. The entire store is sure. So if you don't mind." The guard answered and seemed to be getting annoyed by Joe's mockery.

Joe then put his arm around the guards shoulders, the guard followed Joe's arm as it rested upon his shoulder. The guard seemed to be a little nervous as Joe moved him a few inches from where they were standing.

Joe looked down at him and whispered to him in a sarcastic yet serious manner, "Do you know what's under our glasses? Are you absolutely certain that you want me and my companions to take them off?"

"Sir," The guard said. "It would be appreciated if you and your friends shop through the store in a manner that is comfortable for everyone."

Joe turned to us and smiled wickedly and said with a small laugh, "He called me sir." He then turned back to the security guard. "Okay, okay," Joe answered in a transparent state of defeat. "You win, we wouldn't wanna tangle with a guy like you." The guard stood and watched as Joe removed the glasses from his face.

Joe stared at him turning his pretty blue periwinkle eyes to penetrating vicious red eyes and condescendingly asked again, "Now are you absolutely positive that you want us to take our glasses off?" Joe also exposed his fangs as well, making sure that the guard was the only one able to see his true appearance.

The guard was terrified, turned whiter than...us and stood motionless as he stared at Joe in hypnotic shock.

"I thought you would see it my way," Joe said, dropped down his glasses, retracted his teeth and patted the guard on the shoulder before he strutted away. The rest of us silently laughed and crookedly smiled as we went off in separate directions to shop. We weren't being followed or scrutinized any longer. Humans are like domesticated pets, you have to let them know who's the boss, instill a little fear and watch them cower in the corner until the master says it's okay to come out.

Shopping during the holidays was anything but pleasant. Dianna and I were both being pushed and shoved by hostile, inconsiderate shoppers. It took a lot for me not to hurt someone. I think we lasted about an hour before we all threw in the towel and went home. We did however manage to buy a few things for ourselves. We all had our fetishes. Dianna bought a bunch of shoes. I bought her a long black leather coat that she absolutely hated and didn't want, but I wanted her to have it. She was part of our clan now and I wanted her to feel like she belonged. I also bought myself a few expensive brimmed stingy hats that Dianna hated also, but I liked wearing and having them. Joe bought several pairs of high priced sunglasses and overly priced hair brushes. Joe was very vain about his appearance and he had a thing for sunglasses. Helena bought jewelry, specifically rings, to satisfy her compulsive addiction. Richard bought a lot of cologne to add to his collection of two hundred different fragrances on his dresser top. Ava loves cosmetics and bought the latest look from the Mac and Urban Decay counters.

Ultimately, the end result was that Joe, Richard and I had Crissy do all the shopping for us. I don't think she minded because she made out like a bandit between all of us. After all, she was only human and took what ever she could get her hands on.

16

Christmas and New Years came and went without a hitch. The Christmas tree survived our living room rumbles. Crissy did a good job shopping for gifts. Everyone was pleased and surprised with the things she bought. Within time she did the Christmas shopping for all of us. Dianna, Ava and Helena also gave up shopping in New York City during the holiday season and passed the duty onto Crissy as well. The shopping experience was over rated and not one of us, not even Dianna, wanted to do it again.

Dianna went to her shop to remove holiday decorations and have her day in the sun. Dianna having sunlight in her life meant a lot to me. Dianna took the sunlight for granted. She doesn't realize how fortunate she is. I'd give up a lot of my strengths just to have a day in the sun with her. I wanted her to enjoy it for the both of us. I envied her and wished that I could share the morning sun with her.

She kissed me before she set out to into the human world. I did, however, have one condition for Dianna to walk in the day, and that was to be back home by 3:00 P.M. Anytime after that was too close to sunset and she would be vulnerable in the darkness. Dianna was too unique and too tempting to resist among my kind and I don't trust many of them. Vampires, myself included, are a heartless, ruthless and sinful breed. We don't hold ordinary qualities such as compassion and mercy. Dianna alone and susceptible in the darkness was an invitation to disaster.

Dianna was also a little bit to trusting of humans. She was unaware of the many masks that humans wear and how deceitful they really are. Humans aren't a loyal species among their own and most of them would use, sell and destroy their own family for a taste of immortality.

It was my true belief that Dianna did have the ability to protect herself, but she didn't know how to use her gifts. She was afraid of them, and having a conscience didn't help matters either. It was a scary thought of how out of control her powers could be if she ever unleashed.

As for right now, her vampire skills were feeble and untamed and her magic was changing direction. No one could say for sure what Dianna was capable of. She was the only one of her kind and there wasn't a species on earth that wouldn't love to get their hands on her. Dianna is a confused and needy individual and guiding her through her transformation wasn't going to be an easy task. I would have to teach her as I saw fit although some would question my methods. Dianna is exceptionally childish and sometimes needs to be disciplined like a child. I don't take pleasure in being an authority figure in her life as well as her lover. I was torn as well.

That particular morning I rested longer than average. I turned over in my bed to put my arm around Dianna. She would always crawl into bed with me when she came in from her daylight outings. Dianna would lay in bed with me all day and night without ever leaving. This time she wasn't there. *Strange*, I thought to myself. *Too strange.*

Something deep within my gut made me jump out of bed frantically. I couldn't feel her or sense her. I began to get nervous and frantic, she was in danger that much was certain. She wasn't dead, if she was, my ties to her would have been severed immediately. My connection to her would have disappeared instantly, although her death would scold my soul forever. This is why vampires only mate once in an eternity. The loss of one's mate is just to intense to relive, and when the bond is broken so is the individual. The connection of one's mate may vanish but the memories never do. Everything a vampire feels is excessive beyond reason.

Dianna was scared, that much I could feel. I couldn't get a read on where she was or who she was with, I only knew that something was wrong.

I quickly got dressed and raced into the living room where the others were involved with their daily routines.

"What time is it?" I asked aloud to anyone who was listening, but no one responded.

I asked again, "What time is it?" As I was putting on my shoes.

I couldn't fathom what was happening. I was scared and angry at the same time. If anything happened to Dianna I would be ridden with guilt. All I can think was, *why did I let her go?*.

Today was the day when my dreams of walking in the sunlight ended. The sun was the cause of Dianna's demise. I trusted the sun to light the way for Dianna and watch over her in my place. Dianna often talked about the moon and the sun in her culture. How the sun is the essence of life and allows her to grow, stay warm and guide her home. She claimed that the moon watched over her when the sun couldn't. She trusted the sun and its qualities and talked me into trusting it too. That was my mistake.

Helena looked at her new watch that was a Christmas gift, "It's almost 3:30."

"Did Dianna come home yet?" I asked hoping that I was just being over dramatic.

"No, she hasn't come in. We haven't seen her all day," Helena answered.

"Is she with Sebastian?!" I said hysterically loud.

"He's resting," Helena replied. "What's going on?" Helena seemed to be genuinely concerned about my current state and walked towards me.

I was losing control of my rationality. "I want her home now!" I screamed and punched a hole in the wall.

Helena attempted to console me, she placed her hand on my shoulder, "Dan, you have to calm down."

I shook my head, "I have to find Dianna, something isn't right. I have to go. I want you and Ava to stay here in case she comes home," I said in a panic.

"You can't go anywhere the sun still hasn't set, you'll be at risk," Helena cautioned.

"Fuck the sun! It won't stop me from finding her," I said and searched for my car keys.

Richard and Joseph didn't question my motives. They both got up from the couch and stood behind me ready to follow me in my desperate hour of need. Richard and Joe are loyal, all of them were, even Ava, as I was to them as well. Humans should take lessons from my kind when it came to loyalty. Whether I wanted them there or not, they were going to be at my side and do what ever I asked of them. We didn't let anyone walk alone in their hour of need. It wasn't because I was head of the household, it was because we were all connected by bonding blood. Our rebirth existed in each other. As dysfunctional as we were at home, in a time of crisis...we always knew how to pull it together and organize.

I raced out the door and into the garage at top speed. Richard and Joe followed quietly and speedily behind me. I got into my car swiftly and let down the roof so we can get in and out faster. The roof down in a convertible in New York City in December was odd, even for this city.

I stomped on the gas and burnt the rubber off the tires as I pulled out of the parking garage. I set a course to Dianna's shop. I was in the middle of New York City during rush hour and I was racing against time. Every second wasted felt like a thousand burning needles plummeting into my brain. Dianna needed me and I wasn't there to protect her. I promised her that I would always keep her safe and...I let her down. She was hurting and scared and I didn't have any power to stop it. This was my first experience of not having any control over my own destiny.

The traffic was in gridlock. I doubled parked the car a few blocks from her shop and ran the rest of the way at lightning speed. I wasn't concerned about the sun or how weak I would be when I got there, if I was weak at all. As I said earlier I wasn't going to allow the sun to pose a threat to me. There's something to be said about adrenaline and nothing was going to stop me from bringing her home. At our intensified pace the three of us were only seconds away and the sun didn't have time to do much damage.

We stepped into the shop and everything seemed to be in order. It wasn't ransacked. The safe and register wasn't tampered with, but Dianna wasn't there. I wasn't surprised, I knew she wouldn't be there, we all did, but I had to see with my own eyes. I was able to smell her aroma the moment I stepped inside. Her scent was strong and lingering, she wasn't taken all that long ago. We scanned the small shop and Joe reached down and found a wet cloth on the floor. He handed it to me and the first thing I did was smell it.

"Chloroform," I said somewhat calm and threw the cloth back on the floor.

I was astounded that something so predictable as chloroform was the culprit. I was disappointed in Dianna's senses and disappointed in myself for not teaching her better. She had to have known the individual who did this to her. It just didn't make sense that she could be taken so easily.

"Chloroform doesn't work on us," Joe said suspiciously.

"Dianna isn't like us. She isn't undead. Her heart beats, and her lungs breathe. She has a lot of the same physical weaknesses as humans. She's just supposed to be more intuitive, so I thought." I said in disgust with myself.

She was gone, that was a fact and I didn't have a clue as to where she was. It was evident to all of us that Xavier was behind Dianna's disappearance. When I find her, Xavier will pay beyond reason for what he has done. *This I promise.*

"Let's go, this is just a waste of time and she doesn't have much time. If X doesn't kill her first, her hunger will. I seriously doubt he'll take the time to make sure she feeds. I have to find her." I said fearfully.

We were about to walk out when we all heard someone call for help quietly in the stock room. We rushed in and one of Dianna's workers was locked inside with his hands tied together.

"Where's Dianna!?" I screamed. I wasn't concerned about his well being I only wanted information on Dianna's whereabouts. The thought of untying him never entered my mind.

Richard untied him and helped him up. On a normal day we probably would have left him there or fed from him but we needed any help he could offer.

"I don't know...where Dianna is. *Huff, huff,*" he panted. "Someone, *huff,* came in and took her. When I went to stop him, *huff, huff,* his partner grabbed me and locked me in here," he replied nervously.

His answer wasn't enough to help me find Dianna, but considering that he attempted to help Dianna during her struggle he got to live another day.

I was about to leave and Joe pulled me back when he asked the stock boy another question.

"Do you know who took her? Have you ever seen them before?" Joe asked sternly.

"They've been in here a few times over the last few months. They were always very friendly and curtious to Dianna. I don't know why they would do this."

"What did they look like?" Joe asked again.

"Like...like...Goths, trying to look like Dracula..." He stumbled with his words with fear in his eyes.

He asked if he could leave. It was apparent that our presence made him nervous.

"Go ahead," Joe answered and waved his hand to let him pass.

"Xavier's day walkers. I didn't think he'd have the balls to bring his day walkers into Manhattan," I threw one of the many books across the room. "This is all my fault. How the fuck could I underestimate that son of a bitch! How could I be so careless?" I kicked down the front door as I left the building in a rage of fury.

I left my car behind. I really didn't care what happened to it. Time was ticking and I had to get home and think about my next move. I had to clear my head. Thousands of thoughts were running out of control in my mind. I was losing touch of all my senses. This was the first time that I ever felt completely powerless.

I stomped into the house flustered and frantic. I was kicking and throwing anything that was in my way as I headed twords the kitchen for some much needed solitude. I leaned over the kitchen island just to have a moment to think reasonably and nothing came to mind. Not one realistic thought of how to get her home came into my head. I was infuriated by my limitations. I threw the microwave and lifted the kitchen island from its cemented base and tossed that as well. I was frustrated and disgusted with myself for my lack of leadership and my carelessness as Dianna's guardian. She was not ready to walk alone, and I knew that, but yet I let it happen. *I'll never forgive myself for this.*

Sebastian was in the kitchen. I don't know how long he was standing in the doorway, I stared at him pathetically.

"Sorry, I'm wrecking the house," There just weren't any words only vivid and frightening images of what Xavier and his clan were doing to Dianna.

"That's alright. This is a time when I expect you to wreck the house," Sebastian said in his calm and controlled manner.

I leaned over the sink. I didn't want to look at him as I spoke.

"I want her back, Sebastian. I want her to come home and I don't know what to do," I spoke tenderly and docile.

"You'll get her back, but you have to gain control of yourself. You're not of any use to Dianna if you do anything in haste. Don't let your temper control you," Sebastian said.

"That's easier said than done," I answered.

"I know you will get her home safely. The prophecies say…"

"Sebastian!" I said trying to keep my temper in control. "I really can't do prophecies right now. Now is not the time."

"Okay then," he said acceptingly. "Let's concentrate on Dianna, can you sense her at all?"

"No. Which leads me to believe that she's doped up and they're moving her around," I acknowledged.

"Now you're thinking with head. Just stay in that mode and you'll bring her home. Don't let Xavier get the better of you. Keep in mind that this is about you, not Dianna. It's not her he wants, it's your status," Sebastian reminded me.

"That's a big part of the problem also. I will never bow to Xavier or give in to any of his demands. Not even at the expense of Dianna's life. I just can't and I won't," I said coldly.

As much as I wanted that statement to be false it wasn't. As much as I loved Dianna and wanted her home, I could never allow Xavier to run my life or the life of everyone else who dwelled here. There was more to it than pride and ego. I was responsible for the well being of everyone in this house as well as Dianna's.

"That's not as unreasonable as you think," Sebastian stated. "Just conduct yourself as the leader I know you could be and were always meant to be and you will prevail. I guarantee it."

"Only time will tell," I answered and walked slowly back to my room.

Everyone was in the living room conferencing with one another and the rattle of their voices fell quiet when I entered the room. I didn't pay much attention at their attempt of discretion. My cell phone rang before I walked two steps. I took it out of my pocket and threw it across the room. Joe quickly raced to grab it before it smashed.

"Dan..." Joe called, concerned.

"Not now," I said solemnly as I walked down the hallway slowly. "Just let me know when it's sunset."

I stepped into our room and slammed the door behind me. I wanted to be alone. I sat at the desk holding my head in my hands. I was feeling so completely numb. I opened the desk drawer and began to rummage through it. I wasn't looking for anything particular. It was only an impulse that seemed vital now. There were many useless things in there. Scraps of paper, pens and computer games. However, among the rubble, as instinct would have it, I came across the necklace that I had given to Dianna so long ago. I had forgotten all about it. I must have tossed it in there the night she threw it at me. I smiled at the memory of her behavior and the shock I was in when she unleashed a small part of her rage for the first time. As I held it in my hand, I began to rub the diamond moon in hopes that it would put me in tune with her. But it didn't. Many memories came thrashing ashore in my head like a tidal wave. As I held the pendant, I remembered that the only reason it was in my possession was because of the pain I had inflicted on Dianna. I hurt her so much that night. I dismissed and humiliated her. I hated myself for that and I couldn't believe I still had the privilege of her love.

Reminiscences of the good and bad times we shared were running simultaneously through my mind with each passing moment as I gazed upon the pendant. I thought of her standing at the main counter of her shop the very first day I met her, she was pretending not to notice me, but she couldn't help herself. When our eyes met, we instantly fell in love with each other, we both felt it. It was uncontrollable. The capacity of our love was unlimited. Yet her face grew jealous, resentful and angry with me whenever she heard Lizzy's name.

The way her big stormy gray eyes lit up the sky when I gave her the pendant nearly could have killed me cause she never looked so happy. When I walked away from her, intending to never see her again a couple of hours later, the sadness in her eyes struck me like a slow and painful suicide. I remembered the way her face glistened with intrepidity when she drank from me for the very first time after she was scared and helpless because of what Joseph tried to do to her. The way her vibrant white teeth beamed when I agreed to take her to Vermont and give her Christmas. The way she felt so honored that I would tattoo her name on my body, but she should only know that it was an honor for me that she would even allow a monster like me into her life after all the pain and suffering that I had inflicted on her. I thought of her sadness when I left her alone in the world that would take her away from me. Although, I couldn't feel her or sense her, I knew she was in pain and afraid, more than she has ever been. She needed me to hold her, to carry her. She couldn't sleep unless she was snuggled in my chest. She couldn't eat unless I wiped her mouth and she couldn't cry unless my shoulder was there to comfort her and dry her tears.

This was tearing me apart.

She believed I was capable of anything. I knew that at this very moment she was wondering where I was and why I hadn't come to save her. She was depending on me and I was letting her down with each passing second. Who would ever think that a vampire was able of feeling so much love for just one being?

As I continued to hold the delicate pendant in my hands, something peculiar came over me. Something I didn't have any recollection of. One single tear drop fell from my eye and fell onto the pendant. I touched it and wondered why this was happening. Then I instantly thought of the many tears that Dianna was crying at that very moment. I leaned my head back only to find that both my eyes were clouded up by many more tears. The tears gushed like a broken damn down my face. I tried to hold them back but I couldn't, it was almost instinctive. They just kept flowing and flowing, endlessly. I lost control of my entire being and broke down. I was crying Dianna's tears. I could taste her as they ran down to my lips.

Dianna...where are you?

My body ached and my soul yearned for her touch.

I felt colder than I ever have before.

It took everything inside me to compose myself. Whatever fragments of human instincts that were dwelling inside of me were released with each one of Dianna's tears that I cried for her.

For every tear I cry, Xavier would pay in triplicate.

I gazed upon the pendant one last time and my final salty water tear drop turned into a viscous, crimson drop of blood.

The bits of humanity that I had sitting inside me all these years were officially gone. Darkness had loomed over me. I restrained myself, set the pendant back into the drawer and went into the bathroom to wash my face. This was unacceptable behavior. I looked in the mirror and I saw someone different, someone transformed. I was colder, pitiless and unfeeling. Something happened that night, I was reborn again. As monstrous as I was before, it was nothing compared to what I was at that moment. I was merciless. I wanted blood, anyone's blood. I never had much tolerance for humans but now all of them would pay the price for the two men that took Dianna.

I dried my face and gained composure. I was reasonable and controlled. Dianna was coming home, there wasn't anymore doubt about that. My clan would be safe, and I would keep my status and be feared among my own kind. I wasn't looking at the situation as ending it was a new beginning. I was going to turn the tables and anyone who was involved would pay dearly.

I looked at the clock and it was almost sunset. I walked out of my room with my head held high and my confidence was soaring.

"It's time to go," I commanded. "Helena and Ava I want the two of you home in case she miraculously comes home. Joe and Richard the two of you come with me."

Sebastian watched my actions from the corner of the room and seemed proud of the way I was handling myself and everyone else. It was time for me to stop playing around and feeling sorry for myself. I finally reached out and took hold of the scepter that Sebastian handed down to me.

I lead the way out of the building and Joe and Richard stayed a few paces behind me. It was a strange feeling. I didn't feel like their friend or brother anymore. For the first time I felt like the leader Sebastian expected me to be. I was changing and I welcomed it. Richard and Joe felt it too.

Joe brought me to date by telling me that the phone call I received during my frantic episode was from the New York City car impound, they towed my car. I heard him say it, I just didn't acknowledge it. I continued to walk at a steady pace.

As we walked the dark city streets. I lead the way assertively. The first stop on my journey was Dianna's book shop. I hated this place. In my eyes, if it didn't exsist this wouldn't have happened. This was her link the outside world. This was her only purpose to be without me and on her own. This place put her at risk. She trusted anyone who walked through the doors. That was going to change when she came home. Fate was going to change, Dianna was going to change, and a lot was changing now, right before my eyes.

I stared at the building in torment. I thought of Dianna being snatched out of a place she felt safe in. It infuriated me. I gave my first order of the evening.

"Torch it," I instructed to both Richard and Joe and they did as directed. Joe removed his shirt and Richard doused it in lighter fluid. Joe stuffed the drenched shirt in a beer bottle that he found on the ground, leaving a small portion of the shirt out of the opening to use as a wick. I watched Joe light the phony wick and toss it into the building. I turned and walked away calmly without regret, never looking back as I heard the crackling of the flames.

It didn't take Richard or Joe long to catch up with me. I was in a hurry to find Dianna but not in hurry to lose my concentration and do things in haste.

Next on the list was Dianna's apartment. I wanted the past removed. I didn't want anymore reminders of hurtful times for either of us. It's been months since I've seen the place. I looked around and saw all the things she left behind. I smelt every fiber of her being within the walls. I looked beyond the dust and the broken furniture and thought about the last time I was here. The night Dianna bound herself to me. The night I promised to keep her safe. I thought of the first time I was here. We were both so cocky to one another, playing games of wits. The way I ran back to her after standing her up for some human trashy woman, and she thought she was so tough. I thought of the moment we almost bounded ourselves to one another on the first night we were alone together and how we were so fated to be together from the very beginning. I was thinking about how she was trying her best to seduce me but I wouldn't allow it. She should only know how hard that was for me. I wanted to make her mine the day I turned her so many years ago. I smiled and rejoiced in those memories until I turned to Joe. I glared upon his face, his baby blue eyes and his sneaky, sultry grin. Joe is a con artist in disguise, and he fooled anyone who didn't know him. I remembered when he tried to take what was rightfully mine. He fooled Dianna and put her in a state of fear and helplessness. Probably much like what she's going through now. I wanted to kill him all over again, but I had to restrain myself.

"You need to wait outside," I said to Joe, cold yet calm and stared at him with beaming red eyes of hatred.

"You don't belong here," I added.

Without hesitation, he did as he was told.

The memory of Joe forcing himself on Dianna coursed through my brain like nails to a chalkboard. I remembered when Dianna saw him for the first time after that night and the genuine fear that she felt when she looked at him. I became angry at myself for allowing him to live. If it was anyone else, they would have been dead. However, he was indebted to me for a lifetime of servitude. Joe couldn't make a move without my permission. Death might have been the better option on his behalf. In spite of the fact that this was where Dianna and I shared a lot of special and intimate moments, Joe's attempted rape took the innocence and prudence away from all those precious memories. There wasn't anything good here. Nothing but heartache for Dianna, and I felt nothing but antipathy.

"Burn it until it falls," I commanded to Richard solely.

I walked outside and grabbed Joe by the arms and pressed him against the brick building.

"If you ever call her princess again, I'll kill ya," I said with rage and released him. "Go and help Richard."

Joe didn't question me or utter a sound he did what he was told without a second thought. Joe expected how I was going to react the moment we walked through the door. He didn't hesitate to burn the building with perfection. I waited and watched as I began to see the curtains burst into flames and watched the windows implode. There were other tenants in the building but I honestly didn't care. The three of us walked away unfeeling and kept a steady stride.

It was well pass feeding time. I was hungry and so were Richard and Joe. This wasn't a night where I was going to have us go out of our way to feed on the vagrents in the subway. That was never going to happen again. The first human in my sight was going to be my victim from this day forth. Young, old, man, woman or child...it didn't matter. As I said, any stitch of humanity that I possessed was nonexistent. As for Joe and Richard they could feed how they saw fit. I intended to feed as the savage I was created to be.

I walked down the street and at first sight I saw a hooker. She was tonight's dinner. Without warning, I grabbed her from behind and pulled into a dark doorway and quenched my thirst more viciously than I have ever fed in all my years as a vampire. She didn't have time to scream or panic, I went straight for the kill and bit down into her jugular, killing her instantly. She never saw it coming. When I was done feeding I maliciously ripped her lifeless body apart. I wasn't going to worry about disposing of her properly. I mangled her up so immensely and so destructively that there wasn't any evidence of a vampires existence. Bits and pieces of her body and blood were scattered throughout the rough city streets.

Joe and Richard never saw me so behave viciously and carelessly, nor did they ever see me this angry. They didn't dare comment about it, I read their thoughts and they were weary of me and my irrational state of mind. They were both concerned for their own lives. They didn't question any of my antics, they were afraid of stepping out of line and ticking me off.

they If they didn't agree with the way I was behaving they could take their chances, walk alone and hope I don't seek revenge on them for being disloyal to me. This is the way things are now. Everything was going to be done my way. I didn't want anyone's opinion at inopportune times. The only opinion I would take into consideration at this time was for the whereabouts of Dianna. That was the only thing open for discussion. Joe, Richard and the others were part of **my** clan, not the other way around. They all belonged to me. They cleaned up whatever mess I left behind, take my orders and deal with my moods, as it should be.

I may be cold and uncompromising but I'm not cruel to my own, they still needed to feed. It was in my best interest that they were energized and rejuvenated. Joe and Richard didn't want to take any time to find or look for a particular human to feed on. They also weren't going to take any chances of annoying me and wasting precious time. They fed on the first human that was in their sight as well. The only diffrence was they were much more diplomatic and neater about it.

I walked to the Brooklyn Bridge and just gazed upon the old historic structure. Somewhere beyond the water was Dianna waiting for me to bring her home. Nothing would have given me greater pleasure than that. I wanted to touch her, smell her, taste her and love her. I wanted to hold her tightly and never let her go, I wanted her safe in my arms. As much as my anticipation was gnawing at me to take her back, I couldn't just waltz into Brooklyn unarmed and unprotected. I had to devise a plan to destroy and conquer who was responsible for touching and taking what was mine. Xavier's clan has grown, thanks to Ava and Christopher, and there was power in numbers. Something that I lacked at the moment. I had to see Adam about joining forces.

I turned and walked away callously and headed to Midtown. It was inevitable that Xavier would seek me out on his own. This was the moment he's been longing for. I had to sit back and wait. He had the upper hand and he had to make the first move.

17

Gambling

When I stepped one foot into *Hell on Earth*, all eyes turned to me. News travels fast among my kind. Adam approached me immediately, tapped me on the shoulder and motioned for me to follow him. We walked straight into our private office. Our office was typical of any other office. A cluttered wood desk, disorganized file cabinets, a high tech computer, a sturdy safe and a few stained chairs. There wasn't any décor at all. It was there only to serve its purpose.

Lidia, Adam's mate, followed us in but Adam dismissed her immediately. Lidia was an obedient, stable, and experienced mate. Lidia did as she was told and left the room on command. She was nothing like Dianna. Who was untamed, unstable, inexperienced and stubborn. Despite Dianna's flaws, I loved her, missed her and wanted her back. Dianna's flaws weren't going to last forever, and even if they did none of that mattered, I wanted her home. I would deal with her inadequacies when she was safe and secure at home. I would make certain that she was going to be more intuitive and less trusting from now on. She was going to learn how to live up to my expectations weather she liked it or not. I was going to be hard on her to adapt to my way of life because the dilemma that she was currently in was never going to happen again. Dianna had to become more self sufficient and I had to guide her.

Adam and I both sat down, and he asked, "How are you holding up?"

"I'm holding up just great, it's how Dianna is holding up that I'm not sure about," I answered.

"Xavier has been bragging all over the city. How you'll fall to your knees and he'll have control of both uptown and midtown. He's has openly taken the credit for Dianna's disappearance." Adam confirmed my suspicions.

"He's in for a rude awakinging if he thinks I'd ever fall to my knees. I'm just waiting for him to show up so I can see what he's up to and make a move. I'm counting on your back up when it goes down," I told Adam.

"You always have my back up. It would be a pleasure to bring that pussy down. He causes too much trouble. It's time for him to perish. It's unfortunate that something like this had to happen for us to do what should have been done ages ago."

"Xavier played it smart for a lot of years. He never crossed the line until now. He kept himself safe. He crossed the wrong line when he took Dianna. He will suffer above and beyond that of anyone I've ever killed before. He'll feel all her pain and mine," I was determined and strong willed when I made that vow.

"We'll get her back, try not to worry too much," Adam assured and I simply nodded.

We finished our private conversation and joined the general public. Adam and I stayed focused as we leaned against the small untidy bar that was used for liquor and beer for the small amount of humans that were allowed to be among us. Both of us waited patiently for Xavier to arrive with our arms folded and our thoughts clear.

Lidia joined Adam and stood by his side fondling his fairly long disheveled blonde hair. I was envious; I wanted Dianna at my side as well. I scrutinized the room to see that Richard and Joe were running the pool tables. I didn't have a problem with that until I saw Crissy hovering around Joe. This I wasn't going to allow. It may have been selfish and childish of me but he wasn't going to have his affectionate woman attached to his hip while I ached for Dianna. I turned to Adam and asked him to dismiss Crissy. She was Adam's day walker, I didn't have the authority to force her to leave, but Adam did. Now was the time when Joe was going to start to repay his debt to me. I ignored Dianna's attempted rape for far too long and Joe was getting too comfortable. As of this moment, Joe would be reminded of his past actions frequently. Adam did as I requested and Joe was aware that I was behind Adam's actions. When Crissy walked away I waved Joe over to me, of course he obliged.

"This isn't the night to be cuddling up with your lay of the month. We're here for one reason only. Get your head out of your ass, stop thinking with your dick and stay focused. Xavier won't come here alone and anything can happen. Get your priorities straight and we won't have a problem. You're my right hand and your place is here, behind me. As boring as it may be it's where you belong," I was cold, arrogant and forceful.

Joe didn't argue with me he only agreed and nodded. Although my comment about Crissy being his lay of the month seemed to disturb him. It was apparent that Crissy was more to him than just a one night stand but it was my intent to degrade her as he degraded Dianna. I wanted him to feel the things I've been feeling for so long. A slick comment on my part wasn't nearly as equal to the humiliation that he instilled upon Dianna. That would come in time but not by my hands.

An eye for an eye, I thought to myself. Unfortunately for Crissy, she would ultimately pay the price for Joe's ineptness, disloyalty and addiction in due time. Crissy's shame and discord would be irrelevant to my kind because she is only a human. When the time comes for her to suffer my wrath she should consider it a privilege that a vampire, such as myself, would take the time out to use her as a decoy to avenge someone who was well above her in status and class. That would be Dianna.

I'm positive that Joe sensed that I was being more spiteful than serious, but the fact of the matter was this night was strictly business and not pleasure. I'm the boss and my word is law whether Joe agreed or not. We had to appear strong, loyal and confident when Xavier arrived. Joe and Richard both accepted the terms and silently took their rightful and privileged place behind me.

Time wasn't ticking fast enough while I waited for Xavier to make his grand entrance. When he finally did arrive it was about ninety minutes before sunrise and he strutted in proud as a peacock. His clan was not present in it's entirety. The three drones that Christopher turned weren't there nor was the biggest and the strongest of his posse. Apparently, they were assigned to keep watch over Dianna in Xavier's absence. I could smell Dianna scent all over Xavier and the rest of his clan and it sickened me. The thought of their hands on her infuriated me. Trying to keep my cool wasn't going to be easy. However, her scent was so potent that it was evident and refreshing to know that she was definitely alive. It was hard to inhale her so deeply and not be able to touch or see her. I missed her so much. I couldn't let Dianna's sweet fragrance distract me from the current circumstances. Her life was in my hands.

It was game time. I had to put on my best poker face and play the game precisely. This meeting was nothing more than a battle of wits. However, the stakes were high and I was gambling with Dianna's life. It took everything inside me not to kill him right then and there. However, I played it cool and leaned back against the bar, arms folded and stone faced. This was Xavier's game and it was up to him to make the first move.

He was greeting everyone boisterous and catty before he approached me.

"Hello, one and all," he said. And his clan were dressed in their coats of arms. They followed gallantly behind him. "How is everyone tonight?" Xavier and his mate Carla were arm in arm when we met face to face. We stood only inches apart as he continued with this masquarade.

"Dan," he said sarcastically. "You look distraught this evening. Maybe I can help ease your tension." I remained composed and let him continue.

"I see you have new ink on your arm. It's a pity that Dianna isn't here to appreciate what you do for her." He reached out to touch the tattoo of Dianna's name on my crossed arm as he spoke.

I pushed his hand off my arm and said, "I don't recall saying you can touch me."

"Watch that temper of yours," he gloated. "As I was saying….ahhh…yes, I was talking about Dianna. I do understand why you find her so appealing, she is…absolutely…delicious." He turned to his mate Carla, pointed to his lip and said, "Oops, it looks like I missed a spot," Carla then wiped a small spec of blood from his lips and smiling wickedly. This was Xavier's way of telling me he was feeding from Dianna.

I was enraged. I'll never know how I contained my anger at that moment. I quickly avoided the conversation and moved on to the matter at hand. If I dwelled on his comment I would have fell into his trap and I couldn't allow that to happen. This was a delicate situation and it had to be handled with precision.

"Let's cut to the chase without the theatrics and tell me what you want," I was calm,cool and collective in my mannerism. I was a better actor than I thought because all I wanted to do was rip him apart, limb from limb.

"You already know the things I want. We've been over this already. So just take your place on your knees and you can have Dianna back," he said smuggly.

"Every time we talk you add something new to your list of demands. So I just want to be sure what we're negotiating. Enlighten me and tell me what you want and maybe we can reach an agreement."

I was arrogant and cocky. I wasn't showing any signs of anger or heartache. I took control of the conversation and I was playing the game correctly. I rarely lose when I gamble and tonight wasn't going to be any different.

He made a dramatic huff, as if he was inconvenienced by my request. This was the moment he has been waiting for, he wanted to give me his list of demands in the presence of many Manhattan vampires.

"*Humph*, okay, I'll tell you yet again," he said clasping his hands together. "I want you on your knees at my feet and apologize for all your superior humiliation through out the years. I want you to succumb to my wishes. I want control over Midtown, Uptown and this place. I will then allow you and your minions to be part of my clan and walk with me as my body guards."

"And if I agree to these terms, what's in it for me?" I asked in a condescending tone.

"You get Dianna back...alive," he answered wickedly.

I nodded my head up and down as if I was pondering his demands. Pretending to be lost in thought for a few short seconds before I gave him my answer.

"Well X," I said. "You drive a hard bargin and you give me no choice." He began to smile just before I finished my statement.

"Kill her," I said coldly.

The smile that was on his face suddenly vanished. And his eyes widened. My clan, Adam and his clan stared at me with astonishment. I unfolded my arms and started to walk away before Xavier stopped me,

"I can see your very distraught and you're not thinking rationally. I'll give you forty-eight hours to think about my terms before you commit to your decision," he said anxiously.

"Forty eight hours is reasonable," I patronized. "Make no mistake X, if Dianna dies I will hunt you and I will kill you. I will destroy that piece of shit city of yours as well. Your mate Carla and I will watch it burn together before I throw her into the flames. If I remember correctly she doesn't like fire."

I saw the dismay on his face. I took control of a situation that I didn't have any control over. I caused a huge diversion in his plot to humiliate me. Through all my years of gambling I've learned that any diversion that you can throw at your opponent is a good diversion. If I could cause an opponent to lose sight of their goals, even just for a moment, then the tables would ultimately turn in my favor. The same applied to this situation as well. Although he still had Dianna he feared my reputation of viciousness and revenge. Whether or not Dianna lived or died was irrelevant. Xavier sealed his fate the very second he came into my city and took her. He and his crew of misfits were going to die regardless of Dianna's outcome. Dianna was still the primary reason for this war with

Xavier, but it was also about pride, ego and territory and none of the aforementioned reasons were negotiable. Xavier's days were numbered.

"You will not take my moment of glory away from me! Time is your enemy and I will be in touch in forty-eight hours or Dianna dies from hunger and not my hands," Xavier attempted to threaten, but the tone in his voice only proved that he was running scared. He and his crew turned to exit the building. I stood and watched as he approached the door.

"One more thing before I depart," he said as he handed me a sealed envelope.

"Sending me a love letter?" I asked self-satisfied.

"Perhaps," he answered and vanished.

I handed the envelope to Joe and he put it in his pocket. I wasn't going to give Xavier the satisfaction of opening it in front of him. Everyone and I do mean everyone fell silent. I turned to Adam and told him that I would be in touch soon, to let him know what my next course of action would be. We shook hands in agreement and I proceeded out the door. Joe and Richard followed behind me.

During our walk home I was silent and deep in thought. I held my ground but I still didn't know where Dianna was, and it was killing me. Her scent that was so intoxicating just moments ago was fading and so was my patience.

18

The Past

Not acknowledging anyone, I walked straight to my bedroom when I arrived home. Richard and Joe allowed me my silence and recluse without asking me questions that I didn't have any answers to. The house was silent and lifeless. There wasn't anyone in my sight and I was thankful. I wasn't up to recapping the events of the evening. I only wanted to be alone.

When I entered my bedroom it would be an understatement to say that I was surprised to find Helena and Ava inside hovering over my desk and talking. I noticed Ava sitting at the desk chair clinging onto Dianna's pendant and Helena leaning against the wall. I was outraged to say the least. We respected one another's privacy, this was inexcusable. They were so engaged with conversation that they didn't even notice I was in the room until I spoke.

"What the fuck are the two of you doing in here!" I screamed

They both were taken back by my sudden appearance, and suddenly became speechless.

"You better fuckin' answer me now! Why are you in here and touching Dianna's things?"

Richard and Joe came rushing in to see what was the matter. Richard saw the anger in my eyes and gazed at Helena with concern hoping that there was an extremely good reason for her to be in my domain.

"Tell him, Ava," Helena said nervously.

Ava warily dropped the pendant and stared at me with fright in her eyes. She tried to speak but couldn't get out the words. Ava's fear of me was that intensifying.

"Somebody better fuckin' tell me something soon because my patience has reached its limits." I said furiously shaking my hands as if I was going to strangle someone.

"Ava can see the past!" Helena jumped in immediately somehow convinced that this was something I wanted to hear.

"How the fuck does that affect me? If this doesn't have anything to do with Dianna, I don't want to hear it. So everyone get the fuck out!" I snapped.

"It has everything to do with Dianna!" Helena snapped back sharply.

I instantly settled down and attentively stared at the both of them.

"Okay…" I said calmly and leaned against the wall. "You have my attention. Talk."

Helena pushed Ava on the rolling chair lightly toward me and told her once again to tell me what she knows.

"I'm not going to hurt you Ava, just fuckin' tell me already or I will hurt you and Helena too. You're both getting on my last fucking nerve and I want answers right fucking now!" I screamed as I punched yet another hole in the wall.

Richard looked worrisome and concerned about my threatening words and my terrifying actions. He was afraid for Helena but stayed quiet, knowing that she was out of line just being in my room. He was hoping that what they had to say was significant enough to appease me.

Ava was nervous and anxious when she spoke to me. I remained patient and allowed her to talk to me in her own time. After all, if this was prominent enough to rescue Dianna she would be in my good graces once again. Although, if it weren't for Ava and her stupidity Dianna wouldn't be in this mess.

"As Helena told you, I can see the past. All I need is something of significance of the person I want to look back on. Nothing worked for Dianna. I've been sneaking around trying to find anything to give me a read on her. Then just a while ago, Helena and I found this," she said and held up the crescent moon pendant.

"Do you mean to tell me that you know where Dianna is?" I asked with disbelief.

"Yes," Ava replied.

"How deep in the past can you see?" I asked with much interest.

"I can see from approximately twenty-four hours ago until right now and then it subsides."

"I want to know everything," I ordered. "Tell me where she is."

Ava took hold of the pendant and closed her eyes as she tried to get a fix on Dianna. She tuned in almost immediately and began to tell all of us what she could see.

"They moved her around a lot. Bringing her back and forth over the bridges so you could lose her scent. They keep her drugged constantly. She's here in the city. Xavier doesn't think that you would look in Manhattan for her. He's not going to move her any more."

"Can you see the exact place where she is?" I asked excitedly.

"Yes. She's in the abandoned fabric warehouse on South St, near the Seaport. Most of that is area is condemned already."

Ava looked at me with sadness in her eyes. It was apparent that she didn't want to see anymore, but I wanted to know everything

"Don't stop now Ava, I want to know what's happening to her. Don't be afraid to tell me. I'm not going to hurt you. I have to know…please," I pleaded.

Ava nodded and continued.

"Xavier left, he doesn't stay there. He and the others leave an hour before the sunrises to be sure they have enough time to be out of the suns rays. Xavier is very afraid of the sun. Right now she's with four males from his clan. When Xavier is with her the four that are with her during the day go to feed. He comes in with numbers, about six or seven are with him. Just in case we show up. Some of them are from other Brooklyn clans. They have her hidden and blind folded. They keep her blinded and break her fingers daily so she can't use her magic. They won't give her time to heal knowing how fast we do that," Ava suddenly stopped speaking.

She knew more but didn't want to tell me. I don't think it was out of fear it appeared that she felt pity for Dianna and it hurt her to see the things she saw.

"Okay, Ava, I won't taunt you, but there is just one thing I have to know and I'll leave you be. Are they *all* drinking from her?"

Ava nodded her yes and said, "They all are. She's already been drained." She placed the pendant on the desk and bowed her head down to revive herself from her visions.

I picked up the stereo and threw it across the room. I was livid. Everyone jumped back as the stereo broke into pieces against the wall. Everyone except Joe, who was already settled in the back of the room. He knew me well and my reaction didn't surprise him at all. He was waiting for it. The sun had already risen and there wasn't a thing I could do about it. I did, however, restrain myself and took control over my being once again. Since I now knew where she was, I could devise a plan to bring her home. Dianna's safety and well being had to be my first concern.

Joe inaudibly walked over to me and handed me the envelope that Xavier gave to me earlier. I had forgotten all about that. I knew for a fact that it was going to be something dramatic I didn't want to open it, but my curiosity got the better of me and I opened it. It was nothing more than a piece of paper with a *YouTube* web address on it.

More theatrics.

Without haste, Richard nudged Ava out of the desk chair and sat down in front of the computer and logged onto the website. When the video popped up, there was a red piece of posterboard with Dianna's name written across it. Mozart's Requiem Mask was playing in the background. The video stood silent for a minute or two and then I heard Dianna's screams of pain and torment. I heard them take a blunt object and slam it onto something and Dianna screamed frantically. They made sure Dianna was awake when they fed from her, I heard them nibble on her body her screams faded as she was being drained. They spoke about the taste of her blood and suggested bottling it. Xavier laughed and yelled into the camera, "If you don't agree to my terms, Dan, the only thing of Dianna that will be left is her bottled blood, hence, your blood is in the mix and ruins the taste." He laughed sadistically, I lowered my head and put my hands on my hips.

They laughed as she cried and I heard them tear off her clothes and made vulgar comments about her ass, breasts and skin. She begged them not to hurt her and screamed my name, yelling for me to save her. I knew she was weak from hunger, I heard it in her voice and any impulse to fight back would be useless. I heard her begging and pleading for them not to cover her mouth with the chloroform cloth. They only laughed at her and blamed me for the position she was in. They drugged her repeatedly and beat her while she was unconscious. There wasn't anything being filmed other than the red poster board. It was nine minutes and forty seconds of Dianna screaming in agony, crying and calling my name.

Richard shut the compter off half way through the video. We've heard enough and got the message. Everyone was stunned and shocked. They all expressed sorrow on their faces but remained speechless.

Amazingly enough I didn't go into a full blow rage. I was devastated and numb. I didn't have the energy to lose my temper.

"Everyone get out, I need to be alone and think," I ordered serenely. They did as they were told without insult, only sympathy.

I lay in my lonely bed replaying her screams over and over again in my mind. Hearing her call my name cut through me like a sword. It was difficult to bare but I didn't let it cloud my judgement. I couldn't let it. If I wasn't able to think straight then I couldn't save her. I had to keep myself together for her sake, not mine. This was more than a rescue mission, it was going to be a blood bath. I put Dianna's fears aside to think of something tormenting and cruel to instill on Dianna's captors. Her suffering wouldn't go unnoticed. I wanted to be sure that they all screamed with the same fright as she did and felt everything she did without the pleasure of being unconscience. Xavier was going to watch everyone in his clan perish before I killed him...slowly.

As I lay alone, I remembered the picture I took from her photo album back at her parents house. I took it out of my wallet and stared at it for inspiration. Her smile captivated me and I was going to make sure that she would share that smile with me again. I put the picture on my chest and began to think of how I was going to bring her home and take Xavier down as well. There were many ideas flashing through my mind. I could just go there in the morning and get her, but I wanted Xavier's blood. I wanted each and everyone to feel my wrath. I wanted them to encounter the element of surprise. I wanted them all to have a long and lingering death.

Then suddenly, without warning or much thought I put everything into perspective and came up with a very simple and sure way to satisfy my thirst for blood, mend my broken heart and save Dianna as well.

I leaped out of bed and banged on everyone's door, even Sebastian's to wake them from their rest. I wanted to go over all the details with them before I put my plan into action. I had to be sure that things were going to be done my way and done without mistake. Once I was convinced that they were prepared I would call Adam and tell him the part I wanted him to play.

I was excited and anxious as I everyone followed me into the living room struggling to wake up from their slumbers. I gave them a few minutes to settle on the couch and make themselves comfortable.

"First things first," I said to Sebastian just to get it out of the way. "Sometime today you have to get my car out of the impound." Sebastian, of course agreed.

I looked at everyone else and informed them that we were going to make a move, Unfortuantely; Dianna will have to suffer another day. I couldn't attack until one hour before sunrise when Xavier leaves to go to back to Brooklyn. I had to take them out one shift at a time to assure Dianna's safety. Somewhat like a chess game. I was going to take out the pawns first before I slaughtered their king.

I explained to everyone that we would make our first move in twenty four hours. They seemed concerned that I was only allowing one hour to take out Xavier's four clansmen. We had to move fast to make this work, so their concerns were irrelevant to me. I did, however, set their minds at ease when I explained that three of Dianna's captors were new and inexperienced. Only one of them had experience and strength. I would take care of him personally. One hour was more than enough time to eliminate them. I told Sebastian that he was going to accompany us as well. I wanted him to wait outside in his van to transport Dianna home while the rest of us took care of business. My priority was to get her out of there and out of harms way immediately.

To make sure this plan worked with precision, I had to have pictures of the warehouse that Dianna was being held captive in and the other surrounding buildings. I picked up the cell phone, walked into the other room for privacy and called Adam. I told him the whole story of Ava's gift and how she found Dianna.

I went over my two part plan and told him that his services would be required tomorrow when the sun sets. I would meet him tonight to let him know the details. He agreed without hesitation. I also asked his permission to borrow Crissy. I needed her to take pictures of the warehouse that Dianna was in and the other buildings in the surrounding area. I needed a human who blends in and could go unnoticed and Adam agreed. It had to be a human, a human who can be trusted, who wasn't very popular in our world and a scent that wasn't known. Crissy was a day walker, not a donor, so she fit the description perfectly. I couldn't take the chance of Sebastian taking the photos because of his scent. If they sensed him alone and unarmed they would probably kill Dianna. I had just one other request for Adam, I wanted him to allow Joe to give Crissy the order to do so. I was being vengeful. I wanted Joe to be in a situation where something he cares about was in danger by my hands. It wasn't nearly enough to make up for what he did, but all in all it fed my ego and taste for revenge. Adam agreed and laughed. He knew exactly why I made such a request. I finished my phone call and walked back into the living room.

"Joe," I said. "I want you to call that girlfriend of yours and have her go to South St. and take pictures of the fabric warehouse and everything else that is in the area."

"Why Crissy? She isn't part of this. She's human." he answered with concern in his voice.

"I don't owe you an explaination, but I'll give you one any way. It has to be a human who can do this. Pictures need to be taken in the sunlight and she doesn't have a vampire scent."

"Doesn't something like this have to go through Adam first? She does belong to him," he debated.

"That's already been done. Now call her and give the fucking order," I commanded voicterously.

Joe reached into his pocket with irritation to get his phone and call Crissy.

"Just one more thing Joe," I said as I interrupted his dialing. "Tell her to shower thoroughly to get your scent off her. I don't need any fuck ups."

Joe, without enthusiasm, nodded and did as he was told. He attempted to go to his room to speak to her privately. I stopped him before he took one step from the couch.

"Sit down. I want to hear the conversation," I told him. "This isn't the time for you to whisper sweet nothings into her ear. Do that on your own time. Tell her what needs to be done and hang up."

I was nasty as I dictated to him, but at least he was able to call her on the phone and talk to her. I didn't have that satisfaction. I couldn't touch, see, smell or hear Dianna. I could only wish at this moment that I could talk to her on the phone and tell her to take pictures. I was taking all my frustrations out on all of them. It was wrong but if I wasn't happy nobody was going to be. They were aware of how vengeful and vicious I could be, this didn't come as any shock to them. Up until now I usually looked the other way when it came to Joe, I favored him slightly above the rest, considering I am his creator, but he won't be teacher's pet anymore. Joe sat down angrily and he did as he was told. It was apparent that he was upset that I involved his playmate and he wasn't used to me being firm with him. Joe knew me better than anyone and he was aware that this was an act of resentment and power. He dialed the phone with a sour puss and he flung his silken mane from his face in annoyance. His conversation was brief and to the point.

Crissy was confused by Joe's short and indifferent conversation but agreed anyway and was honored to be a part of something crucial and historic among our kind.

19

Warriors

We all had a long rest, we were well aware that one hour before sunset we would make our move. We had to be alert and focused. Taking out Xavier's babysitters was going to be the easy part of the game. We didn't need to carry an arsenal to stop Dianna's spineless captors. That would come later when we faced Xavier and the others. The four thugs that were watching over Dianna were not a threat. Xavier's first mistake was trusting Dianna's fate to unproven vampires. An hour was more than enough time to do what we had to do and bring Dianna home.

Sometime during our rest, Crissy came by and gave Sebastian the many pictures that she took of the warehouse and its surrounding area. It was an industrial area that was mostly condemned. This was better than expected because I didn't have to worry about human interference. This was Xavier's second mistake.

When we awoke, we were silent among each other and proceeded to put our minds into perspective. Despite our arguments, disagreements and acts of selfishness, we are unified and we take care of our own. We are all well trained and disciplined soldiers. Losing is never an option. We all obtain qualities that make us the fierce predators that we are.

Before we left the house, Sebastian advised us to be careful and not to get too cocky. He assured us that he would be waiting in the van outside Dianna's prision one hour before sunrise. Sebastian used his van when he had to play the role of a day walker, not to be noticed and blend among humans. I reminded him to bring human food, water and someone or something, that contains human blood for Dianna to drink.

We walked the streets dressed in our coat of arms, prepared to desecrate our enemies. There was also something to be said about our facade, it gave us the confidence and ability to be victorious. I led the pack while the others walked with loyalty and precision behind me.

Like great athletes, vampires were also superstitious and always carried or wore something of personal luck before battle.

Joe wore his *"Charles Manson for President"* T-shirt, Richard wore his platinum black sapphire crucifix around his neck, Helena wore her emerald rosary beads around her neck. She held them in her hands while laying in the hospital bed the night Joe turned her. Back in her human days, Helena was raised a good Catholic girl.

Ava wore her black bandanna as a do-rag. As for me, I wore a pewter ring with an enlarged hooded face of the Grim Reaper on my left ring finger. The ring was suitable and lucky. My hands were lethal beyond measure. Inside my pocket I kept Dianna's pendant, for her own personal luck as well. If it weren't for that unspoken piece of jewelry, I don't know how I would have found her. From this day forth it would always stay with Dianna to watch over her.

More importantly than items of luck and chance, we had to feed. Blood was our fuel, this wasn't the time to let that go unnoticed. We went to Penn Station—where there was a large population of homeless alcoholics and junkies. It made more sense to feed as a group upon many victims in one secluded gathering, and we did just that. We were incapable of mercy, empathy and pity on this day of days more than usual. Any human within reach was instantly a target. We fed more than usual, we were revitalized. Along the abandoned train tracks, was where the degenerate humans dwelled and slept. We intruded on their territory. We slaughtered and butchered them, making them unrecognizable and there wasn't any need to dispose of the bodies we left behind. We devoured and shredded each and every one of our victims. We killed anyone else who was within sight, just for kicks and preparation. We acted in this vulgar manner as a training technique. Helena used her shape shifting powers to attack her prey; Richard used his hypnotic gift before he killed the innocent to prepare himself for the true battle. Richards's gift was amazing. He was the only one known among our kind that could hypnotize another vampire. There wasn't any doubt that his power would be useful during combat.

Joe tied his hair back to be free of annoyance and distraction. He rehearsed his agility by running rapidly along the tracks, along the tunnel walls, onto the ceiling, and leaping backwards in the air. His coat flowed when he mounted behind an unsuspecting victim and fed before they were aware of his presence.

Other than her gift of seeing in the past, we also learned that Ava has the ability of hiding. She was able to hide in the shadows of anything and anyone, stealthy, unnoticed and unheard. She practiced her gift among the many inept humans that were lurking along the train tracks. Ava never used her gifts often, there was never a need to so she kept them hidden. I was impressed with Ava because none of us were aware of how beneficial she is as a warrior. *If Ava would only have used her powers as opposed to her stupidity, we would not be in this predicament.*

As for me, mind reading among humans was easy as it is for all vampires. However I can read the mind of a vampire also, a rare gift that requires some effort. More importantly, I can block out anyone or anything from attempting to read my thoughts at any given moment. I am literally "thick headed" however, should I open my mind to others they can see my thoughts if I allow them to. I have total control over this unique gift that I've been blessed with. I can block out memories and enhance them, which was already proven. There wasn't anything living or undead, that could figure me out even in the most ordinary of circumstances. However, my true and beneficial power was my strength. I could decapitate a human, a vampire, even an animal with one hand in a split second. There wasn't much of anything that could contain me. I couldn't be immobilized by anything short of a God. The infamous stake through the heart theory can't kill any of us, but it will immobilize vampires until the stake is withdrawn. We are immortal after all and the thought of a piece of wood taking the life of a vampire is ludicrous. Once the stake is removed, we could heal immediately. As for me, I would be able to withdraw it myself because my strength would hardly be affected by the infliction and I don't become immobile. Not to boast, but I *am* the definitive killing machine, even among my own kind. Instant decapitation by surprise is the only way I could be stopped. Even that would be a challenge, because of my enhanced telepathy, I have keen, superior senses that keep me alert, aware, and on the defense. For me to rehearse my strength against a human wasn't much different than a puppy tearing apart a shoe. There wasn't any challenge for me, but I rehearsed anyway. As I said, it was going to be a massacre and a well deserved buffet.

As for Dianna, no one knew what she could do and what she couldn't. She didn't even know. Only time would tell. However, I knew for certain that there was a dark side to her and I just had to sit back and wait for her abilities to surface.

We were all feeling invigorated and ready to do the deed at hand. We went to meet Adam and his clan at the club of the undead. An eerie silence fell upon the room when we stepped inside. Adam was there with his followers and we gathered in the middle of the room. Adam stood alone, face to face with me, as his clan stood behind him and mine behind me. Adam and I shook hands and began to talk. Both clans were disciplined and we stayed solely among each other. This wasn't a night of frolic and fun. Tonight it was all about business.

Crissy approached Joe with a beer in her hand. I was impressed how Joe handled her. She glided towards him in her cute flirtatious way. She stood in front of him waiting for him to acknowledge her. Joe stared at her almost demonically, shrugged his shoulders and said, "I didn't call for you, now go," he pointed to the door.

He was cold and domineering. He turned his head from her and she walked away confused. Joe was all business and I was pleased. When two clans are uniting as one to save one of our own, it was customary to socialize and strategize among ourselves. Outsiders were forbidden to enter the circle. Although Crissy belonged to Adam, she wasn't a warrior and she isn't a vampire. Her place within our world was that of a maggot. She does not belong with us, but she didn't know any better. That is why Adam forgave her for stepping out of her bounds.

It was January, the sun would rise at approximately 7:20 A.M. Xavier would be departing for Brooklyn at 6:20. It was almost showtime. I informed Adam that once the deed was done, I would be in contact with him to go over the details for later this evening. He wished me luck and we set our plan into motion.

I informed my clan that once we were inside, things had to be done fast and quick, or Dianna would surely die. My orders for them were to immobilize their combatant, in whatever way they saw fit. I also insisted that they feed from them as well. Depriving a vampire of their own blood wouldn't kill them, but it would drain them and make them weak for a substantial amount of time. Eventually, they would be doomed to slip into a state of madness. I wanted them to be alive and suffering. Under no circumstances, were they to have a fast and painless death.

As we approached our destination, I was becoming more eager and determined to have my revenge and get Dianna out of their clutches. I closed my eyes and cleared my mind. I had to set my mind into the right mode so I can bring my baby home.

We stood about two blocks away before moving full force into conflict. I handed Ava Dianna's pendant for her to read. I had to be sure that Xavier was gone and only the four body guards were present. It was imperative that they were in a deep state of slumber or they would kill Dianna before we walked though the doors. Vampires are at their most vulnerable in a deep state of slumber. It's not only our bodies that rest, our senses and powers are dormant also. Ava went into her swift trance and locked into the recent past. She told us that Dianna was incoherent and the four bodyguards have been resting for almost an hour. Xavier had left earlier than anticipated and was surley back in Brooklyn. He was too far away to catch our scent, especially over water. I took Dianna's pendant from Ava for safe keeping, "You did good," I complemented and she smiled bashfully.

We approached the old dilapidated warehouse in a perfect chess formation. Pawns in front and the knight behind them guarding the king. There was a lock on the door. I was actually offended to think that Xavier would believe that a two dollar lock could keep me out. "Need help with that?" Joe asked.

I wasn't amused with Joe's attempt to humor me. This wasn't the time. I ripped it of the latch with my finger, and we busted inside still standing in our chess formation. The sound of our footsteps awoke Dianna's captors abruptly. For a few moments, they were oblivious. Their eyes keyed in on us and they instantly jumped into an attack formation. Everyone stood face to face with their chosen opponents simultaneously and then attacked in perfect sequence. Joe was the first to seek out his prey. Joe liked to play like Tom and Jerry before he killed. He liked to show off, taunt and tease.

He circled his rival rapidly to confuse and mesmerize him before tapping him on the shoulder from behind. When the unskilled vampire turned his head and flashed his fangs, Joe said casually, "What up," and smiled crookedly. He allowed his foe to punch him in the face to keep things upbeat. Joe licked the small drop of blood that dripped from his broken lip and smiled devilishly once more. He then flashed around him in a complete circle and lunged at him like the cunning, sly fox that he is. Joe's speed is really incredible, his swiftness is too fast for an untrained vampire to compete with. Within a tenth of a second, he had Christopher's creation up against the wall and locked his fangs into his neck, draining every drop of blood from his undead body. The untalented abomination fell to the floor weak from blood loss. Joe bit into his own wrist and exposed his blood to the abomination. He waved it over the fallen vampires mouth and watched him struggle for a taste. As the first drop of blood began to fall from Joe's wrist, Joe quickly pulled his arm back, laughed and sarcastically said, "No candy for you!" As I said, Joe liked to tease his victims. Then he ripped the fangs out of the mouth of the bloodless creature, just to be dramatic. I enjoyed that sight and I was satisfied with Joe's performance and loyalty.

Helena moved in next. She isn't very strong or fast. Therefore, when Helena attacked our kind she would use her shape shifting abilities. She could shape shift into anything just by thought, she didn't need to touch what she wanted to be. As soon as she entered the empty warehouse, she turned herself into a hungry cheetah, pouncing on the first unknown vampire that she saw. She leaped onto his neck and ripped out his jugular and spit it across the room. She changed back to her standard form midway through her feeding until he fell to the floor weakened by her appetite. She stood over him making sure he didn't heal. She pressed on his chest with her foot to hold him down. If he should regain any strength back she would drink from him again.

Richard walked in quiet, calm and scoped out the room for his prey. The last of Christopher's' creations leaped in front of Richard, screaming and hissing like a lunatic, flashing his fangs trying to intimidate him. Richard looked at him in bewilderment and turned to Joe, "What the fuck is this?" As he pointed to the crazed one.

"Better you than me," Joe shrugged.

Richard huffed and rolled his eyes, "Why do I always get the loons?" He muttered to himself.

Richard locked his eyes on the maniacal vampire, who was obviously unaware of Richard's gift. Anyone who was worth knowing in our world knew about Richard's extremely rare skill. Within seconds, a green beam of light shot from his eyes and his enemy was sedated, serene and stunned. Richard walked over elegantly and eminently and bit into the neck of his untrained combatant. Once he was weak and non threatening, Richard plucked the fangs of his enemy and released him from his hypnotic state to watch him writhe in pain and humiliation.

The strongest and oldest of Xavier's foursome pushed Ava to the side like a rag doll. As I was scanning the room to find Dianna, I saw an old stained curtain hanging from the ceiling in the back corner of the warehouse. It was obvious that Dianna lurked behind that curtain. I could smell her scent and it reeked with fear. I began to walk rapidly toward Dianna's cell, my senses still keen and ready for any sudden moves by my enemies. Suddenly, Xavier's best warrior leaped in front of me. Without stopping my rhythm, I reached out my left arm, snapped his neck, pulled his fangs, pushed his nasal bone into his brain and tossed him across the room. He slammed down to the concrete floor. It wouldn't be long before he would heal himself. I shouted out to Ava, "Drain him!" As I pointed to Xavier's "best". She did as I directed promptly and viciously.

Joe called from the other side of the room and yelled, "What do you want us to do with them?"

"Nothing yet. Keep them down. I'll tell you when," I said with authority.

My pace grew quicker as I stood within inches of Dianna's hiding place. I was anxious to see her. The others remained quiet while hovering their prey.

I pushed the curtain to the side and I found Dianna's bare body laying face down on the cold dirty floor. Seeing her that way tore me apart. She was always shy about her body being exposed and this was probably the hardest thing for her to handle during her captive.

"Dianna, how could this have happened?" I whispered.

She was in a state of comatose.

I crouched down along her side, untied the blindfold and gently moved her long hair off her back to see what damage has been done to her. She had been bitten everywhere. There were multitudes of vampire bites all over her back and buttocks. I noticed that Xavier carved the letter X into any spot that was clean of a bite mark. They treated her like an everlasting buffet and suddenly I felt a sense of regret. I thought about the day when Dianna threw the pendant at me and what I had said to her,

I'll order a feeding frenzy on your blood and it will be a buffet, and I'll take the first bite, I promise you.

I curled my lips and closed my eyes in repulsion.

Dianna, I am so sorry.

I examined her hands and fingers, they were bruised and broken, but beginning to heal. I was sickened and disgusted by what I saw. I would have preferred her to be dead than to be like this. I turned her over see what damage has been done to the front of her body and it was a replica of her back. She opened her eyes briefly and looked into my eyes before closing them again.

"Don't worry baby, I'm taking you home," I whispered, unaware if she heard me.

Her lips were blue, dry and cracked from thirst. Her skin was dehydrated. There was swelling under her skin and her body temperature was below normal from hunger. I reached inside my pocket for her pendant and placed it around her neck. I removed my coat and wrapped it around her gently to conceal her body.

I called to Helena, "Is that pathetic excuse for a vampire that you're with drained and weak?"

"Yes," she answered.

I then asked Ava the same question, she also confirmed that he was still drained and weak as well.

I called both Ava and Helena over to me. They were at my side in less than a second.

They were shocked and appauled by Dianna's condition as was I.

"Sebastian is waiting outside in his van. Get Dianna home. Make sure she's fed, washed and comfortable. We have to finish up here. I don't want any of you to be a part of it. I need you both to take care of Dianna now. We won't be long," I explained.

They accepted their orders without question. Helena gracefully lifted Dianna up lightly and kept her wrapped tightly in my coat. I stood and watched them race out the building with Dianna's limp body in Helena's arms.

I heard Sebastian start the van and pull away. I wanted Dianna to be out of harms way before we did what was next. Joe and Richard stared at me waiting for me to give an order.

"Before they die, I want you to feed from them through out their bodies. Break their bones and then tear off every limb. Save the head for last. Do it slowly and sadistically. Show no fucking mercy!"

Without question and without surprise they did.

I stomped on the Xavier's "best" with my steal tip boots breaking his hands, arms and knee caps before I drank from his neck, arms and face in excess and ferociousness. I ripped his limbs from his body with my one hand and let them hang by a thread before I detached them. He was writhing in agony and screaming in fear. The sound of his fear illuminated me, but it could never make up for what they did to Dianna. I ripped out his jaw and tongue, so he couldn't have the pleasure of releasing his despair. Then I spit his own blood into his face before I crushed it with my fist.

Richard wasn't as nonchalant and elegant as he was just moments ago. He feasted upon his enemy. He ripped out his neck with his fangs and tossed his larynx across the room with his mouth. He broke his arms by pulling them around in a complete cirlcle. He listened to him scream before he dismembered him.

Joe wasn't being cocky anymore. He too was enraged by his small glimpse of Dianna. Joe is a glutton for blood. He drank from the pathetic excuse of a vampire, in excess. He pulled apart his limbs slowly, skinned his arms and legs with his retractable fingernails before dismemberment.

The three of us stood in front of Helena's casualty. We watched him nervously crawl to the wall and curl up in a fetal postion while begging for mercy. Richard pulled his legs and laid him on his stomach. The three us feasted upon his back, neck, arms and legs. We looked like a pack of wolves feasting on a lamb. We listened to his screams fade to tears. *What a pitiful group,* I thought to myself. Joe took his right arm, Richard took the left and I took hold of both of his legs. We were about to pull him apart when Joe asked, "Hey Dan, heads or tails?"

I managed to crack a smile, "You're a dick," I said humorously.

Richard laughed as well. We simultaneously pulled on the victim's limbs and dismembered him.

Once they were mangled and dismembered we severed each of their heads with our bare hands. The entire warehouse was a pool of blood and we took delight in the massacre that was caused by our hands. This was way beyond any fight for revenge that I have ever seen. This was a slaughter house. A wolf couldn't do this much damage to a lamb.

Since Xavier liked to leave messages for me using the internet, I thought it would only be fitting to leave him a message as well.

We took all the limbs and heads and aligned them in the shape of an "X" in the center of the room on the floor. "When Xavier comes here tonight to humiliate Dianna, the first thing his eyes will see is his disintegrated army in pieces," I said to Richard and Joe before we departed.

I think our message was loud and clear that Xavier would be next.

20

Reunited

I could finally sense Dianna. I was able to feel her presence burning inside me like an inferno. I didn't feel empty any longer. She was out of her comatose state and alive again.

We headed home from the gruesome warehouse with thirty minutes to spare before the sunrise. Things went better than expected. I was pleased with the outcome and with my entire clan. They are deadly machines of precision and obedience.

Richard, Joe and I entered our building through the parking garage. It was morning rush hour and manuvering through so many humans in the lobby wasn't worth the effort. As we walked through the garage, I called Adam on the phone. I told him about our success and that the services of him and his clan were still required at sunset. He concurred to meet me on the rooftop of an abandoned tire warehouse that was just one block away from Dianna's prison. In return, I agreed to send Sebastian to his place during the day to give him the pictures of the precise location. Adam was at ease with the arrangements and we ended the civil and brief phone call.

We entered through the basement doorway, I was able to smell Dianna's scent and it was exhilarating. I removed my bloody t-shirt. I didn't want Dianna to visualize the brutality that occured. I would to do anything to put this ordeal behind her and make her recovery as easy as possible. I was actually a little nervous about seeing her. I didn't know how she was going to react when she saw me or how she was going to handle the nightmare that she lived. I wasn't quite sure how I was going to approach her at our first glance.

I hesitated before I opened the front door that led into our apartment. I sauntered inside and didn't acknowledge anyone before I turned down the corridor. Dianna must have sensed my arrival immediately, because I heard rampant footsteps coming closer. By the time I turned to go down the corridor she was racing down the long hallway as fast as she could in spite of her frail and weak condition. Her eyes were filled with tears, and she was wearing one of my many concert T-shirts, she looked so cute. I smiled brightly at the sight of her.

Dianna was strong enough to leap into my arms and straddle herself around me. I twirled her around and she hugged me tightly with her head rested upon my shoulder. "I missed you so much," she whispered.

"Me too," I caressed her hair. We tilted our heads and our eyes met. We had the same spellbound look on our faces like the day we first met at her bookshop. Our first kiss since her imprisonment was gentle and lingering. I didn't remove my lips from hers, nor did she. Her arms were wrapped tightly around my neck. I walked down the hall, her frail body railed up against mine, our lips still locked. I carried her into our bedroom as we remained entwined with one another. I slammed the door behind me with my foot. I wasn't going to let her go and neither was she.

Without parting we stumbled onto the bed gently. I placed myself on top of her as tenderly as I could. I was afraid to aggravate her battered body. I detached my lips from hers for a brief moment, she was breathing heavily as her lips ran down my neck. I struggled to unbutton my jeans and pulled them down as far as they could go without separating myself from her. I only wanted to be inside her and revive our bond. Dianna's instincts told her the same. Nature forced us to become one and rejoin with each other once again. We didn't have any power or control over our emotions, gestures and destiny. I spread her legs gently with my knees. Before I entered inside, I wanted to taste her lips against mine again. She looked so beautiful. Her beauty shined brilliantly through all the ugly scars and bruises that was inflicted on her body. I lightly penetrated my many inches of manhood inside her, pulsating in and out of her as carefully as I could. Her fragile hands were stroking my hair and chest, and she gripped tightly with her legs around my back to hold me deep inside her. Without a glimpse of consciousness, we simultaneously recessed our fangs into each other's necks and began to drink from one another. Our instincts forced us to share blood so our life essence could surge through each other's veins and replenish for the days that we were apart. It is almost imperative that mates such as Dianna and I, drink from each other daily to nourish the bond and keep it flowing. This was a magical moment between us. The thought of getting laid, reaching an orgasm was irrelevant. The short yet lingering time she was gone nearly devastated me. I had to drink and be inside her again so we could rekindle our love. The days without her seemed to be an eternity and was tearing my damned soul apart. It was at this moment, I knew for certain that Dianna and I were destined to be with one another for eternity.

After we were able to regain control over our instincts, I pulled myself out of her and comfortably laid myself beside her. I told Dianna repeatedly how much I loved and missed her. I confessed how empty and lost I was without her. Of course, I didn't confess that I cried. That would make me appear weak and my male pride and ego wouldn't allow such a travesty. I just couldn't bring myself to tell her. I stroked her hair, her face, her neck and then down to her pendant, I don't think Dianna realized she was wearing it.

I held it up,

"Where did you find it?" She asked weakly.

"It was in the desk drawer," I answered. "That little piece of jewelry saved your life."

She rose an eyebrow and gave me a puzzled look. I told her about Ava's psychic gift and how that pendant was the only thing that kept us in tune with one another.

She touched the pendant with her hands and rubbed it lightly. I noticed her fingers were still black and blue even though she was able to move them. I removed her hand from the pendant and kissed her fingers gently and caressed them.

"Does it hurt when I touch your hand?" I asked with concern.

"No, they're much better now. I can move them a little. See," she replied as she wiggled her fingers to show me that her motor skills were still in tact.

"Do something magical. Use your fingers to make something move. Something small, so I know that you're healing," I insisted.

Dianna looked around the room. She set her sight on the bedroom door and magically locked the door with a simple point of her index finger. I was elated that her magic wasn't affected and she was getting better every minute she was with me.

My eyes squinted, "Are you locking me in?" I asked with a flattered smile.

She smiled cutely and said, "Yes. I don't want you to leave. I don't want to ever be without you again. Please don't leave me alone. At least not tonight," her smile turned to a pout as she waited for an answer.

I got up from the bed and pulled up my pants and leaned against the adjacent desk. I didn't know how I was going to tell her that I had to leave in a few hours to end her nightmare.

I cleared my throat, "Dianna, I have to finish this thing with Xavier tonight. I have to leave when the sun sets. I promise this will be the last time we'll be apart," I said firmly.

She rose from the bed and latched onto me.

I pulled her close and she looked up at me, "Can I go with you?" She asked.

I shook my head, "No you can't come with me. You need to rest and not concern yourself with this." I answered.

"Okay," she said with disappointment. "Just be careful."

She let me go and proceeded to walk towards the bed with her down and sulking. I lightly pulled back her arm and hugged her warmly.

"Don't be like this baby," I said. "This will all be over soon. Besides, Sebastian will be here and the two of you can polish each other's nails or something."

She managed to crack a smile, "I understand why you're leaving. I even want you to go and hurt him, hurt them all. I just would have liked to be a part of it to watch them suffer."

I never heard Dianna speak like that. I was impressed by her taste for revenge. Her dark side was surfacing a little. Although, I didn't think that Dianna was aware of how much suffering, brutality, and blood thirsty damage was involved when vampires kill. Her conscience would probably keep her from that part of our world forever.

"Can you tell me what you did to save me?"

I hesitated for a moment and began to talk with my hands, "We walked in the place. We had a little rumble and I took you home," I answered vaguely.

"Little rumble? So you're not going to let me in on any of the gory details are you?" She asked with sheer disappointment.

"No, I'm not," I said sternly. "Just trust me when I say you won't have to worry about them hurting you ever again." I hugged and kissed her to end this conversation. She melted in my arms and responded to my affection on impulse.

I asked Dianna if she was hungry and of course she was. Dianna is always hungry, especially for human food. Before we exited the bedroom, I told her to put on her robe or something over the long T-shirt to cover up. I didn't want her body exposed in such an explicit way. She decided to get fully changed instead. I stood against the desk, just watching her get changed. When she removed my T-shirt, I was able to see all her inflictions. I stopped her from getting dressed to examine her. She was uncomfortable, but I needed to see everything that was done to her. She was healing but the faded wounds were still defined. I noticed for the first time that Xavier had *branded* a letter X on the back of her neck. I was furious but I had to contain myself for Dianna's sake. When I was finshed scoping out her body I hugged her tightly and said, "I am so sorry I couldn't get to you sooner."

"I knew you would come. I wasn't worried," she answered. "You don't have to be sorry. You didn't do this to me. My own trusting stupidity got me into this mess."

I couldn't argue with that so I just held her tightly before we adjourned to the kitchen. Dianna wasn't herself, she was acting different. Xavier didn't just drain her blood, he drained her spirit as well. Her spark—that fire—that made me attracted to her seemed to be extinguishing as my own fire and fury was becoming a raging blaze of flames. Xavier and his pathetic group of insufficient vampires were going to pay severe consequences for their actions.

She continued to get dressed in an old sweat suit that covered up everything. We walked out of our sanctuary and into the living room where everyone else was awake and quietly socializing about the earlier events with Sebastian. They all fell quiet when we enetered the room. I could sense that Dianna felt uneasy and the tension in the room was thick.

"Good morning, Dianna!" Sebastian clasped his hands. "How are you feeling?" He asked cheerfully.

"She's hungry," I answered for her. Dianna turned to me, and rolled her eyes angrily and turned away.

Sebastian nodded, "Well then, let me make you something delicious to eat," he offered.

Dianna shook her head, "Oh, no. I can make myself something to eat, thank you," she said sternly, "This way all of you can continue to talk and I won't be able to hear you from the other room, because it seems that I don't have the ability to do that any more either. Then if you want to know or ask me anything, you can just ask him!" She said pointing her finger to me. The rest of the clan was pretending not to notice the sudden roar in Dianna's voice, "Because Dan has all the answers and knows what's best. Don't ya!" She then gazed at me harshly and strutted with her head held high and slammed open the kitchen door. *She's acting like her mother.*

My reaction was to follow her into the kitchen. The way she behaved wasn't called for and I didn't like it. I wouldn't yell at her but I wanted to calm her down and talk to her.

Sebastian stopped me and said, "Danato, let her be. She's been through a lot. It's normal for her to take out her anger on those she's with the most. She'll come around, just be patient."

He was right. I couldn't argue with him. I let her be in the kitchen while I stayed in the living room with the others. They started to ask questions about tonight's rendezvous but I ended it as soon it started. I didn't want

Dianna to walk into that kind of discussion, nor did I want her to feel tense again.

Joe put on the Nintendo Wii. He and Richard started to play "*Punch Out*", a boxing game. Helena, Ava and Sebastian were sitting together on the couch discussing redecorating. As for me, I was leaning against the fireplace just taking everything in while I waited for Dianna to come out of the kitchen. I wanted to go in there, but I also believed that it would probably be for the best to let her come to me when she was ready.

I have never seen her act like that, to snap so suddenly. I know that Dianna can yell and be nasty, but never so quick or without good reason.

I guess she got her spark back, I thought to myself.

After about twenty minutes she walked out of the kitchen. The others continued to stay focused on what they were doing at the time. Dianna walked over to me and put her arms around me and apologized for the way she behaved.

"Don't sweat it. It's no big deal," I said and kissed her on top of her head and held her closely.

"So are you feeling better dear? What did you have to eat?" Sebastian asked trying to make Dianna feel as comfortable as possible.

"Froot Loops," she answered. "I'm sorry for how I spoke to all of you. I shouldn't have snapped and been so nasty." Her apology was genuine.

"Nasty?" Joe said humorously. "Darlin, you've been here long enough to know that's how we talk to each other normally. I think you should get meaner, start breaking things, *except for the T.V*, slap around the big guy a little—even slap me." he said as Dianna started to chuckle.

"You should *definitely* give me a beating too. I deserve one," Joe concluded.

I let the "*darlin*" comment slide because it made Dianna laugh.

"How about *I* give you a beating?" I patronized to Joe humorously.

"If you can catch me," he said in his cocky way.

I faked going after him by taking one step forward and backing off. He jumped from the couch and was across the room in seconds.

"That's you're defense? You're going to run away?" I said demeaning and jokingly. "You're such a pussy."

"I may be a pussy and I get a lot of pussy, but I ain't stupid!" Joe answered and laughed. We all had a good laugh at Joe's expense, even Dianna. Joe threw a candle stick at me to start up a living room brawl. Sebastian intervened and caught it, "No! Not today! No more breaking household objects," he said seriously.

"Speaking of breaking things," Dianna infringed. "What happened to the kitchen island?"

Everyone turned to me, smiling wickedly and I answered, "I was a little upset when you were gone and it was the closest thing to me at the time."

She shook her head, "You should stop doing things like that."

I kissed her on the cheek and said, "I really need to get some rest. We all do. We have a busy night ahead of us," I stressed.

Everyone agreed and scattered into our resting chambers.

Neither Dianna or myself took the time to undress as we settled into our bed. I held Dianna and we lay on our sides like a puzzle. I moved my hand from her waist to her neck and lightly moved her hair so I could see the branded letter X that Xavier put there. I touched it and began to rub it as gently and inconspicuously as I could.

"You can't erase it, you just have to wait for it to go away on its own," Dianna snapped without facing me. She got up from the bed and walked over to the black leather recliner and sat down. She began to cry.

I was confused and concerned. I kneeled down in front of her and asked softly,

"What's the matter?" And took hold of her hand.

"All these bruises and marks on my body, they repulse you. I repulse you. You won't even make love to me." "What the hell are you talking about? We were just together an hour ago," I said baffled by her accusations.

"That was different. That wasn't being together because you wanted to, it was because your body forced you to. That was some kind of weird ritual instinct thing that just happened because nature insisted upon it. Now I'm home and laying next to you in bed and all you can do is look at that stupid mark on my neck," she said disturbed and began to cry harder as she continued.

"I'm sorry it's there. I'm sorry that they did this me and that it sickens you. It sickens me too. I feel dirty and ashamed and I don't know what to do to make it go away." She broke down and tears streamed down her face and her body was shaking frantically as she spoke.

I pulled her up from the chair and held her close and tight and kissed her head. She nuzzled her head deep into my chest and tears poured from her eyes drenching my bare chest. As she cried all I could think was how *that mother fucker is going to pay for Dianna's anguish, my grief and torment, upsetting the flow of my household and for putting all our lives at risk*. My rage was indescribable, at a moment when I had to be compassionate, sympathetic and considerate.

"Dianna, I hate that this happened to you. I don't like the marks on your body, but not because I'm repulsed by them. I hate them because of the pain you endured and because I couldn't get there soon enough to take your pain and torment away."

She looked up at me and said, "You once told me, when I wanted a tattoo…that I couldn't get one because you like my body clean and untouched. Now look at me. I'm anything but clean and untouched. I don't even know if they raped me while I was unconscious. So why would you want to touch me?"

She was hysterical and scared and I tried to somehow set her mind at ease,

"They striped you but you weren't raped. I would have smelled the scent immediately."

"Then why won't you touch me? Why did you go to bed dressed? Since when do you do that?"

"I don't want you to rush you into anything. I only want to love and care for you without putting any pressure on you," I answered. She was beginning to compose herself.

"Please don't treat me like a fragile piece of glass. I won't break. I just want things to be normal, as if this never happened. I don't want what they did to me to come between us.….literally," she smiled and so did I.

"So what do you mean by normal? We're anything but normal," I asked.

"Just be yourself. Please," she begged.

I pondered her request, let her go and walked towards the bed. When my head was turned from her I said in my usual condescending and demanding way,

"Get that raggedy ass sweat suit off and get in bed," then I laid down sprawled across the bed, "Does that make you feel better? Are you happy now?" I asked humorously.

Dianna smiled, removed her sweat suit and sat her bare body on top of me. I looked up at her and said, "Females are a strange breed." I pulled her head down to face me and kissed her gently. I caressed her hair, whispered to her that I loved her as I tenderly rubbed her back and kissed her compassionately.

"Stop it!" She yelled.

"What did I do now? I'm just trying to love you," I said firmly, a bit loudly and very baffled.

"Don't *try* to love me, just love me the way you always have," she insisted.

"I'm so confused!" I shouted out loud. "Do you want me to be rough with you? Is that what your asking?"

"I want you to be yourself," she answered sternly.

"I give up. Do with me what you will," I said as I spread my arms out in a crucifix pattern. "You're the boss."

"I'm the boss? Since when?"

"As of right now because I don't know if your going to laugh, yell, cry or hit me. So just this once you can call the shots," I smiled as I answered her.

She smiled seductively as she slapped my face jokingly. Apparently I gave her that idea. She kissed me deeply on my lips nearly choking me with her tongue.

Dianna was very aggressive that day. I wanted to make love to her romantically, lovingly, but she had other ideas for our reunion. She had her way with me and I didn't have any regrets or complaints. I let her be the aggressor, something I wasn't accustomed to. Dianna may be shy outside the bedroom, but when we are alone together, she becomes a sexual demon. We spent an hour of romping, wrestling, headboard banging and screaming with ecstasy as opposed to sighing quietly with romance and passion.

I was able to understand why she felt the way she did. She wanted her life to be like she never left and that her nightmare never happened. She fell asleep curled around my body and she felt safe once again. I rested peacefully with thoughts of revenge and murder, waiting patiently for the sunset. I was going to avenge Dianna's mental and physical suffering and Xavier was doomed to feel my wrath.

21

Blood

I awoke from my well deserved rest. I tried my best to let Dianna sleep, but her senses were acute and she woke up right along with me. We were quiet as we got dressed. She put on her old sweat suit again to spend an evening at home, while I got dressed for battle. I wore nothing out of the ordinary, jeans, T-shirt, steel toe work boots and my lucky ring. I felt her staring at me. She was nervous about me leaving.

"What's wrong?" I asked as I was pulling my shirt over my head.

"Why can't I go with you?"

"Because I said so, let's just leave it at that," I ordered.

It was obvious she didn't like my answer, she put her head down with sadness in her eyes. Shockingly enough, she didn't press the issue. Instead she walked over to me and put her arms around me.

"Please be careful."

"Don't worry about me Dianna, I'll be fine. They can't hurt me," I answered confidently.

"They're very mean and I don't want anything to happen to you," she sobbed.

I gave her a twisted smile at her and laughed impishly at her concern. She was still so naive as to what I am and to what she is as well.

"They're mean?" I ridiculed. "And what would I be considered, a nice guy, the boy next door?"

She didn't seem amused before she rebutted,

"I've seen and lived what they are capable of. I don't want them to hurt you or maybe kill you."

I stared at her intensely. "What do you think I'm capable of?" I asked seriously. I wanted to know if she was aware of what she is in love with.

"I don't know, you won't tell me or show me. So I have no other choice but to be worried."

"Touché," I answered. She looked at me with dread and wanted me to reassure her of my safety.

"Dianna, they can't hurt me, there isn't much of anything that can. I'll be fine and so will everyone else. This has to be done. It's been a long time coming, even before he took you. Trust me."

She hugged me tightly and I held her close for a few moments. When we detached our grasp from one another, I had an idea that could benefit me and make her feel included.

"I need you to do something for me," I asked.

"Anything," she answered quickly.

"When the sun begins to rise at 7:20 A.M., I want you to make it shine brightly, without clouds across the city. Then after about ten or fifteen minutes, fill the skies with clouds, keep the sun hidden so we can get home without feeling weak. Will you do that for me?"

"Of course I will, but why?".

"Good soldiers don't ask questions, they just take orders and do what they are told," I answered firmly.

"I'm not a soldier," she said snobbishly.

"And that's why you can't come with me," I said coldly, as I put on my coat of arms.

She was struck by my answer and for the first time she was speechless.

"So will you do that for me?" I asked again.

"You know I will," she answered with defeat.

We walked out of the bedroom and into the living room. The other's were gathered around, scrutinizing the television.

"What's going on?" I asked whoever was listening.

"We're celebrities!" Joe answered. He was standing in front of the TV, with his arms folded, dressed in his full coat of arms, hair tied back, wearing his Manson T-shirt, jeans and black biker boots. He was ready to go.

Dianna and I joined them and stood behind the couch listening to the news anchor,

"It appears that there has been a brutal massacre among the homeless along one of the derailed tracks at Penn Station..."

We all smiled.

The news anchor continued, "Officials believe that the massacre could have been gang related or perhaps a wild animal attack. Medical examiners found remnants of wild cat DNA, a cheetah..."

We all turned our attention toward Helena, and she smiled proudly.

"Officials are checking into the local zoos for any reports of missing animals to confirm the strands of DNA found on the many victims. However, officials are not discarding the possibility of gang related violence that used machetes as their weapon of choice because there was also bloody shoeprints that seem to run up the tunnel walls and on the ceiling. It's a mystery how they got there..."

We turned to Joe, he held his head high with flare. He seemed thrilled that humans took the time and analyzed his agility. The camera zoomed in on his footprints for the viewers to see.

I didn't want Dianna to see or hear about the slaughter, so I covered her ears with my hands and pulled her face into my chest. She released herself from my grasp and attempted to push me—unsuccessfully, I might add.

"I've been blindfolded long enough. Stop it!" She yelled and stared at me furiously. Her eyes manifested from an innocent tint of gray to a vehement chroma of black. Every breath she let out, caused pictures on the wall to fall and glass to shatter.

"Dianna!" I shouted to break her from her trance. Her eye color toned down and the menial damage she was causing seized. She didn't have any idea what just occurred.

"What the fuck was that all about?" I asked.

She looked around confused and nervous.

"I don't know," she said slightly higher than a whisper.

The room fell silent for a moment. The others looked at her, bemused and stunned. All except Joe.

"Good job, Dianna. I told you breaking things would make you feel better. Now tell me how you did that?" Joe cracked.

Dianna and I just ignored him, we didn't find him funny. We just stayed focused on each others faces. She had a look of fear and concern. I had a look of irritation and apoplexy.

"We need an arsenal," I told the others—without taking my eyes off Dianna. I heard the others footsteps scurry along down the hall. Dianna and I were having a staring contest. I didn't like how her untamed and uncontrollable powers affected her. I wanted her to be more in control of her abilities. This wasn't the night for any kind of distraction. I broke our trance by walking away from her, without saying a word and turning to follow the others.

The others walked down the hall off the kitchen and proceeded to our arsenal closet. A vampires arsenal isn't the same as human weaponry. We had guns—but they are just for fun, complete amusement. Guns don't work on vampires. We can walk through bullets. Our arsenal is very simple. It consisted of wooden stakes, Molotov cocktails, lighter fluid, matches and a machete. The machete was for a vampire who didn't have the guts to behead an enemy with their own hands. Not one of us here ever needed to use the machete, we are all capable and willing to rip heads off with our bare hands. None of the other items can kill a vampire but they all can immobilize or weaken one.

Fire won't kill a vampire because of our rapid healing powers, but it will weaken and bring one to a halt. Our bodies are able to revive even if we are burned or dismembered. Not to say we can grow limbs back, of course we can't, but the socket of where the limb was once located is able to seal itself and heal. All except the head. Once the head is removed, we die—instantly.

Draining an opponent of blood weakens and immobilizes because our blood can't renew and replenish on its own. This is the reason why we have to drink daily. If we don't, we become so weak from the deprivation that we would go mad from the lack of blood in our bodies. Sunlight is the only thing other than beheading that could kill a vampire. The sunlight would disintegrate us completely. It isn't like the movies where we would burst into flames the second the sun hit our bodies. We weaken gradually, ultimately collapsing and lay helplessly in the sun's rays as they drains us and eventually the rays turn us to ash. The sun was a long, lingering and sufferable death for a vampire. However, Xavier's body couldn't handle the sun at all, he is the exception to the rule. He was more like the fictional vampires where he would collapse and just burst into flames the very second the suns rays touched him.

We used lighter fluid and matches to burn our meals, however in times of battle, my clan preferred making Molotov cocktails to burn our enemies. It made more of a statement. A rag dipped in gasoline and then placed in a bottle filled with gasoline as well. Once ignited and tossed onto an enemy, the small explosion of fire would quickly immobilize them-and cause a lot of damage to its surroundings. Xavier's mate, Carla, would be joining me for a cocktail tonight.

We concealed many stakes within our coats and Joe carried the duffle bag that contained the pre-made Molotov cocktails. We all carried lighter fluid and a lighter, just in case we didn't have time to launch a cocktail party.

We finished gathering the supplies that we needed and walked back into the living room. Dianna was sitting on the couch with her head down. Sebastian was sitting with her. She looked distressed. I kneeled in front of her and lifted her chin to raise her head.

"Hey," I said in a calm demeanor and removed my finger from her chin. "Everything will be alright. This will be over soon. I don't want you to worry about me. Just be awake when I get home and don't forget about the sunlight and clouds. I need you to do that."

She nodded with her head down, and said, "Just be careful and I'm sorry for my little outburst."

"We'll talk about that later, now kiss me," I said. She kissed me tenderly on the lips for a few minutes.

The others were getting impatient and Joe interrupted,

"Okay, that's enough kissing, we got to go. I'm thirsty and our favorite restaurant is closed due to low inventory, so where are we dining tonight?"

"Midtown tunnel," Helena said. "Let's go there to feed."

I got up from Dianna's side and turned to Helena, "No, there are too many people and not close enough to where we have to go.".

"What's the big deal? "Helena said. "We have time. It'll take Xavier at least forty minutes to get here from Brooklyn."

Before I could reprimand Helena for her bossy intolerance, Richard decided to take control his woman and intervened,

"Helena, shut up! And do what your told!"

We all looked at him startled. He never spoke to Helena like that before. Helena was taken back by surprise. We stood silently staring and waiting for Helena to explode, but she never did. She did as she was told.

"I didn't think anything could shut her up. Not even me and I'm her creator," Joe said to Richard.

"That would explain why she never shuts up," Richard rolled his eyes. "Your such the role model," Richard said sarcastically and turned away.

"Okay, enough bullshit," I intervened. "We have things to do. Joe don't be *too* cocky to tonight. I need you to focus. I don't know who this other clan is that Xavier runs with or what they're capable of."

Joe nodded in agreement, "I'll be on my best behavior, but we really need to feed right now if we're going to come out victorious." Joe was legitimate for the first time in a long time.

"We'll go under the Brooklyn Bridge. There's a lot of vagrants there. We just need to dispose of the bodies and not leave a mess. It's Adams territory and we're only guests," I said as we left the apartment and onto the streets. I didn't look at Dianna's sad face when I walked out the door.

Since our two clans were joining as one force at this time territory limits were suspended, but we still had to be respectful.

On our way to the Bridge, I stopped at a hardware store. I didn't forget the puny lock that Xavier had on the door of the warehouse and I was still insulted. Yes, I hold grudges too. So I bought another lock to replace it and make a statement. Xavier was wrong to underestimate and challenge my ego. When we reached the Bridge, there was a decent variety of vagrants on the menu and we fed. We were neat and we didn't drink with our mouths full. We disposed of the bodies in the usual, non-conspicuous manner, one news story was enough.

Before we met up with Adam, I went back to the warehouse to put the new puny lock on the fabric warehouse door. We noticed Adam and his clan of six were waiting for us to arrive on the roof of the adjacent warehouse.

We scaled the walls and leaped onto the roof, Adam stood tall.

"We looked inside the warehouse before you got here, your message is loud and clear," he smiled. "It looks like a slaughter house in there."

I could tell by his expression that he didn't expect things to be as brutal as they were. If Adam ever underrated our killing strategies and techniques, he was proven wrong.

I let his comment go unnoticed without explanation or a longwinded story about our previous battle. After all, I never once told him to enter Dianna's prison without us. I didn't have to justify anything about that episode to him. He knew he over stepped his ground when he entered the warehouse and changed the subject.

"So what's the plan of action for tonight?" He asked.

"Once Xavier is inside—we follow in immediately. I want to get him from behind. There isn't a plan. Just go in there—find your opponent and do what you do. The only thing I want to make sure is that Xavier dies by my hands and he and his mate die last," I answered.

"How many does he have?" Adam asked with concern. He wanted to know what we were up against.

"Eleven or twelve," I answered. "Do you know anything about the other clan he's running with?" I asked sternly.

Adam shrugged his shoulders, "I only know that they have a fearless reputation in Brooklyn. They don't follow by any rules and feed on violence and murder more than they feed on blood."

"So they're bullies? Stupid mother fuckers who are feared more by their reputation than their actions. That's good," I wisecracked.

"Won't Xavier sense that Dianna isn't there?"

"Of course he will. He'll be expecting us to be waiting inside, which is why I want to ambush him from behind. He'll enter with a dramatic presence among his followers. So once they are all inside—we go in."

Adam nodded with certainty.

The sky was considerably darker than any other night. The moon was no where in sight and the sounds of the city echoed through our ears as we waited patiently on the ledge of the roof, perched, our fangs sharpened and already dripping with thirst. Everyone was eager to get the show on the road. The night crept slowly as I could smell Xavier getting closer. We all narrowed our eyes and were able to see the clans running toward the building. The vengeance that consumed my blood began to boil. I could already taste Xavier's blood.

Xavier was leading the pack and they abruptly stopped at the front door. He picked up the unfamiliar lock, and anger piqued on his face as he looked around to find us. He knew we were there. He pulled it off furiously, threw it on the ground, and began to scream dramatically and violently. He stumbled trying to open the door and entered inside frantically and his minions followed.

Once they were encaged inside the building, we leaped from the rooftop ledge down to the ground, like a falling curtain. Our coats flowing against gravity in slow motion as we coordinated perfectly mounting on our feet.

We entered the bloody warehouse just seconds after Xavier's first scream of torment. Adam and his crew barreled inside first, tossing a Molotov cocktail in before them. The warehouse instantly began to reek of smoke and we heard a loud explosion coming from within.

My clan and I marched in after, faster than any ordinary eyes could see. I immediately noticed two frantic unknown vampires snuffing out the fire.

I turned my head and I made eye contact with Xavier.

Xavier stood frozen.

I barreled through his many protectors, throwing them aside like dice. I didn't even flinch. I watched him cower into a corner as I approached him like the monster I am. I wasn't paying any mind to the my many comrades that were engaged in battle behind me. I clutched him by the throat and slammed him to the hard cement floor, I loomed over him like a victorious Spartan, pressing my foot down on his chest to keep him pinned.

"Dan," he begged, quivering with fear. "I'll stay out of your city. It doesn't need to come to this. I'll do whatever you want. My whole clan will be indebted to you forever."

"Who's groveling at whose feet now, motherfucker? You feeble excuse for a vampire. I can't believe we're even of the same species," I scowled as I pulled a stake from my coat and plunged it into his heart, and made sure I tucked it in deeply with my foot—so no one could pull it out. "You get to watch everyone die before I kill you," I said in a colossal tone as I kicked him in his melodramatic face.

I heard his mate Carla come running towards me screaming ferociously. Before I turned to stop her, Ava was already hidden within Carla's running shadow and grabbed her from behind without ever being noticed. She gauged deep into her neck with her fairly new fangs and drained her till she fell to the ground from weakness. She then staked her next to Xavier,

"You get to watch too, bitch," she said callously as she disappeared into the chaos within the large room.

I was really impressed by Ava's gift, aggressiveness, choice of technique and her fast thinking. She redeemed herself into my good graces. I smiled sinfully at Carla as I poured lighter fluid over her body.

"I'd imagine fire is a fate worse than death for someone who fears it so much," I said, completely omnipotent as I kicked her in the face and broke her jaw. I watched her tremble with fear. She felt the pain of my kick and lingered in it because of her neutralized condition.

I turned away from Xavier and Carla to see what was happening behind me. Everyone, on both sides were engaged in warfare. I scoped out Joe instantly. I sensed he was in trouble. Two of Xavier's unknown clansmen had him pinned against the wall as they were draining him from both sides of his neck. He was beginning to slide down the wall from his loss of blood. I ran to Joe and his assailants. I grabbed the male that was drinking from his right side and ripped his head off with one pull and tossed him aside. When both my hands were free, I grabbed the other one, a female, and bit down forcibly into her neck. Joe was on the floor—drained and feeble. I helped him up to drink from her.

"I know you'll only drink from women," I said considerately as I watched him lunge into her open wound and drink vigorously until she was completely drained and rejuvenating with every swallow he took. It was obvious he had full strength again when he extracted her head from her body with just one thrust with his hands—but not before he called her a *cunt*.

His adrenaline was running rampant as he swung back into action to join the fighting. He was using his lightning speed to toy with our enemies and show off his skills and speedy recovery. He was getting cocky again, and aggravating me.

"Giuseppe! Ti ho già salvato una volta stanotte, smettila di giocare! Voglio che spogli Carla e sazi la tua fame con il suo corpo, e rimani là. Fallo ORA!" I reprimanded.

(Joseph! I saved you once tonight, stop playing games. I want you to strip Carla down. Appease your hunger by eating from her body, and stay there. Do it now!")

When he heard me yell at him in our native tongue, he stopped instantly and did as he was told. I didn't speak the language of my land often but when I did, Joe knew I was serious and wouldn't dare to hesitate to take his orders.

I sensed Helena was in trouble, while the others were standing their ground. She was laying in a corner, paralyzed. Lidia, Adam's mate, was at Helena's side along with Ava. Apparently, Helena has been staked. Richard took notice and raced to her side pulling out the embedded stake from her chest cautiously. Richards eyes filled with rage as he asked Helena, "Which one did this to you?"

She pointed to her assailant timidly. She was weak. It was a soldier of Xavier's clan. Richard pursued the guilty party in a rage that was much like my own. I have never seen him like that before. I followed behind in case he should need assistance.

"Let her feed," I ordered to Ava and pointed to Carla as I walked behind Richard. Lidia and Ava carried Helena's frail body over to Carla and left her with Joe to feed upon Carla.

"Ava," I shouted again. "Make sure Xavier watches. Turn his head so he could see," Ava willingly did what she was told. Adam and Lidia stood in front of Joe and Helena to guard them against any retaliation.

Richard came face to face with Helena's attacker and pushed him with such force and sent him clear across the room. Richard gazed into the eyes of Helena's enemy. A beam of mesmerizing green light flashed from his eyes soaring through the eyes of his adversary, hypnotizing him instantly. Richard didn't need my help, he had this well under control. He decapitated his rival with brutality, slow and suffering, not in his usual classy, aloof manner.

"Go to Helena," I said sternly and he rushed to her side.

The numbers were now even between each of us. I've wasted enough time looking after everyone else. My pawns were where I wanted them to be. The chess board had been set exactly as I wanted it. It was time for me to take all Xavier's pieces before calling—*check mate.*

Xavier began to shout out orders hysterically to his remaining soldiers. "Kill them all! Do it now!"

Carla laid completely drained, defenseless and her body was exposed, "Help me, X…" She whispered faintly to Xavier.

Xavier gazed at her and became frantic trying to release himself from the ties that bounded him.

"Free me!" He hissed.

I smiled maliciously at his cries of hopelessness. It humored me to see him helpless to save the one he loved.

I called to Ava, "He's talking too much, drain him…but not too much, keep him alert." Ava did as directed with gratification.

The battlefield was now six against six. The others were either wounded, dead or standing guard. It was time to end this.

"Enough street fighting," I said as I walked into the line of fire.

I swiftly picked up two unknown clans man and snapped their heads off their necks with a pivot and a push simultaneously with each hand.

Adam's two crew members who were fighting against them looked at me oddly, unable to believe that I was capable of beheading two vampires at once.

I called to Joe, "Let's finish this!"

He jumped up abruptly to join the rumble. He raced at his top speed and reached for the first opponent that he saw. He wasn't toying with them anymore and he took care of business. He pinned down his foe, staked him and ripped the head from his neck with both hands and carried it over to Xavier.

"I believe this belongs to you," he said to Xavier and placed the head on Xavier's chest. He couldn't be totally serious, but that was Joe. "I didn't have time to get it gift wrapped," he added and spit in his face.

Adam's boys had the urge to show off. They didn't want to look useless in front of me or my clan. They both ran into two of the three remaining challengers at the same time and finally did some damage. They staked them in the heart while plunging into them. They dismembered their arms before decapitating them. Then just for a sense of victory they kicked their challengers heads clear across the room and landing at Xavier's feet.

"Looks like you got company," Joe yelled to Xavier.

I looked at him and just shook my head.

One enemy combatant was left he was in the center of a circle made up of me, Joe and Adams two warriors. We stayed still and watched him try to use his speed to escape our trap.

"Finish him," I demanded and left the circle.

Joe and our two allies attacked viciously, tossing him around like a game of catch. They would drink from him one by one, slowly and torturing until he was completely drained. When his blood was gone they dismembered him and burned him before taking his head.

I walked to Xavier and pulled him up and showed him the devastation,

"Look at this…" I said and pointed to all the corpses that reeked of death and murder. "This is all *your* doing."

He looked around the best that he could considering his frail state. I turned his head aggressively toward his mate,

"Look at Carla, you did this to her. Do you feel her drifting away from you?" I asked. Xavier gazed at her with sorrow in his eyes.

"Answer me!" I growled. "Do you feel her drifting from your essence? Do you feel empty?"

"Y…Y…Yes…" He whispered mournfully.

"What would you do to keep her alive? Would you grovel at my feet? Would you give me your territory and be indebted to me for eternity?"

"Yes…" He answered again, whimpering.

"Wrong answer. You're so inept. A coward right to the end," I said in disgust, I took a hold of his neck and threw him against the wall.

"Prop him up. I don't want him to miss a thing!" I ordered to Joe and Richard.

"This is the best part of the show, considering how dramatic you are, you should like this. It's the climax."

I told Adam and Lidia to drag Carla's limp body across the floor and place her in front of Xavier.

"Do you want the honors?" I asked Adam.

He smiled devilishly and took out a book of matches out of his pocket.

"You should douse her in lighter fluid again baby, just in case," Lidia said to Adam.

She handed him the can of fluid and Adam drenched her in lighter fluid from her feet to her knees.

Just before Adam lit the match, I stopped him and said, "Do you have anything to say X before we do this? I may be humbled if you humiliate yourself enough."

"I know you're going to kill me anyway. Just let her live. She didn't cause this, I did," he struggled and sobbed.

"What did Dianna do to deserve your torture? Are you saying that this wretched piece of rat food is more worthy to live more than Dianna?" I screamed as I kicked Carla once again.

"I never would have killed Dianna. I wouldn't have tested you any further than I did. I came here tonight to untie her and just walk away without looking back, and go into exile."

"So you would have left Dianna here naked and unable to fend for herself, weak and helpless? So her blood wouldn't be on your hands.

You're a worthless excuse for any species—much less a vampire," I paused and turned to Adam, "Do it."

Adam tossed the match and half of Carla's body imminently went up in flames. She was screaming frantically, crying for help.

"Ava, you're the one who rendered Carla powerless, you take her head," I ordered.

Ava was jubilant that I trusted her with that responsibility. She had a little trouble prying off her head but managed to succeed after many tugs.

"Adam, if you and everyone else wants to leave, you can. I'll be here until sunrise. That's how he's going to die, but if you want to stay and watch that's alright with me too," I said as I sat on the floor directly across from Xavier.

"I wouldn't miss it," Adam answered and he and Lidia sat next to me as we waited for the sun to rise.

We had quite a few hours before sunrise. So everyone tried to make due and amuse themselves for the long wait. Richard and Helena were curled up in a corner resting on each other's shoulders. Lidia and Adam were conversing to one another but keeping a sharp watch on Xavier. Joe, Ava and Adam's four henchmen were playing dice, Joe always had a pair of dice with him.

I got up and walked to the other side of the warehouse. I took out my cell phone from my pocket and called home. Sebastian answered the phone and that was what I was hoping for. I told him to meet us at sunrise to drive us home. He asked how things went and I told him that things went better than expected.

"Do you want to talk to Dianna?" He asked.

"Is she awake? Don't wake her if she's sleeping," I said.

"She's awake in the living room, pacing frantically. I'm sure she'll be thrilled to hear your voice," he said happily.

"Okay, put her on," I said and waited as Dianna came to the phone.

"Are you alright?" Dianna asked nervously.

"Yeah, everyone is fine, just like I told you. Why aren't you sleeping?"

"I'm not tired. So are you coming home soon?"

"I'll be a little longer. I wanted to remind you to do that thing with the sun."

"I didn't forget. It'll be done."

"I want you to go to sleep, so you're awake when I get home at sunrise. I miss you and I want to see you when I walk in, okay?" I asked humbly.

"Okay," she answered and we both hung up the phone.

Adam also called Crissy on his cell phone. He told her to pick him and his clan up at sunrise also. Everyone was wired and bloody and none of us wanted to walk or run home even though it would be faster.

We waited long and silently for the sunrise. Xavier was getting frustrated by his condition and just wanted to die. He actually seemed annoyed at us for keeping him alive. I looked at him with disgust and asked him,

"Did you really think I was going to make this quick and easy, you stupid fuck?"

"No, but I didn't think you would let the sun do your dirty work. I thought you would take enormous pleasure in killing me yourself," he said with a nasty disposition.

"I'll take great pleasure in watching you die slowly by what you fear the most. Now shut the fuck up, you peasant!" I yelled.

"And if I don't shut up, what are you going to do...kill me? You already took everything else," he said uncaringly.

"No, I'll let you live in that state for eternity, alone and scared. You decide," I retorted.

He didn't stop speaking but his sarcasm disappeared. He was more controlled about his choice of words.

"You know this isn't over whether I live or die. You and Adam will both have to face our allies for killing our kind, some without reason, but if you let me live, I can fix things."

"You never stop thinking about yourself do you?" I asked, "Your allies don't scare me. I'll always be fighting and killing—**it's what I do**," I said sharply.

"Even the mighty fall, Dan," Xavier said.

"Tonight wasn't that night," I answered vehemently. "What do you know about being mighty?"

"Nothing," he admitted.

"I'm curious about something X, did you really think that I wouldn't find her? And did you really think that tiny little lock could keep me out? That lock really hurt my feelings. I thought you knew me better than that," I said pestering.

"I gave it my best shot. I thought for sure you'd crumble to a certain degree and I'd at least get Midtown. I made mistakes."

"Your first mistake was taking what belongs to me."

"And my next mistake?..."

"Thinking that I'd give into your unreasonable demands, and the well being of my clan for the sake of a woman." I said truthfully.

"I thought your love for Dianna was stronger than that. I was obviously wrong. I wonder if she knows how you *gambled* with her life..."

I stared at him angrily and was fed up with his psycho analysis.

"Adam," I yelled. "Shut him up! Gag him with something and then drain his sorry ass." I insisted.

As Adam walked towards Xavier he made one last comment,

"Looks like I hit a nerve."

Xavier did hit a nerve. He may not be the strongest of vampires, however, his choice of words can pierce through someone like knives. I didn't want to hear his voice any more. Adam put on his brass knuckles, punched him in the face two or three times before he clutched his neck with his drooling fangs and drained him viciously.

After a few long and grueling hours, I looked outside to see that the sun was beginning to rise. I never thought I'd be happy to see that. Just as Dianna promised, the sun was shining brilliantly and there wasn't a cloud in the sky. Adam and I dragged Xavier by the feet and put him outside directly in front of the door with his head facing inward.

As the sun was rising, Xavier's skin was beginning to burn and he was screaming ear piercing screams in pain. It was slower than I thought and I had the pleasure of watching him linger in agony. Once the sun had fully risen, it still didn't totally do him in. It just tormented him, scorching and stinging every part of his body. I watched him blister and burn and it was better than sex. I didn't want to take any chances of him surviving so before he turned to ash, I took his head and watched all of him disintegrate in the suns rays. Then the sun turned to clouds, my wrath had ended and Dianna had done her part.

I turned my head to see Sebastian and Crissy waiting along the street to escort us home. We walked out the door calmly and slowly. I held out a Molotov cocktail for Adam to light and one for myself. We simultaneously threw them into the warehouse. There was a small explosion and the flames were erupting fiercely behind us. We walked to our means transportation for our journey home. All evidence of a vampire war turned to ash as did the building and Dianna's nightmare had come to an end.

22

Unleashed

When I arrived home, Dianna was sitting on the couch waiting for me. I opened the door and she came rushing towards me to greet me. She put her arms around me excitedly and then she backed away. She became a little fidgety.

"What's the matter?" I asked.

"All the blood on your clothes," she said nervously. "Are you hurt?"

I had forgotten about the condition of my wardrobe.

"It's not my blood," I stated.

"There's so much," she said and then scanned everyone else as they were walking to their resting chambers. "There's so much on all of you. What happened?"

That was Dianna's first glimpse of our blood thirsty identity and she seemed to be afraid.

I didn't get into the gory details with her, I wouldn't do that to her. However, I was condescending when I implied an answer to her question.

"Well, let's see, we met up with Xavier, had a couple of cocktails and we all had a great time. It was a surprise party for him and he was just thrilled that we were able to attend." I paused, then I said mockingly, "What do you think happened?"

She looked at me angrily, but honestly, I wasn't in the mood for ignorance.

"You're such an asshole!" She scorned and turned her body away from me and went to sit back on the couch and folded her arms like a spoiled child. I walked behind her and kissed her on top of her head,

"I love you too babe," I said as I started to walk down the hallway to our room and she didn't follow me as she usually does. I was immune to her childish and stubborn mind games and I wasn't going to fall for it, not today.

"Dianna!" I said loudly, as I entered our room. "Get in here, let's go."

I walked straight into my private bathroom and took a long hot shower.

After twenty minutes of relaxation, I dried myself off, wrapped the towel around my waist and exited the bathroom and stepped into the bedroom. Dianna was still being obstinate and remained in the other room instead of with me—where she belongs.

I walked my towel covered body into the living room to find her still in the same spot that I left her. I stepped in front of her without saying a word. I bent down and lifted her up and flung her tiny body over my shoulder. I didn't want to talk, argue or discuss anything trivial and things not worth mentioning. I was also cutting corners. It was inevitable that we would make up anyway, so I just moved it along without the drama.

"Put me down!"

"Shut up," I said good-humouredly and smacked her tight ass lightly with my free hand.

I closed the bedroom door behind me when I entered the room. I removed her from my shoulder and threw her on the bed casually. Before she could say a word, I placed myself on top of her and kissed her. Dianna wanted everything to be *normal* between, and for us, this was *normal*.

She turned her head and started to speak.

"I'm mad at you right now, I don't want to kiss you."

"That's okay, I don't mind," I said tuning out her words and kissed her again.

She kissed me once and turned her face again and raised her eyes not to look at me.

"I'm serious," she said trying to force herself to stand her ground.

"Uh-huh, me too. Now shut up and kiss me." I said and continued to kiss her mouth, if for no other reason than to shut her up. She kissed me a little longer this time, but Dianna was a glutton for the last word.

"You really hurt my feelings and embarrassed me," she said cutely.

I put my face down in her pillow in annoyance. I then picked up my head calmly and asked her,

"Do you want to fight or make up? Which one is it?" I said with displeasure.

She smiled at me delectably yet shyly and put her arms around me, she was willful. She wouldn't actually come out and say that this was all a plot for my attention. She wanted me as much as I wanted her. However, when she held me in her arms it was obvious that she didn't want to argue, and conceded to my desires and hers as well.

"I knew you'd see it my way," I whispered with a seductive smile and kissed her forcefully and avidly, Dianna responded with great passion and of course one thing led to another.

Dianna awoke before I did. As I was resting, I felt her poking my cheek repetitively with her finger as she was asking me over and over, *"Are you up yet? Are you up yet?"* This was just to annoy me, but in a innocent and teasing way. I opened my eyes and laughed at her attempt to look guiltless.

"Why are you so cheerful?" I asked.

"You're home and not hurt," she answered.

"I told you that you don't have to worry about me."

"If I don't worry about, who will?"

"Sebastian." I said with a laugh.

I pulled her close to me and hugged her tightly.

"Do you have any idea how much you mean to me?" I asked seriously.

"Hopefully as much as you mean to me," she responded.

We gazed at each other and I outlined her lips gently with my finger before I kissed her momentarily. When our lips parted she got off the subject and asked,

"So tell me what happened last night? What did you do?"

"Let's just say…they won't hurt you ever again and leave it at that," I said sternly and got out of bed to get dressed. I didn't want to have this conversation. I was standing with my back turned to her directly in front of the bed.

"I want to know everything. Why won't you tell me?" She begged.

I turned to face her, I was fully dressed and said, "It's over now and my methods don't concern you. Now enough questions." I was getting more and more irritated by her persistence.

"How can you say it doesn't concern me? I think I have the right to know, after all I was part of the reason why you killed them," she said timidly.

"So if you figured out that they were killed, why do you need to know all the gory details?" I shouted.

"I just do," she stated.

"Not a good enough reason," I ordered as I walked to the door and punched a hole in it. "Now can you please stop testing my patience?"

"Why did you do that?"

"Because I hate this conversation."

"I won't persist any more if that's what you think is best," she said coldly and I wasn't really convinced that she meant it.

"It *is* for the best," I said calmly.

"Okay then. I'm going to take a shower. Are we doing anything tonight?"

"Yeah. We're all going down to the club. When vampires come out of battle victoriously, it's a cause for celebration. Especially when there aren't any casualties."

"Whatever. I'll be ready in a bit," she said in a huff and walked into the bathroom and turned the water on.

I waited for her in the living room hoping she wasn't going to be in spoiled brat mood tonight. This wasn't the night for her childish behavior. The others were almost ready to leave and waiting on me and Dianna so we could leave as a clan.

When vampires go into battle among our own kind, it is customary to celebrate the victory. However, this wasn't a typical battle. As I said, there weren't any casualties from my clan or Adam's. This was an achievement within our circle, and we stood out among the rest as being the first clans ever to walk away with all our soldiers. There hasn't ever been such a conquest in our history. When something as rare as that happens it goes beyond a celebration. It's like becoming immortal among the immortal. We now held a page or two in the books of time. We would always be remembered and glorified. Adam and I now have become feared and respected among our own kind. That was an amazing feat considering all vampires are fearless. Both our clans now have risen above the rest. Although in time, it would be inevitable that we would be challenged by other clans to strip us of our title and reputation. As for now, we only wanted to fester in the glory, feed our egos and flaunt our pride and loyalty for a respectable amount of time. This wasn't going to be an all night affair. It was basically to make an appearance and socialize. It would be considered tacky to be in this powerful position just to boast about our victory and wallow in our glory for an over extended amount of time.

Helena was getting antsy waiting on Dianna, I could sense her frustration through her body language. I must confess that I also was getting agitated, because she was taking her time to be spiteful. She wasn't going to be in a spoiled brat mood, she was going to be in a *bitch* mood instead. I kept my cool. I wasn't going to let her get to me. She came out of the bedroom dressed and ready. She looked gorgeous. For me it was worth the wait, all except her hair. She had it tied back in a long braid. She knew I liked her long silken hair to just hang down. She wore a black lace and silk dress that was held together by many ties along the back. It lifted her bosom to give the illusion that she actually had a voluptuous chest. That could definitely be the reason why it took her longer than usual to get dressed. Her ensemble was true to her identity. She looked like a vampire and a witch and it worked for her.

"Finally!" Helena said annoyed.

Dianna shot her a wicked stare and narrowed her eyes at Helena.

"Why are you looking at me like that? We always have to wait on you and it's getting old," Helena sneered.

Dianna rolled her eyes, snubbed her and turned her face.

I gave her the leather coat that I bought for her during Christmas to wear.

"I'm not wearing this," Dianna said with firm conviction.

"Oh, here we go, now we'll have to wait, so the two of you can fight over a god damn coat." Helena intruded, "Just wear the damn coat, Dianna!"

"You wear it!" Dianna shouted back.

I was just about to scream at Helena for talking to Dianna that way and for putting her nose where it doesn't belong. However, Richard beat me to the punch.

"Helena!" Richard yelled. "Sit down! Shut up! And stay out of it and wait."

Richard has been becoming very aggressive with Helena lately and it suited him. His sudden controlling nature seemed to work and Helena did as she was told.

I handed her the coat to put on.

"Really, it's much too big. I'll trip if you make me wear that thing," she said and it seemed to be truthful.

"Ughhhh!" Joe shouted, "Wear the coat—don't wear the coat. Who cares? Just leave the girl alone. This is all bullshit and not a big deal. Let's just go already."

Joe was right. That was an accomplishment in itself. We took Joe's advice and left. The tension was thicker than the bible and everyone was generally quiet as we left.

As we walked I asked Dianna, "What's with the braid?" I said it low so only she could hear me.

"Fine!" She said faintly above a whisper angrily and pulled out the rubber band and let her hair down.

"I didn't say to take it out. I just wanted to know why you tied it back." I said calmly.

"Because I wanted to, but I wouldn't want to upset you, so now it's down." she said being the bitch that she was determined to be.

Still, I kept my cool. She's been through a lot and we would be around a lot of our kind and I didn't want to create havoc. I could only hope that she would compose herself among strangers.

There wasn't a need to stop to feed because on a night like this, there would be live human hostages drugged and ready for us to feed. It was like an offering from other clans to keep the peace.

When we arrived, the music was blasting, the place was packed, and all eyes were upon us if only for a few seconds. Adam was already there and approached me.

"There's plenty to drink in the back," he said and pointed to the private room that was off limits to patrons.

I led the way as we walked through the crowd holding Dianna's hand. She obliged and kept on a fake smile for appearances.

"Where are we going?" She whispered.

"To feed," I answered.

"Here?"

"You'll see," I said and opened the door to the private room. Once everyone was inside I closed the door behind them. There was quite a large variety on the menu. Men and women. Tall, fat, skinny, gorgeous and ugly. Ready to become food for the undead.

"Dig in!" I said sadistically. Everyone rushed to their victim like rats to cheese and feasted as did I. All except Dianna. As I was drinking from a not so attractive woman, I noticed Dianna's horrified face. She glanced up at me with disgust and said, "This is sick!" and stormed out.

To my kind this was a blessing. We didn't have to hunt or prey. Blood was there for taking and we wanted it all. It slipped my mind that Dianna was just recently drugged and fed upon as well. *Okay, I feel like a complete idiot now.*

I did go after her but not until I finished feeding. I was already going to have to make up for my inconsideration, *so why waste perfectly good food?*

After about five or ten minutes, I left the room and scoped her out. She was actually behaving, I was shocked. She was mingling with allies while shooting pool and drinking a beer. I walked up behind her and put my arms around her waist while she was waiting for her turn to shoot.

"I'm sorry," I whispered into her ear. "I wasn't thinking."

"That's a first," she said cynically but kept a fake smile on for appearances. She left my grasp and took her shot and sunk four in a row.

I had that coming so I just laughed it off and watched her run the pool table, collect her winnings all without cheating. When she was finished with her opponent I asked her,

"Do you think you could beat me without cheating?"

"Probably not," she answered meanly and threw the pool stick on the table and walked away with her fake smile and socialized. *Okay, here it is, the bitch that I was waiting for.* I had to make things right before we went home. I didn't want to argue with her, especially since I would be the one who would come out looking bad, and I'd never live it down.

She was a few feet away from me talking with three females, one of them was human, the two others were barmaids. All of them asking her questions about me and giggling. Such as: How did you get Dan to mate with you? Is he good in bed? Is his "ya know" as big as I think it is?" She just looked at them like they were completely out of their minds and scanned the room for me before she answered them.

It was definitely time for me to intervene. I walked fast and slipped my arms around her waist.

"What's goin' on here?" I asked Dianna and the three females.

"Nothing," one of them answered. "We're just getting to know Dianna."

"Yeah," Dianna continued arrogantly and straight faced. "They want to learn so much about me that they only thing they are interested is how big your dick is." I smiled crookedly and laughed silently and put my head down into her shoulder. Part of me was modestly flattered and she sensed it.

"Why don't you show them?" She instigated and stood firm with her arms folded in my grasp and stared at the three females intensely. I was surprised to see how intimidating she was and the three girls backed down and walked away embarrassed but peeved. Evidently, I wasn't supposed to know the things they asked her.

"Come with me," I said to her, but she waited for the three women to be out of sight before she left her ground. We walked over to the pool table and I sat her down on top of it. I kissed her long and forcefully, her jealous and threatening nature turned me on. She attempted to fight me off but she fell under my spell. There was a little irony in that.

"Are you alright?" I asked.

"I am now," she said and kissed me again and smiled.

The three girls who aggravated her walked by us, so Dianna had to lay it on thick. Once they were in our sights she began to fiercely make-out with me and cupped her hand onto my crotch. She wanted to make them jealous and wanting. She kept her eyes on them as they stared at us through out her territorial escapade. This was her way of letting them know that *I belonged to her* and it would be in their best interest to stay away and keep their hands off. *I fuckin' loved it.*

Joe walked by with Crissy hung over him like a drape.

"What's with you two and pool tables?" He asked.

Dianna and I both laughed. I apologized for my ignorance and she apologized for freaking out earlier. We played a few games of pool. She won two games I won three, and she didn't cheat. The night turned out better than anticipated.

We stayed longer than expected and it was time to go. Everyone was in good spirits on the leisurely walk home, even Helena, who was drunk with affection to Richard more than ever before. He was gloating at her attentiveness. Joe decided to bring Crissy home with him and she walked proudly at his side, while he held her with his arm around her neck. She should be honored to have a vampire of Joe's status to even acknowledge her, much less anything else. Ava even met someone. She didn't take him home and he wasn't human. So I didn't have to worry about her turning him and creating another fiasco. He was a loner vampire from Midtown and seemed quite smitten with her. I carried Dianna home on my shoulders because she is so small that she struggles to keep up with everyone's long strides when we walk at a human pace.

When we got home, we were surprised and stunned to see Sebastian entertaining a few friends in the living room. Three men and two women to be exact. *Who knew he had friends?*

"A party? Why weren't we invited?" Joe asked comically.

"Why are you home so early?" Sebastian asked with annoyance in his tone. "Just go in the game room," he huffed as he waved us off into the direction of the game room.

We walked pass Sebastian and his entourage smiling and snickering, and went into the game room.

This room had everything you needed to amuse yourself. Video machines, pool table, air hockey, foosball table, a stereo, two forty-two inch plasma televisions. One for playing games and the other for movies. We have DVD and blue ray machines. X-Box 360, Nintendo Wii, PS3. A few computers, card tables, craps table and three slot machines and a piano. There was a suede couch and three recliners for conversation.

Joe and Crissy took over the Nintendo Wii. Ava turned on the stereo and blasted the new Eminem C.D. before she joined Joe and Crissy. Helena and Richard were cozy on a recliner, Dianna and I were on the couch talking. She was sitting and I was laying down with my head on her lap playing with a portable play station and she was playing with my hair.

"Tomorrow can we go to my bookshop so I can see how Thomas is?" She asked sweetly.

"Who's Thomas?" I asked, not paying too much attention to what she was saying. I was engaged with the video game.

"He was there the day I was taken away. I want to know how he is. I also want to know if it's been opened since then. So can we go?"

"Thomas is fine," I said still pressing buttons on the portable game controller

"How do you know?" She asked.

I put the controller down and looked up at her,

"When I went there to look for you he was there, locked in the stock room. We let him out. He wasn't hurt," I answered.

"I still want to go. It's the right thing to do," she insisted.

"We can't go Dianna," I said solemnly. "It's not there."

"What do you mean it's not there? Where did it go?" I got up from her lap and stood up in front of her. This was going to be—round two—the moment I told her what I did. So I put the boxing gloves on and got prepared. I didn't know how to tell her tactfully, so I just blurted it out.

"I burnt it down, I got rid of it. There isn't any need for that place. After what happened I decided that I didn't want you there anymore."

"You burnt it down?" She asked shocked and appalled. "Is there anything else that you did that I should know about?" She ordered as she stood up and faced me.

"Yeah, one more thing. Your apartment building, I burnt that down too," I said honestly and uncaring.

"Why? What possible reason could you have?"

"I didn't like the memories there. You never go there anyway. It's not a big deal," I said coldly.

"I had things there for safe keeping. I had books that are centuries old that have been passed down in my family for generations. Then you come along, strike a match and everything is gone!" I attempted to hold her but she pushed me away. Everyone stopped what they were doing and turned to watch the main event, *me and Dianna*.

"Your things in that place have been there for months and now all of sudden these things are so precious to you?" I answered a bit loudly too.

"It's the fucking point!" She shouted. "You just don't stop. You just keep taking and taking. All you ever do is take things from me, even my identity. I don't even know what I am much less—who I am because of you. You shut me out of everything and keep me secluded. You don't even allow me to have an opinion or make a decision. The only time I'm of any use to you is when I'm *fucking* you. If you had your way, I'd be in bed all day with my legs spread just waiting for **you to decide** if you want to get laid or not."

"Dianna, come on, I don't want to do this," I said rationally and made another effort to hold her again.

"Get off of me!" She screamed and pushed me away using her magic. She wasn't able to move me, but there was a force field around her so I couldn't touch her.

"I want it back. I want everything you took from me back!" As she was screaming at me, the art work was plummeting to the floor. The television screen shattered and the card tables were being tossed and smashed against the wall causing them to break apart. Joe and Richard were witnessing her untamed rampage and immediately got up to circle her. This is an instinct among clan brothers. They were there to be by my side and stop her if necessary.

She looked around and saw Richard and Joe on either side of her. She glared and smiled at them diabolically, "What the fuck are you two going to do?" She mocked, egotistically and laughed wickedly. She pulled the wind from the air with her hands and tossed it their way, causing them to bang against the wall.

"Dianna!" I screamed hoping to release her from her state as I did earlier. Her eyes were blacker than a starless night and her powers were surfacing out of control. The wind was around her, protecting her. It was like a raging tornado that suddenly entered the room. She glared at the piano bench and with a wave of her hand, she slid it across the room to face me and then she pushed with her hand for it to come towards me. The piano bench hurled against my knees, but not before I kicked it out of the way causing it to break.

Sebastian and his company came running in to see what was going on. She stared at the door and slammed it shut right in their faces. That didn't keep them out. Sebastian stepped inside and looked at me with eyes full of sorrow. She kept Richard and Joe encaged in her power with control of the wind. She stared at me with pure hatred, a look I have never seen before. She lifted her arms and pulled them back quickly. Then with all her might and concentration, she threw her arms towards me triggering every nick knack in that room to lunge at me at a forceful speed.

"You go out and say your fighting for me and won't even give me the benefit of knowing what you did. I'm just supposed to take your word for it. How can I take your word for anything when you only tell me the things that you want me to hear? According to you, I'm just too stupid and childish to understand. I don't know anything about you. Everything is a secret. Who the fuck are you anyway?" She scowled and threw a video game controller at me. I caught it with one hand and broke it with one squeeze.

"Who the fuck do you think your screaming at? Do you think that you and your magic can stand a chance against me? Stop your bullshit and grow the fuck up!" I screamed and pounded my chest with one hand.

Then with her hands she magically busted the door off the hinges and stormed out of the room.

I somehow managed to let her say all that she wanted without punching her in the face, but I was burning inside and I felt my rage building up. Sebastian told me to calm down, the look on my face must have explained everything I was feeling. I thought about his advice for about two seconds.

"No, not this time. I'm over this shit. This bullshit ends now. I have had it with her and her tantrums. I've restrained myself far too long," I said and stormed out the door after her.

I ran at top vampire speed to the locked door of our bedroom. I kicked it open, causing the door to break into pieces on impact. I must have startled her because she leaped from the floor to the top of the book case and perched, just like she did the day we had our training session.

"Get down! I'm not playing this time!" I screamed as I kicked the bookcase causing it to crumble so she would fall to her feet.

I picked her up by the neck and pinned her against the wall. My eyes were filled with ire and animosity.

"Do you honestly think you can over power me?" I shouted and pushed her back against the wall.

"You inconsiderate little bitch! What the fuck do you do for me besides give me grief?"

I loosened up on her neck, but not enough for her to escape my clutches. She was going to listen to what I had to say, and she was going to find out *who I am.*

"You're going to scream and destroy everything in sight because I took things from you? Do you have any idea of the lengths that I have gone to, that we all have gone to for your sorry ass?"

"You're choking me," she said timidly.

"Good, then maybe you'll listen for once."

"You're being a *cunt,* all because I want to spare you the gory details. I'll give them to you now. Only…I'll start from the beginning."

"You're scaring me," she said with a few tears in her eyes.

"You should of thought of that before you gambled with my patience, I have told you countless times not to test me, but you never stop! Now shut the fuck up and listen, I'm going to give you what you want, the morbid details of my life ever since I met you."

"I don't wanna know," she cried.

"Too fucking bad. Maybe you need to know what has been done for you! Let me start from the beginning, remember the time you went out with your friend and met a lonely vampire who wanted to feast on you? When you were hidden on the rooftop? Joe and Richard grabbed him and I took pleasure in decapitating him and tossing his remains in the river. That happened because of **you.** Your friend Janet, I wasn't sure what I was going to do with her, but the second she tried to seduce me, it made it real easy for me to kill her, that was done because of her disloyalty to **you.** Christopher didn't have anything to do with you, but I'll tell you anyway since you like horror stories so much. When I sent you in the other room, it was because I was in the kitchen beheading him as Joe and Richard dismembered him. He never went away, I murdered him. Xavier and his crew, I decapitated and disremembered eleven of my own kind. I tortured and had everyone feed from his mate before I threw lighter fluid on her and Adam lit the fucking match. Something he'll have to pay for eventually, and I'm in his debt because of **you.** Helena took a stake to the heart because of **you.** Joe has a lifetime of servitude to me because of what he did to **you,** and he was drained the other night for **you.**" I paused for a second. "Now the most gruesome thing of all, was enduring a day with *your mother.* I sat in that hovel that you call a house where I was insulted and disrespected and I took it all in for **you,** but now I can see the family resemblance. According to you, I've done nothing but take from you. You selfish, ungrateful little bitch." I pushed her against the wall again and said, "This whole mating thing can be easily severed and to be honest, I'm only a few inches away from doing so."

She was crying immensely. I still held her up against the wall, but not tightly. The tone in my voice was tamer once I released all that I was feeling.

"Please…let me go…" She pleaded.

I released her from my grasp and asked with conviction,

"Do you want me to *let you go* Dianna? I'll do anything for you and if that's what you want, I will."

She stared at me with fear and regret.

"No, I don't want you to let me go."

"Why?" I asked, "And don't tell me its because you love me. I want a real reason."

"I don't want to be without you. I was just angry," she answered.

"You always have an excuse for yourself. I never thought I would know anyone more self righteous than me, until I met you."

I continued with a twisted smile,

"You know what I don't understand," I said as I was pacing the floor and she remained stationary. "All you want is my attention constantly and you loved to be babied, and it's obvious that you'll do anything to get it. Ever since I got you back home, that was all I wanted to do. I wanted to cuddle with you, pamper you and give you all my attention, but you wouldn't let me, you wanted us to be *normal*. So when I gave you what you wanted, you couldn't handle it. I don't know what to do anymore. I just know that I can't do this anymore. I'm fuckin' damned with you and without you. I'm starting to regret ever mating with you, because your making me fuckin' nuts! You're so fuckin' needy and yet you wanna be controlling, you can't have it both ways." I paused to look at the expression on her face. She looked nervous and afraid that she was going to lose me, and to be honest she was very close of doing just that. I was willing to take the risk of eternal heartache and emptiness than deal with this shit. "So make a decision, you say I never let you make decisions, do it now. What do we do fix things?" I continued and she said nothing, she just cried and honestly it pissed me off.

I smirked at her ineptness to even come up with an idea.

"This is why I have to decide everything, because when the chips are down you can't even think for yourself, then again how can I expect you to make life altering decisions when you can't even drink blood correctly. Not only are you a vampire with a conscience, you're also handicapped. There isn't a gray area with you, everything is all or nothing—and that's going to change. It's obvious you can't make a simple decision. Even a bad decision is better than not making one at all. You're fucking useless. What are you like a thousand years old and this is how you behave? How did you ever survive all these years?"

"Don't mock me!" She yelled through her sobbing.

"You make it so easy. You rant and rave and have nothing to back yourself up. If you wanna stay in this relationship then things are going to be done my way and you're going to do what your told, because you are incapable of doing it yourself. Now I'm only gonna ask you once, do you want to stay with me? Because I will release you if you feel you can't live up to my expectations," I asked sternly and waited for an answer.

"Can you at least answer a simple fuckin' question? It's either yes or no!" I screamed.

"Yes, I want to stay with you," she answered swiftly and meekly.

"Then understand this, you will be kept in the dark about certain issues until I think you are able to sustain them in the correct manner. You will adapt to my lifestyle and my household. I will not allow you to be an outcast any longer. You will fit in, even if you have to force yourself. There isn't anyone in this house who owes you anything. If they respect you it's only because of me, you have to earn respect to get it and you have done nothing but walk around snobbishly. They put up with you and your bullshit for me. You are not better than any of them, you are the less dominant species, you are only high and mighty because of me, always remember that. I'm the only one that will ever put you above anyone or anything and don't forget it. You will learn how to tame your powers, because if you don't, always keep in mind that I have the potential to unleash *my* dark side too. A side of me which you haven't seen, this is only a preview and it ain't pretty," I paused and she stared at me trembling and unable to give a rebuttal.

"Do you at least have an opinion about anything I've said?" I was rude, degrading and arrogant.

She still said nothing. This was the first time I didn't have any sympathy towards her. I wanted my words to hurt her the same way her words hurt me.

"Nothing, not a fucking word. You're pathetic. Until you are able to fend for yourself, you don't get to have an opinion either. This is your last chance, do you have anything to say about my list of demands?"

She didn't mutter a sound.

The only sound I heard from her was sniffling through her tears.

I turned my back from her, disgusted with her in just about every aspect. I looked up and exhaled. I turned around and grabbed her by her upper arm, "Let's go," I said.

"Where are we going?" She asked timidly.

"No questions, just get your coat." I commanded.

"Your hurting my arm!"

"I'm going to hurt it more if you don't shut the fuck up!" I yelled.

She didn't question me anymore.

I grabbed her coat as we walked into the living room. I was tugging Dianna along ruggedly. Everyone was sitting around pretending not to be eavesdropping on Dianna and myself. Before I stepped outside the front door I shouted to all of them,

"I don't want to be disturbed for at least twenty four hours. Not one phone call, or there will be consequences. I'll call you," I instructed.

I walked expeditiously down the hallway to the garage with Dianna struggling to keep up as I had her gripped by the arm tightly. We walked through the garage and reached my car. I opened the door and put her inside discourteously. I walked around and started it up and raced out of the garage like a bat out of hell. Dianna quickly put on her seat belt and she didn't say one word. She was holding on to her seat for dear life. It was the best decision she has ever made.

23

Reckless

We drove through the city at ninety miles an hour. I put on a loud, monstrous, heavy metal CD and turned up the volume, so loud that it might have popped her eardrums. I was making sure that I couldn't hear her speak because Dianna's silence is usually short lived. I wasn't taking any chances.

When we finally reached the open highway on I-87, I tested the car to its max. I was driving recklessly at one hundred and sixty miles per hour. Dianna was panicking as the speedometer was jolting. That was my initial plan. I wanted to instill fear into her. She never feared me and perhaps it was overdue. She wanted to know who I am and what I am. I gave her a small taste of what it's like to deal with reckless behavior.

I turned my head to watch her squirm in the passenger seat and I was gratified by her fear. She reached over and lowered the music.

"Slow down...please!" She begged, horrified.

I looked at her and smiled sinisterly and pressed on the gas even harder.

Two hundred and fifty miles per hour...maximum speed.

"Danato! Please!" She shouted. "Slow down!"

"Why, what's the big deal?" I asked rationally and swerved the car to enhance her nervousness.

"You're going to crash into a wall or something! Please slow down!"

"So what if I do? We'll get a little mangled up, shake it off, heal and be on our way. It isn't like we'll die. So why are you so scared?"

"Because I don't want to get mangled up at all!"

I eased up on the gas a bit but nothing too significant,

"Are you afraid to die, Dianna?" I asked stealthy. She looked at me horror struck. She definitely thought that I was going to kill her.

"I don't want to die," she answered cowardly.

"That's not what I asked. I want to know, *if* you're afraid to die?" I asked again formidably.

"Yes," she whispered.

"Why? We're both walking death. Everything about us is death. So how different can death be from what we are now?" I asked.

"I'm not death. I *hate* what I've become," she pressed.

"Whether or not you hate it—is irrelevant. It's what you are. I can admit it. Everything about me is death, I *am* death, are you afraid of me?" I intimidated.

She glared at me and said, "Only right now I am."

"I won't crash, I don't want to fuck up my car," I said shrewdly.

I turned my head from her and slowed down my speed. I turned down the music to a reasonable volume.

Then as luck would have it, I heard police cars. Apparently they didn't like my speeding tactics. I looked through the mirror and saw two blue flashing lights behind me. I had three choices;

One: I could kill them both and be on my way.

Two: I can let them lock me up in jail for the night, leave Dianna to fend for herself and have a good rest and a meal on death row and breakout.

Three: I could hypnotize them to yield at my will.

Needless to say, I was in a reckless mood so my plan was to go with option one but not until I toyed with them for a few minutes.

I pulled the car over and the two police cars pulled up behind me. One of the officers walked over to my window and asked me to step outside the car. I did as I was told. The cop told Dianna to stay put. They threw me up against the car and started frisking me and reading me my rights.

I was laughing silently to myself through out this charade. Suddenly, the clouds rolled in and it began to drizzle. The wind started to pick up and the rain became torrential. I turned my head while standing in my arrested position and smiled at Dianna. Then the rain turned to hail and the wind was blowing their little hats off and their cars were moving from the forceful breeze. The officers were trying to keep themselves on the ground. A small twister was in the distance and they were frightened. They told me to get going and to slow down. They jumped into their police cars and went in the opposite direction of the small funnel of wind. I strolled into my car and started it back up and took off in a civil manner.

"Why did you do that?" I asked Dianna.

"Impulse. I didn't want them to hurt you, even though you're being a complete dick."

"Watch your mouth, I don't like it," I said strictly. Then asked, "Did you do it for my safety or theirs?"

"A little of both," she answered.

I rolled my eyes, "So I can't even depend on you to be on my side completely. You claim that you didn't want them to hurt me—so you caused this great diversion just so they wouldn't die by my hands. So who were you really trying to save, me or them?"

She sat silently and turned her head out the window and put her head down.

"Of course, you don't have a fucking answer. You never do when you come out looking bad. All I can say is—if it were the other way around, regardless if you can take on a bad situation yourself or not, I would have been by your side and ripped them apart. Where's your loyalty Dianna? Do you have any at all?"

"You know I'm loyal to you," she said convincingly.

"I didn't ask if you were faithful, I asked if you were loyal. There is a difference."

She gave me a baffled look. She seemed really confused by my line of questioning.

"Let me put it another way. I forget what I'm dealing with," I said condescendingly. "Would you die for me?"

She sat quietly for a few moments and said,

"I suppose I would."

"You *suppose* you would? Hmm, that's an interesting choice of words, considering you hesitated to answer. As for me, I'd die for you without even thinking about it. That's loyalty, something that you don't know anything about. I misjudged you. I thought I could trust you with my life, I was wrong."

We were silent for at least an hour. Neither of us looked at one another. I just drove. I didn't even know if any of this was even worth it anymore. At that moment, I regretted having Dianna in my life, I regretted being eternally bound to her and I regretted my decision to turn her instead of killing her.

Dianna broke the tense silence.

"I'm hungry. Will you get me something to eat?" She seemed nervous to ask me.

I didn't answer. I pulled off the next exit where there were twenty four hour fast food restaurants. I went to the first one that I saw, McDonalds. I pulled in and parked the car.

"You can eat inside. I don't want that junk smelling up my car," I said, uncaring.

"Aren't you coming in with me?" She asked cowardly.

"I *suppose* so," I answered.

We went inside and walked up to the counter. Dianna was pondering the short menu, unsure of what she wanted to order. I was getting annoyed that she couldn't even decide what to eat. Just as she was about to order, I ordered her a number one hastily—what ever that was. She didn't argue. She quietly took her tray to a table and sat down. I didn't sit with her, but I stood close by. I was making a phone call home just to check in and see if anything was happening. I still had a responsibility at home also. Dianna often forgets that. I stayed on the phone with Joe and Sebastian until she was done eating. I didn't want to look at her, much less when she's eating human food. I noticed she got up and threw away her trash and was walking towards me. I hung up the phone and proceeded out the door and she followed behind me. Dianna was transparent and she regretted everything she said and didn't say. She was getting scared by my authentic coldness towards her. I could sense that she feared she was losing me and I feared the same thing.

I didn't even open the car door for her. She opened it up and jumped in quickly. It was as if she was afraid that I was going to leave her there. Despite her hurtful actions and words, I would never do that, because I am *loyal* to *her.*

We were about thirty minutes from my intended destination and on the road for about an hour since McDonalds.

"I'm still hungry," Dianna said again.

"You just ate," I said disgusted.

"Not for food, for the other thing," she said.

"What other thing?" I asked loudly.

"You know what I mean," she said meekly.

"Just say it, Dianna. You're hungry for *blood.* It's what you are. The sooner you can admit it and act like the blood thirsty predator you are, the sooner we can get on with our lives." I said.

"I'm hungry...I'm...hungry...for blood," she confessed.

"I have to find a rest stop for that. It's at least five or ten miles. Will you be alright until we get there?"

"I'll be okay," she smiled, and I melted whenever she smiled sincerely. I smiled back and took hold of her hand for the first time since we've been in the car.

Sure enough there was a rest stop five miles away. Rest stops were always crowded, day or night. Blood was easy to get. I parked the car and we both got out. I began to walk ahead of Dianna to prey for food.

"Let me do this," she insisted eagerly.

I extended out my hand for her to lead the way. I stood a distance behind her so we wouldn't look like we were together, but close enough to keep her in range. She was scoping and preying for a victim. She made a quick sharp turn and turned her head towards me and smiled hungrily. She found her prey.

She strutted and stood in front of two men in their twenties. They looked like punks. Dianna was alluring and seductive, especially to humans. She was using her feminine wiles. She was bending down and laughing and smiling. She lured them to the back of the restaurant that was on the premises. I was with her the entire time, just out of sight and watching her use her "femme fatale" talents. She was leaning up against the wall across from the convenient dumpster with her one leg up and exposed. I found it comical to see Dianna acting in such a way. She was anything but a temptress. The two men stood in front of her. One of them unbuttoning his pants, thinking he was going to have his way with her, and the other one standing face to face with and about to kiss her.

When he reached in to kiss her lips she lunged into his neck viciously.

Before the other guy could scream, I was already pried into his neck and draining him.

When we finished I took the next step and tossed my dinner into the trash. I told Dianna to the same thing.

"I can't," she said.

"Dianna, just do it. This is getting played out. You already killed him. Now get rid of the body," I was getting annoyed.

"No…I mean, *I can't physically do it*. I don't have vampire strength and I can't lift him, so can you please help me?" She asked.

I smiled and shook my head. *Handicap*, I thought. *One more thing to add to the list.* I picked him up and disposed the body. Then of course, I had to wipe her face because she still couldn't drink properly.

"You really need to learn how to eat," I said.

"I'll try. For you. I'll try for you," she answered, trying to make up for some her misused words during our drive.

In an attempt to make a stand for herself and make me proud of her as well, she magically lit the dumpster on fire with an intense glance before I could find a match and lighter fluid. She smiled proudly at herself and we both walked from around the building and into the car.

Before I started the car she leaned over to kiss me. I made an effort to kiss her, but it was hardly a kiss. I turned the ignition and got back on the road.

She leaned back against her seat and looked at me pathetically and asked me,

"Will you ever kiss me again?"

"Yeah Dianna, I'll kiss you again. This just isn't the time. We can't just kiss and make up and think that everything is alright between us and pretend that nothing ever happened. Things aren't what they were three hours ago. Too much has been said and we have to work things out and come to an understanding so this don't happen again," I answered truthfully.

"So we're not okay?"

"No baby, we're not okay, but we will be. I promise," I answered honestly and stroked her cheek gently.

She sat back contently and put the radio on.

I drove and reached my destination. I owned a little ski Chalet in Windham, New York. It is my sanctuary. It's secluded and quiet. A perfect place to work things out with Dianna and have somewhat of a clear head.

24

Windham

The place is small and set in a serene setting. It sat high in the mountainous region of New York. I didn't have neighbors and the solitude was what I liked best. The Ski Resort was close enough to get a bite to eat. It is my perfect get away. When you first walk in, you enter into the large living room with a small kitchen combo within the same area. It has one small bedroom that was up the stairs in a loft area. The fire place that was in the living room is huge and the mantle was made of cobblestone. The bedroom fireplace was much smaller and the mantle was white marble. The décor was mostly rustic. It wasn't my first choice, but that was how I bought it two years ago. It sat on two acres of wooded land. Only a small portion of the land was cleared outside the back door, where I had a large hot tub sitting on a wood deck. I was satisfied with the condition of the place when I entered the premises. I hired a caretaker to watch over it and keep it maintained. They have orders not to enter if there are any cars in the driveway.

"Whose house is this?" Dianna asked, skimming the room and its trinkets in awe.

"Mine. I bought it about two years ago."

"Why didn't you ever tell me? This place is great," she said as she was walking around touching everything, like a child in a toy isle of a store.

"It never came up," I said.

"I love this place. Let's live here, just me and you," she said with her adolescent smile.

I smiled subtly and said, "I couldn't live here everyday. I need the city life, besides there isn't enough food here unless you're one of those pussy vampires who will only feed on animal blood."

"This place is great, it's so peaceful," she said happily.

"Since you like it, we'll come here more often."

She approached me and stood up on her toes to kiss me and I responded with enthusiasm. She reached down my pants and unbuttoned them, slipping her hand inside and arousing me significantly. She dropped to her knees, pulled my jeans down enough and put her mouth over my well endowed cock and sack. She began to bob her head slowly as she sucked, licked and stroked it with her hands. She squeezed onto my ass and dug her nails deep in my skin as she indulged me with every motion of her head. I moaned and growled with ecstasy while holding her head firm against me.

"That...this...isn't going to make things better," I struggled to say, and she stopped, looked up at me and began to speak.

What was I thinking? Why would I stop her from giving me great head? I'm such an asshole.

"I know it won't make things better, but it's a start. You were so distant driving up here and I was able to feel the emptiness and I hated it. Please don't take from me the only thing that you don't have any complaints about," she said innocently.

I laughed at her theory and I pushed her head back in place to finish what she started. And she continued to give me the best blow job I ever had. I fought to keep myself from having an orgasm. I continued to let her taste me and stroke me with her tongue and lips until I just couldn't take it any more. I wanted to climax inside her, together as one, so I stopped her. I removed my jeans completely and lifted her up to carry her upstairs to the bedroom. I made love to Dianna that night the way I wanted to when I rescued her from Xavier. We were tender and loving as opposed to destructive and wild. I lay on top her most of the night just to look at her gorgeous face and kiss her over and over again during our intimacy. Dianna reciprocated without reprieve. For the first time, we were behaving like two lovers in love. It was a feeling of perfection and gratification. We shared blood lovingly and passionately and savoring every drop of blood with affection. Dianna didn't spill a drop, and her face stayed clean.

I spoke to Dianna in my language without realizing that I was doing so.

"Ti amo, Dianna. Siete il mio mondo. Desidero che potremmo sempre essere come questo."

I love you Dianna. You are my world. I wish we could always be like this.

Then much to my surprise, Dianna answered back in my native tongue.

"Ti amo anche, Danato. Morirei senza voi e morirei per voi. Non lo danneggierò ancora le mie parole."

I love you too, Danato. I would die without you and I would die for you. I will not hurt you with my words again.

"You understand?" I asked enthusiastically.

"Yes. It's a gift. I can speak all languages," she answered.

"I'm not sure I wanted you to know that," I said with suspicion.

"I'm glad I did," she replied.

We kissed each other compassionately and uncontrollably before we peaked and rested in each others arms.

I awoke a few hours later to find that Dianna had made herself at home and was relaxing in the hot tub. I was aware that Dianna was trying to avoid any confrontation about our quarrel. She was hoping that our evening of loving each other passionately would have erased any further conversation. Unfortunately, it didn't. After all, the things we said to each other previously left a nasty scar. I couldn't just put things aside and let them go unnoticed. I didn't want things to be like that any longer. I had to put aside my feelings towards her as a lover and became her teacher and guardian.

I opened the back door, "Dianna," I called.

She looked at me and smiled.

"Come inside and get dressed, we need to talk," I said with humble authority.

Her smile faded and her hopes of moving forward without repercussions were gone as I closed the door and waited for her on the couch.

She met me on the couch and sat on my lap, giving my weakness for her one last try. It didn't work. I gently removed her from my lap and sat on a chair across form her. She stayed put and waited tensely for me to speak to her.

"I can't take back a lot of the things that I said to you last night. I meant most of my words. I could only apologize for the cruel way I said them," I said without flexibility.

"I said a lot of hurtful things too, and I'm sorry," she acknowledged.

"Let me speak, I'll give you a chance. I don't want you to apologize," I said as she sat comfortably back and listened.

"I know you've been through a lot since you've met me. But that doesn't excuse you from the way you behaved. I do have other responsibilities. I'm responsible for everyone. I have to make life altering decisions that affect us all. I don't need any pressure from you, when you're the one I depend on to comfort me, keep me strong and tame. Things are going to change. You will listen to me without argument, and do as you're told. I'm not doing this to hurt you or make you feel inferior. You forget that you are living in a world that you know nothing about, and I only want to guide you and teach you our ways. The right way."

I stopped for a moment and noticed the disappointment in her eyes.

I continued, "I want you to be able to fend for yourself, and make a decisions for yourself. The only way that is going to happen is if you listen to me and my words. I am *NOT* going to put up with the fighting and you testing my patience any more. I'm not going to tolerate it, and there will be consequences. I could go on further, but do you understand what I am trying to tell you?"

I waited for an answer. Then she glared up at me,

"Yes, I understand," she said as she bit her lip. "But I do have one question, if that's alright with you?"

I nodded for her to go on, "If all you want to do is change me, why do *you* love me?"

"I'm not trying to change you, I'm trying to tame you. Your powers are strong. So strong that you cannot behave recklessly among a world full of killers. You have to understand that your careless actions can have a domino effect on our whole way of life. If we are exposed for what we really are, our extinction is inevitable. Remember the witch hunts and what happened to them when they were exposed?"

I hit home when I reminded her of the witch hunts and what happened. I think she understood completely.

"I understand, but now tell me...why *you* love me?"

"I love you because from the day I saw you, I looked into those pretty eyes and I had light in my life for the first time in over a century. There is something about you that I can't do without." I confessed as I reached to wisp the hair out of her face.

"Oh...and also because you have a great ass," I grinned and she smiled shyly and replied, "So do you."

"Now, why do you love me?" I asked.

"I don't know why, I only know that when I'm without you, I can't breathe and I'm hollow. You make me whole. You fill the emptiness that has long been a part of me."

"Then you need to trust me with your life and understand that anything I tell you to do or not to do, is for you. Everything I do and don't do is for *you*. Do you trust me, Dianna?"

"Yes," she whispered.

"Are we going to do things my way, without you crying like a spoiled baby? Without constantly testing my patience?"

"Yes, of course."

"Then we're good."

Unexpectedly, she raised her hand as if she was a fourth grade student, nervous about asking a question in front of the class.

I grinned and snickered, she was too cute.

"You don't have to raise your hand, Dianna. Just tell me."

"Do you think there is anything to the prophecies that Ruth and Sebastian spoke about?"

"I'm starting to think so. I'll have to get into that more with Sebastian when we get home," I answered and she agreed.

We spent most of the evening, relaxing in the hot tub, just talking and getting to know each other again. I went over the traditions of our world and filled in a lot of unanswered questions for her. I agreed to be less secretive and include her more often.

Dianna, of course, was hungry and I had to find a place in this one horse town that delivered. The sun was still shining and I couldn't take her anywhere, and there was no way she was attempting to drive my car, not even by magic. After numerous phone calls, I did mange to find one delicatessen that delivered. Dianna ate like the glutton she is before going to sleep.

We rested for a long amount of time and we stayed longer than anticipated. I awoke from the ring of my cell phone. It's been exactly twenty four hours. While it was ringing I thought about the reality that was ahead of me when Dianna and I left this tranquil place. We would be going back to a world of love and hate, tragedy and comedy, and life and death.

As I picked up the cell phone, Dianna woke up and asked me who it was on the other end. I hung up and told Dianna that it was time to go. She stuck to her word and didn't pursue her questioning when I disregarded her question. She got up and got dressed without argument or any attempts at sarcasm.

During the drive back home, I was thinking about the things that I would have to endure when I got back to the city. I would have to become a teacher to Dianna, I would have to be hard and possibly cruel to the only thing I ever loved—for her own sake. I would have to answer to slayings of certain vampires and possible retaliation. I would have to confront Sebastian about these so called prophecies and see what Dianna and I were in for. Things were getting a little too surreal. We were going back to the place called home that we would be forever bound to.